THE PRINCE OF ORANGE COUNTY

Kareem Tayyar

Pelekinesis

The Prince of Orange County by Kareem Tayyar

ISBN: 978-1-938349-92-8

eISBN: 978-1-938349-94-2

Layout and book design by Mark Givens

First Pelekinesis Printing 2018

For information:

Pelekinesis, 112 Harvard Ave #65, Claremont, CA 91711 USA

Library of Congress Cataloging-in-Publication Data
Names: Tayyar, Paul Kareem, author.
Title: The prince of Orange County / by Kareem Tayyar.
Description: Claremont, CA : Pelekinesis, [2018]
Identifiers: LCCN 2018036708 (print) | LCCN 2018043137 (ebook) | ISBN
    9781938349942 (ePub) | ISBN 9781938349928 (pbk.)
Classification: LCC PS3620.A99 (ebook) | LCC PS3620.A99 P75 2018 (print) |
    DDC 813/.6--dc23
LC record available at https://lccn.loc.gov/2018036708

www.pelekinesis.com

The Prince of Orange County

Kareem Tayyar

For Charles McCall and Joe Robinson

It might be a Norman Rockwell painting, if there were room in Rockwell's world for a more complex American suburb. Walk four blocks in any direction and you'll find enough cul-de-sacs to make you think you're in an episode of *The Brady Bunch*, but lace up your high-tops and head out to the Matsuya Middle School playground where Thomas Kabiri is working on his cross-over dribble, and you'll see a trio of day laborers walking to the bus stop after a day spent painting houses for under-the-table money. You'll see a 1982 Dodge pickup illegally parked in front of a blue fire hydrant that, for reasons which no one in the area can fully explain, has long been referred to as "Buddha." You'll see enough graffiti currently spray-painted onto the wall of the school that you might think it's a street-artist's version of "Guernica." But what difference does it make? Southern California never existed in Rockwell's America anyway.

Thomas has been out here for hours, the sun disappearing behind the rooftops of the Sunwood Apartments across the street, and the barrio dogs that belong to Jorge's older brother and are fought for money in the after-hours backyards of Santa Ana and Westminster have already begun howling at a moon that has yet to appear. Their barks compete with the pump organ from St. Sebastian's Church, located on the other side of the wall from the courts, and which formerly featured a stained glass window of the Messiah that

Tom Willis broke with a towering home run a few days back. The window's boarded up now, with Christ's dangling feet sticking out from the bottom of the wood planks like that unlucky witch at the beginning of *The Wizard of Oz*. So much for the Resurrection, the joke in the neighborhood goes. Jesus couldn't even keep himself from getting beaned.

Thomas catalogues his moves. The stutter-step. The pump-fake. The up-and-under. The crossover. The behind-the-back dribble. The 360. The finger-roll. The step-back jumper. The runner in the lane. He works on his reverse layups, strengthens his off-hand with a series of dribbling exercises, makes certain not to let his free throws become frozen-ropes by always reminding himself to bend his knees as he shoots.

He gets himself to his favorite spots. The right corner. Two steps to the left of the top of the key where, a few months back, he won the city championship for his team with a pull-up jumper with three seconds left on the clock. Midway down the lane, that free-fire zone where he can loft a floater over a larger defender's outstretched hands, a vital skill considering Thomas's size, which is nowhere near five feet or one hundred pounds. He lets one go and imagines he's about to put the Celtics down for good, send them back to Boston to cry on Red Auerbach's shoulder. When the shot falls he raises his hands in the air in celebration, imagines that Pat Riley, current coach of the Los Angeles Lakers, is pointing in his direction and telling him, "I knew you'd make it."

Some kids have imaginary friends? He has imaginary teammates. A cross-section of the best from the professional ranks hang with him on these courts whenever he would have otherwise been alone, their nicknames making them seem like a hoops version of the Justice League: Clyde the Glide, Akeem the Dream, the Human Highlight Film, the Doctor, the Round Mound of Rebound, the Ice Man, the Mailman, the Chief, the Microwave, the Worm, Zeke,

Sleepy, Pearl, Magic, Chocolate Thunder. They run five-on-five with him, retrieve his rebounds, offer moral support when he's in a slump or on a water break, help him celebrate when he's just mastered a new move, or hit a shot that he figured had no chance of going in. These guys are why he'll never really consider himself an only child.

And that's to say nothing of the flesh-and-blood buddies who are always showing up, like, just now, James Bianchi, who hops the chain-link fence to come and join him. James is five-seven in high tops and two pair of socks, with hair he's cut into a flattop that he thinks gives him an extra inch. Looks like he's never run a day in his life, with an extra ten pounds he doesn't seem interested in shaking, but he's still the starting two guard for the high school team. "If I'm in the gym I'm in range", James tells anyone who will listen. Hell, if he's in the country he's in range, Thomas thinks. James is wearing jeans and past-their-prime white high tops, and his mother has a thing for Kenny Rogers. Photos of him hang on the Bianchi apartment walls as if the Gambler were an extended part of the family, a beloved uncle whom, against all odds, somehow made it big.

Thomas throws James the ball as he's walking towards the court. James catches it and immediately lets fly. Of course it's good. Thomas has seen him make twenty-eight shots in a row from that exact spot. Entire months often seem to pass without James missing. It's a shame the high school team is as bad as they are, Thomas thinks, James having to toil away surrounded by a bunch of non-talents, getting an empty twenty-five a night as the Blue Raiders go down to another defeat. Thomas wishes he were five years older. Fourteen going on fifteen instead of ten going on eleven. Then he could run point for the squad, get an easy ten assists by simply getting James the ball in his favorite spots. They'd be the best backcourt in the county, Thomas figures, a high school version of Maurice Cheeks and Andrew Toney.

Immediately they slip into their routine. Thomas is the Magic Man, slipping past imagined defenders before kicking it out to James, perpetual Byron Scott, spotting up. Ten, twenty, thirty times they do this, James talking throughout:

"I'm telling you, kid: MTV isn't going to last. Enjoy it while you can."

Swish.

"Black Sabbath was never the same once Ozzy left the group."

Swish.

"Of course, Ozzy wasn't either."

Swish.

"Ronald Reagan? Please. Some day they're going to find out the guy had amnesia or something."

Swish.

"Who shot J.R.? Who cares?"

Swish.

"Now who shot John Kennedy? That's something else."

Swish.

"You really think Oswald could have done it alone?"

Swish.

"No way."

Swish.

"And don't even get me started on the grassy knoll."

Swish.

"Eddie Murphy is funnier than Bill Murray."

Swish.

"Richard Pryor is funnier than both of them."

Swish.

"Forget New York. It's basically an active crime scene with a giant park in the middle of it."

Swish.

"Chicago? A second-rate New York."

Swish.

"St. Louis? A third-rate Chicago."

Swish.

"New Orleans? Now we're talking."

Swish.

"Of course Christ walked on water."

Swish.

"But Moses parting the Red Sea? Never."

Swish.

"The secret to women? How would I know?"

Swish.

"Just kidding. Of course I know."

Swish.

"They need you to be sensitive."

Swish.

"But not too sensitive."

Swish.

"Independent."

Swish.

"But not too independent."

Swish.

"They need you to be smart."

Swish.

"But not too smart."

Swish.

"Any questions?"

Swish.

Thomas retrieves the ball as it comes through the hoop. He turns to see Dave Hamilton jay-jogging across the street. His Quicksilver hat turned backwards, in a neon tank-top that shows off the muscles surfing has given him. Dude has a perpetual sunburn. Skin peels from his nose and lips like the bark from an albino tree.

"That guy's already died of skin cancer," James says as they watch Dave hop the fence. "He just doesn't know it yet."

Dave who doesn't have much game but rebounds like people are trying to steal his lunch money. A good enough leaper to make Thomas reconsider gravity. Dave breaks into a sprint as he hits the blacktop, and Thomas lofts the ball up into the air for him: Dave rises, seems to stop, look around, check his waterproof watch, and eat a couple of burgers before finally grabbing the ball and stuffing it through the hoop. For good measure he does a couple of chin-ups on the rim as well. Dave Hamilton who will be sponsored by Billabong by the time he turns seventeen. Dave Hamilton who will surf the U.S. Open at nineteen. Dave Hamilton who will vanish in Baja the year after and never be heard from again.

The three of them take turns shooting trick-shots, playing HORSE. They pause to watch a woman in Daisy Dukes roller-skate down the street. She's got long brown hair with killer bangs. She's a music video come to real life. A pinup girl in need of a photographer. She's from a world Thomas doesn't belong to yet. Dave wonders what her name is.

"Out of your league, that's her name," James says.

The two of them shadow-box, trade headlocks, two wild rams

showing off for a ewe who isn't watching. Thomas has seen her around though. Every time she skates past the courts he tries to muster up the courage to at least wave to her. He hasn't yet. He never will.

After James and Dave have stopped, the talk turns to the Four Kings. It's the era of the Middleweight. Thomas Hearns, Marvin Hagler, Sugar Ray Leonard, and Roberto Duran, who rumor has it goes to jail to get in shape, to stay off the liquor and away from the women.

"Duran fights the murderers," James says. "The worst of the worst. Three, four times a week. They've got a special ring set up for him down there in a maximum security-place south of Juarez. My brother knows a guy who knows a guy who did time with him. Duran spent the whole time saying Leonard was a phony. A dancer. Apollo Creed with a glass jaw and no willingness to mix it up."

"Then he isn't Apollo Creed," Thomas says. "He's Clubber Lang."

James ignores this, and Dave doesn't want to hear about Duran.

"Duran's got nothing on Hagler. Best pound-for-bound boxer since Ali," he says.

At this both James and Thomas lose it, in disbelief at the insanity they have just heard.

"I feel like I don't even know you anymore," James says, throwing up an off-balance jumper that finds the bottom of the net anyway.

"Hearns can throw sixteen punches in a second-and-a-half," Thomas insists. He's read it in *Sports Illustrated*. And besides, he saw Hearns dismantle Duran, dropping him in the second round in the open-air heat of Las Vegas, while it took Marvelous Marvin the full fifteen to squeeze out a split decision. Thomas's mother came home just minutes after the fight to find her son standing in the center of their small living room, jabbing, countering, ducking before landing a series of hooks.

"Who won?" she asked, not really interested, despising fights, violence.

"Hearns. By knockout. You should have seen it," and Thomas was off. Playing both parts from memory. His mother watching, grocery bags still in hand.

"It must have really been something," she said, after Duran had been counted out.

But here, on the Matsuya courts at a little after 6 p.m. on a Tuesday afternoon at the end of June, Thomas just watches as James and Dave top one another with a succession of lies, their performances of a manhood they have yet to fully grow into. All the while Thomas works on his handle, his fadeaway, his pull-up jumper.

Across the street a moving van pulls up, drops its ramp like a landlocked anchor. This happens a few times a week. Sometimes more. Moving vans are as much a part of the local color as ambulances are to a retirement community. Sunwood is a way station, Orange County's version of Casablanca. The place everyone comes to when they've just arrived from Vietnam, from Mexico, from Palestine, from Syria, from wherever the hell Romania is. Thomas's neighbors have come to America by boat, by trunk, by trailers hooked up to semis driven by black-market coyotes out looking for easy money. Thomas spends a few moments wondering who the newest arrival is, but is called back to the matter at hand when James makes the catastrophic decision to say Kareem Abdul-Jabbar is overrated, a one-trick pony, a creation of Magic Johnson.

Dave grabs the ball from Thomas and dropkicks it in the direction of St. Sebastian's. It takes hours to land, probably shows up on NASA's satellite.

"Kareem is the greatest player of all time," Dave says.

"Magic is better," James counters.

"Kareem was a ten-time all star before Magic got to the league."

"Bird is better too."

"Kareem was so dominant in college they had to outlaw the dunk."

"Moses Malone could take him one-on-one."

"Kareem is a six-time MVP."

"He never scored 100 points in a game the way Wilt did."

There's a moment where Thomas wonders whether Dave is going to take a swing, but the moment passes when Dave decides to turn and run in the direction of the ball instead, which is now sitting in the grass on the far side of the soccer field like a crashed meteor. As Thomas and James watch Dave run, James says, "It's too easy with him."

Thomas does what he always does. Files it away. Archives it in that sprawling database that is his silence. "Never make it easy," Thomas tells himself, as James heads towards the water fountain. Thomas turns back to look across the street. The movers carry a large, black sofa up the walkway into the complex. They look like pallbearers, Thomas thinks, just like the funeral he went to the year before, when the kid from his school who had gone swimming during a riptide was being laid to rest, the large men in dark suits carrying his casket up the aisle of the church and placing it into the back of the hearse. All the local mothers crying, the boy's father with a look of grief on his face that Thomas would never forget.

A few moments later Dave is back with the ball, and Mississippi Rod has appeared from around the corner, white wristbands high on his arms, his replica Dominique Wilkins jersey giving away his game: Rod who runs like he's gliding, who seems to walk through the air, who doesn't have much range but what difference does it make when you can fly the way he does? Rod whose got a first step fast enough that by the time you notice he's not in front of you, he's already laying it up and letting you know about it as he runs back down the court.

They call him Mississippi Rod because he's from Mississippi. That's about the extent of the group's imagination. Everyone knows Rod's out here living with his uncle, but only Thomas knows it's because Rod's father was tied to the railroad tracks in Mississippi. "Owed someone some money," Rod told him a few months back, one night after the games were over and they were the only two left. Rod showing Thomas the secret of a strong crossover, telling him "you gotta go north-south, not east-west," demonstrating it for Thomas one, two, ten times before giving the ball to Thomas and watching him while continuing his story. "Gamblers, probably, but I can't say for sure. It was too dark for the conductor to see. By the time he hit the breaks it was too late to stop. So my mother sent me out here, said she wanted me away from all that," but then he breaks off, focuses on a hitch in Thomas's move. "You're showing the ball too much, gotta keep it tight, close to the hip, otherwise they'll snake it," he instructs, forgetting to go back and tell Thomas the rest of the story.

A few minutes later Stark makes five. Shows up already sweating, in matching gray warmups that he thinks make him look like a young Sylvester Stallone. Stark's father is with him, stopwatch in hand, the two of them who have turned the entire city into an outdoor gym. Stairs at City Hall. Sprints up Talbert Hill. Pushups in the park. Sit-ups on the diving board of the empty public pool out behind the hospital. Stark who's certain he's bound for the NBA, or the Major Leagues, or a spot on the Olympic 4 x 100 meter relay team. Problem is he doesn't have it, he never will, and everyone knows it but him and his father.

"Dude is missing the self-awareness gene," James says. "It runs in the family."

"He might get better," Thomas says. "You never know."

"You're full of hope, kid," James says. "It's beautiful. I mean, it's ridiculous. But beautiful too."

All four of these guys are between six and eight years older than Thomas; Thomas who doesn't have any friends his own age. Thomas who wishes he were already sixteen with the type of intensity with which Odysseus once longed for Ithaca.

They form an impromptu layup line, as if preparing for an organized game that is minutes from tip-off. It's impressively democratic, all of them taking turns rebounding, shooting, a constant motion that someone older than Thomas would say looks like a jazz concert. But Thomas doesn't know jazz. He's never heard of King Oliver. He won't know who Charlie Parker is until his junior year of college when he reads James Baldwin for the first time. The line lasts a couple minutes before inevitably fracturing back into someone shooting, missing, and someone else grabbing the rebound. You get your makes back. James, of course, gets on a roll. He hits sixteen in a row.

"It's Halley's Comet," Stark says, when James finally misses.

"What's Halley's Comet?" Dave asks.

"It's a comet," Stark responds.

Thomas laughs.

"You think that's funny?" Dave says, putting Thomas in a headlock and rubbing his knuckles across Thomas's scalp. Thomas fights back, doesn't make it easy for Dave. He keeps his feet moving, his fists flying in the direction of Dave's midsection. When Dave releases him Thomas says, out of breath, "In ten years I'm going to get you back, Dave."

"In ten years I'll be surfing the pipeline in Hawaii and won't even remember your name, kid."

Mississippi Rod takes the ball and runs down to the other end of the court. The rest of them instinctively fan out. He's channeling Julius Erving at the 1976 ABA dunk contest. All he's missing are the red-white-and-blue ball and the afro large enough to have been its own planet. Rod breaks into a run, carrying the ball like a running back, before he takes off at the free throw line and attempts to dunk. He crams it through the hoop with a level of force that always makes Thomas wonder if the rim will someday snap from the backboard completely.

Around the corner comes a blue jeep. It looks like something in one of those Vietnam movies Thomas has seen on Sunday mornings with his father when his mother is at church, a couple of guys standing up in the back. They're not regulars. Maybe nineteen, maybe a little older than that, and all of them, except for the driver, hop out before the jeep has even stopped moving. They take the other half court and start getting up shots. It's clear right away they can't play. They've got the gear, of course: new shoes, new ball, wristbands fresh out of the pack. All of them wearing polo shirts in bright colors. Thomas already hates them. Even before he sees the *Be An American, Kill An Iranian* bumper sticker. We're seven years on from the hostage crisis but who's counting? The Ayatollah like a Bond Villain, "ruining it for the rest of us," his father says, "those idiot mullahs who spend their lives worrying what Allah might think if they shake hands with a woman on her period, and get their feelings hurt when an expat novelist has made fun of them in his book."

A couple of minutes go by before one of the new guys crosses the no-fly zone of half court and asks if they want to play. Dave shrugs his shoulders, Mississippi Rod pays no attention, but James, ever the Carnival Barker says, "Hell yes." As Polo walks back to his side James says to Thomas, "if you look up 'Mail Fraud' in the dictionary, there'll be a picture of that guy's face."

"What's mail fraud?" Thomas asks.

"It's what they got Al Capone on," James says.

"My dad said it was tax evasion."

"Same thing."

The ball is an oversized yo-yo in Thomas's hands. The first defender tries to press him and Thomas puts it behind his back. Suddenly his defender has no idea what's happened. It's some David Copperfield sleight-of-hand, Thomas already in the lane and throwing a no-look bounce pass between three defenders to Stark before the defender can even attempt to recover.

The next several times are no different. Thomas gets James so many open looks that James tells him he's going to include him in his will. Mississippi Rod responds by saying, "you're the brokest brother I know, what are you going to leave him? Best wishes?" And then they're laughing, and Polo and his crew are getting frustrated. It's straight to 11 by ones and they're already down 7-3, and that's before Thomas steals the next pass and drives in for an uncontested layup. Now they're splintering, arguing amongst each other, and as Thomas runs back down the court he sees the moving van has pulled away, and on the sidewalk the largest man Thomas has ever seen in person, dressed in dark pants and a dark t-shirt beneath which Popeye-level biceps bulge, is watching them. He's got a bald dome and a ring shiny enough for Thomas to see it from here, the kind of thing a superhero might have that provides him with special powers.

10-5. Thomas stands at the top of the key. He dribbles around a pick Stark has set for him, stutter-steps, pulls a three-sixty, and throws the ball over his right shoulder to James, who's already laughing before the pass even touches his hands.

Game.

Immediately Polo goes down, faking an ankle sprain. This gives him and his buddies cover to pull out two minutes later to avoid a rematch, the jeep tearing off in the direction of Green Valley, back into the bassinet of multi-story homes on the other side of the school.

"Looked like the evacuation of Saigon," James says a few minutes after they have disappeared. "The only thing missing was the helicopters."

Dave laughs while Stark and his father confer on what Stark did well and what he needs to work on. Mississippi Rod readjusts his wristbands and asks Thomas where he gets his vision from.

"That's some Superman, X-ray stuff you've got there, kid."

Thomas feels like he's levitating.

"Seriously. I'm going to get you a cape," Rod continues. "A phone booth too. You step into it like a mini Clark Kent, you step back out and you're flying around the court like it's Metropolis and you're running Lex Luthor straight out of town."

"Thanks Rod," Thomas says.

"Don't be flattered, kid," James counters. "Batman would kick Superman's butt any day of the week."

"Are you crazy?" Thomas says. "Superman has super-strength. Batman is just a rich kid with a car."

"Kid's got a point," Dave says.

"Don't you guys watch the news?" James asks in disbelief. "Rich kids with nice cars run this country. Those guys we just beat? They're going to go home, have the maid fix them some food, beat up their little brothers, and go to bed. Tomorrow they'll graduate from USC, pay their respects at Richard Nixon's house in San Clemente, and then get elected to the U.S. Senate."

"Superman would never let that happen," Thomas insists.

"I don't think Superman knows a lot about the finer points of congressional elections," James says.

"Ok, then I'll be the Hulk," Thomas says.

"Just a science nerd with an anger problem," James says.

"Iron Man."

"A legacy kid with a chemistry set."

"Spider-Man."

"Judas in a funny costume."

"Judas?" Thomas asks, confused.

"He got Uncle Ben killed."

"He didn't mean to," Thomas says.

James shrugs his shoulders.

"I just call 'em like I see 'em."

"Captain America then."

James pauses, considers.

"A senior citizen in a young man's body? Ok, kid. I can see that. Captain America it is."

"You've got too much time on your hands, Bianchi," Rod says.

"There's no such thing," James says. "Considering time doesn't exist."

"What do you mean, time doesn't exist?" Thomas asks.

"Don't take the bait, kid," Dave says. "It isn't worth it."

"Ok, I take it back," Thomas says to James.

In the next couple of minutes the load-out begins. Stark and his father go home to watch *Rocky* and drink raw eggs for dinner; James says he's got two girls waiting for him near Lifeguard Tower 32; Dave doesn't say anything, simply does what he always does: breaks for a sprint back in the direction of Sunwood, hopping the fence with such ease the joke in the area is that he could join the circus as an acrobat if his parents weren't so strict. By 8 p.m. it's just Thomas and Mississippi Rod, the two of them getting up another couple dozen jumpers before calling it a night.

"One of the things I miss about Mississippi is the music," Rod says. "There's nothing like that out here. I'm talkin' swamp guitars. I'm talkin' John Lee Hooker. I'm talkin' bass lines that sound like they've been deep fried before serving. You can't get that here. Not even in Los Angeles. You get too close to the sea and the ocean just swallows everything. Gives it back to you with twelve-strings, singalong choruses, people holding hands and saying they can't wait to get to San Francisco. In Mississippi all you have to do is stand on any corner and just let the songs swallow you whole. You're Jonah and Jackson City is the whale. I miss that. Even though the place is so small-time they don't have a single professional sports team."

Thomas is back in archival mode. When he gets home he will ask his mother who John Lee Hooker is, where Mississippi is located, what a twelve-string guitar looks like. But for the moment he's just got his eyes and ears open, and Mississippi Rod Johnson is turning the half court into a one-man all-star game. He may say he's a man of the blues but Thomas thinks he's more like that rookie for the Bulls, Michael Jordan. The only things missing are the gold necklace and the Number 23 on his jersey.

"I hope I get to travel someday," Thomas says. "The only place I've ever been is San Francisco."

"Not a bad first trip," Rod says. "Where else you think you'd want to go?"

Thomas chases down a rebound. When he returns with the ball and throws it back to Rod, he considers, and then says, "New York. I'd like to see a game at Madison Square Garden."

"Good choice," Rod says, lofting another jumper. "The Mecca of

Basketball."

"Maybe I'll even get to play there someday," Thomas says.

"Wouldn't surprise me," Rod says. "You've got all kinds of adventures awaiting you, shorty."

"You think so?"

"Absolutely," Rod says. "You ever see *Scarface*?"

"My mother won't let me."

"Can't blame her for that," Rod says. "Just for the chainsaw scene alone. But there's this great scene where Al Pacino looks into the sky and sees this banner that says 'The World is Yours.' That's going to be you."

Thomas smiles and then tries to catch Rod off guard and steal the ball from him. No such luck.

"Kid's got a sense of humor all of a sudden," Rod says, as he blows by Thomas for a layup.

2

Iᴛ's 4:17 ᴀ.ᴍ. ᴀɴᴅ Tʜᴏᴍᴀs ɪs ᴀʟʀᴇᴀᴅʏ ᴏɴ ʜɪs ʙɪᴋᴇ. A Schwinn Phantom with yellow mag wheels and chrome handlebars that catch the moonlight like nothing else he'll ever see, not even that lake in Yosemite Valley he'll go swimming in with his wife twenty-five years later, the two of them playing Adam and Eve on the Autumn Equinox. Thomas's got 17 Sunday editions dangling from the canvas sack on his handlebars, *Los Angeles Times* stitched into both sides of the bag. He's been up since 3:45, when he pedaled out to the carports to begin sorting the sections dropped off by the delivery truck into their proper order. Already Thomas's got it down to a science, fifty-two minutes from start to finish, a one-man operation that would have impressed Richard Petty: top-speed pedaling, no wasted motion, no doubt he'll be done and back in bed by 5:15 at the latest.

Riding through the winding paths of the complex makes Thomas think of all those western films he's watched with his father. *The Searchers. Red River. High Noon. Pale Rider. The Good, the Bad, and the Ugly. Butch Cassidy and the Sundance Kid. 100 Rifles. Stagecoach. McCabe & Mrs. Miller. A Fistful of Dollars. Jeremiah Johnson.* He figures this job makes him a modern-day John Wayne. Or a cycling Clint Eastwood, riding through the complex before sunup to deliver the scores from the previous night's Dodgers game to the locals. Thomas finds himself wishing he'd been born earlier, in time for him to have joined the Pony Express.

He speeds past the laundry rooms that local vagrants often sneak into after-hours to sleep, past the large blue dumpsters where old men from the barrio forage for aluminum cans, past the first-floor apartment where Eric Channing shot himself the year before, leaving behind a note that said it was time to finish what Laos had started. Thomas hadn't known where Laos was until he'd heard about the note from a bunch of the other kids in the neighborhood, and asked his father to help him find it on the map.

Thomas has Run-D.M.C. on his headphones, that hip-hop Holy Trinity hailing from Hollis, Queens. The songs have electric guitars, possess rhymes that seem to head down blind alleys only to acrobat themselves back onto the Brooklyn Bridge just in time, and spin narratives witty enough to have made Mark Twain jealous. Jam Master Jay's backbeat sounds like a basketball being dribbled in double-time, while Run and D.M.C. sound like Old Testament prophets that grew up listening to Gil-Scott Heron and The Last Poets.

Thomas is so invested in the music that it takes him a moment to notice that the newspaper he's just thrown has knocked the second-floor door open on impact. He slams on his breaks, backs the bike up, and tries to figure out what to do. It doesn't seem to have awakened anyone in the apartment. No sudden lights have been turned on, no shouts of "what the hell?" have come from inside. But Thomas knows he can't leave the door like that. He'd feel like an accomplice if whoever's now living in Apartment 217 got robbed.

He tries to drop the kickstand but the bike, top-heavy with all of those newspapers, is setting to tip. Instead Thomas tests the bike's weight against the wall, hoping that will do the trick. No dice. Finally, reluctantly, he lays the bike gently on the ground as if it were an injured horse about to be shot after breaking its leg in the final turn at Churchill Downs.

Thomas slowly climbs the stairs. When he reaches the top he hesitates, worried that someone will think he's doing something he shouldn't be, before taking one step into the house to take hold of the handle and quietly close the door.

"The point of breaking into a place is to take something on your way out," a voice from the bottom of the stairs says.

Thomas is too surprised to jump. Instead he turns around to see the big man Thomas saw on the sidewalk the evening before, the man who'd stopped to watch them play hoops for a few minutes before heading into the complex. He's even taller up close. 6'10", 6'11"at least, though he might even be a full 7 feet.

The man's got a paper bag from 7-Eleven under his arm. As he climbs the stairs, Thomas notices that he's dressed in the same black khaki pants and fitted black t-shirt Thomas had seen him wearing the previous evening. Thomas has no doubt he's in the presence of the coolest man this side of John Shaft he's ever seen.

"Door kept sticking," the man says, showing Thomas. "Maintenance said they'd be out later this morning to fix it, but I have my doubts."

"They'll get around to it," Thomas says. "In another five or six years."

"Sounds about right for what I paid."

"The newspaper knocked it open when I threw it," Thomas says, gathering up his courage to explain what happened. "I wasn't trying to steal anything."

"Newspaper? I'm only here for ten days. The previous tenants must have forgotten to cancel their subscription."

"Clara Bowers. She moved last month. She left most of her stuff when she took off."

"That explains the Fleetwood Mac albums on the shelf."

"The rumor is she went to Miami to get back with her ex-boyfriend."

"Lucky her. Miami's a great city."

"They have alligators there."

"They have South Beach too."

"What's South Beach?"

"You know what Heaven is?"

Thomas nods.

"It's like that, but warmer."

As Thomas considers that maybe Miami should be his first trip instead of New York, the man stands beside him, looks down, and says, "What's your name, kid?"

"Thomas."

"I'm Earl," the man says, as the two of them shake hands.

"Did you just move in?" Thomas asks.

"A few days ago. Just a short-term thing, through this week and next."

"I've lived here since I was eighteen months old."

"Oh yeah? How old are you now?"

"Ten. I'll be eleven next February."

"You like it here?"

"It's the best," Thomas says. "There are four different places to play basketball within five minutes of each other."

"You've got a great handle, kid. Not just for a ten-year-old either. I've seen college point guards who didn't have your skills with the ball."

"You think so?"

"I know it, kid. Keep working at it."

"Thanks, Earl."

"Nothing to thank me for. It's a fact. You made those frat boys turn tail so fast they probably left their wallets behind."

Thomas laughs.

"Did you see that one guy faked an ankle sprain so they didn't have to play a rematch?"

"Course he did. He'd just been shown up by a fifth grader. You gave the guy no choice. But," Earl continues, lowering his voice a bit. "You've got to settle for the jumper once in awhile. Against a clown like that it doesn't matter. But against a smarter defender a few jumpers will keep them honest. They'll have to come out and challenge you. Otherwise they'll just sag, and you'll be stuck. No driving lanes to speak of. And that's your bread-and-butter."

Thomas nods, aware that Earl is right.

"You should come out and play," Thomas says.

"You and me on the same team? It wouldn't be fair to the rest of them."

"I'd make you look good, Earl," Thomas says. "I'd get you the ball in the post all day."

"Of course you would, kid," Earl says. "Any smart player would, and you're a smart player."

Then, before Thomas can answer, Earl says, "Good looking out on the door, kid. And thanks for the paper."

"You're welcome, Earl."

They shake hands again, before Earl disappears into the apartment, making sure the door closes and locks behind him.

Thomas spends the rest of his route thinking about what Earl has said. In fact, Thomas has been thinking the same thing for awhile. He's going to have to improve his range. Make them pay from twenty. This realization causes Thomas to race through the rest of his route. He needs to get home, get a little more sleep, and then get out to the courts so he can work on extending his range.

But he doesn't sleep. He's too excited. Instead he drops some bread into the toaster, pulls a jar of peanut butter from the fridge and a banana from the dangling wire fruit basket that looks like it might have been a birdcage in a former life. Then he pours himself a glass of orange juice.

Toast up, Thomas puts the moveable feast on a plate and carries it down to the sofa. Though there is technically a dining room table, it was long ago turned into an unofficial storage area. This morning the phone sits on top of it, as do a couple of Thomas's recent drawings, his mother's purse, and his father's books of poetry. But it's better this way, Thomas thinks. It gives him an excuse to sit in front of the television while he eats. This morning that means spending some time with the Road Runner, before Thomas is reminded that the wild bird is too manic a character to handle in anything other than small doses. Besides, the show always leaves Thomas with more questions than answers. Why, he wonders, does the Road Runner never move on, go west, put some distance between himself and the Coyote, who obviously has an axe to grind he's never going to get over? Thomas simply cannot understand the bird's lack of geographical imagination. If the definition of insanity is doing the same thing over and over again and expecting a different result, Thomas is certain the Road Runner qualifies. If it were up to him, he'd outfit the bird with a straightjacket and send him to Arkham Asylum. He could room with the Joker.

Next Thomas rides shotgun for awhile with the Pink Panther. But the Panther is too laid-back, too detached, too quiet for Thomas's tastes. It's never entirely clear to Thomas whether the Panther even knows what's going on around him. He'd be a terrible teammate, Thomas thinks. He'd never know the score, never look for the open man, never alert a teammate to a screen that was about to be set. You can't win with a guy like that.

Further along the dial he settles in for an episode of *The Odd Couple*. He can't believe that Oscar gets to write about sports for a living. Other than actually being a professional athlete, it seems like the next best job in the world. Thomas hangs with Oscar and Felix through a few commercial breaks and walks the streets of Chicago with the two committed bachelors, the Windy City looking glorious on a summer afternoon as they head to a day game at Wrigley Field. Thomas thinks about the story his grandfather told him, about the time he got to see Ernie Banks in person at the Polo Grounds.

"He hit one so deep that it completely left the park," his grandfather had said.

But it is when the rerun ends that he finds what he's been hoping for. It's 1986, after all, which means his favorite actor is always to be found somewhere along the dial, twenty-four hours a day, seven days a week. Yesterday it was *Smokey and the Bandit*, Burt Reynolds in a 1977 Black Trans Am turning the American South into his personal NASCAR track, leaving the Bull Connor-like sheriff played by a bloated Jackie Gleason in his perpetual dust. The day before that it was *The Longest Yard*, Burt as a troubled ex-football star who rediscovers his love for the game while serving time in a state penitentiary.

This morning it's *The Cannonball Run*, where Manifest Destiny's been reframed as a gigantic road race, and everyone—whites, blacks, Iranians, priests, women—are all having too much fun to be interested in hurting each other.

It's deep in the narrative, with Reynolds and Roger Moore

battling it out on the streets, when Thomas's father steps into the living room. He's still half-asleep, with his dark black hair going seventeen different ways at once, and his eyelids looking heavy enough to double as doors for a bank vault.

"Burt should run for President," his father says.

"You think he could win?" Thomas asks.

"Reagan did," his father answers. "So it's a pretty low bar."

His father follows this up by walking into the kitchen and proceeding to rinse a handful of grapes while singing a Persian aria in an off-key Farsi so painful to hear that Thomas turns the volume up on the television to drown him out.

The credits roll. Burt does what he always does: wins with a smile, and afterwards Thomas's father stands in front of the television and begins to manually scroll through the channels until landing on his desired location. Seconds later the two of them are watching a newsfeed with enough static to make it seem like it's being broadcast from the moon. On the screen a sober-looking man is reporting live in front of an assembled crowd several thousand strong, all of them hitting themselves with the same book while an angry-looking, Middle Eastern Darth Vader in a black robe and long beard presides over the entire spectacle.

"What're they doing?" Thomas asks.

"Setting modern civilization back two thousand years," his father responds.

"Why?"

"Because they don't know the difference between intellect and imagination."

When Thomas doesn't say anything, his father looks at him and clarifies, "They think God is a judge instead of a friend."

"What do you think he is?" Thomas asks.

"I think he's one lazy bastard."

He sits and watches the news with his father for another few minutes. There are images of women in headscarves wailing over the dead bodies of young men in the streets, many of whom are missing limbs, all of whom look much too young to have met such fates. Thomas looks from the screen to his father, in need of some further explanation as to what it is they are seeing, but his father has vanished into himself, beyond anyone's ability to reach him.

A few moments later Thomas reconsiders. His father hasn't vanished at all, because to vanish means that one's present whereabouts are a mystery. After all, Thomas knows where his father is. His father is back in the country of his birth, there in the streets with those wailing women, blessing the bodies with a series of prayers. Thomas doesn't attempt to pull his father back by breaking his concentration with a question. Instead he laces up his high-tops, puts on his purple-and-gold Lakers cap, pulls his basketball from the balcony, and heads across the street.

The twins, Gregory and Nathan, are already out there when Thomas arrives, attempting to train their two puppy akitas not to bite people's hands off. They don't seem to be having much luck. Instead the brothers spend the next several minutes seeking to corral the dogs whom, having slipped free of their leashes, are sprinting in the direction of the parking lot on the other side of the school. Within thirty seconds, all four of them have disappeared around he corner, not to be seen for the rest of the morning.

Other than that it's quiet until, a half an hour later, a man dressed in a green plaid skirt and the kind of hat Thomas has only seen on a deck of playing cards appears. He's carrying a bagpipe in his arms, and he sets up shop a few hundred feet from the courts. The moment the man begins to play, an otherwise quiet Sunday morning suddenly turns into *Ivanhoe*.

Or, as Thomas's father will say later on that night, "It sounded like King Arthur's funeral."

"Who was King Arthur?" Thomas asks.

"Just another sucker who thought the good times would never end."

Thomas will have a follow-up question, but that's not how his father rolls. The man works on a more minimalist level. Cryptic, even. He'll give you three, four sentences at a time, and then disappear into smoke while you're still trying to work out the samurai haiku he's just dropped on you. There are Tibetan monks who provide greater context for their statements than Bijan Kabiri.

But that will be hours from now. At this moment Thomas has begun to work on a jumper which, considering he's still a few years from hitting 90 pounds, isn't really a jumper at all, but more of a set shot he releases quickly enough for it to be unblockable anyway. He's got the wrist motion down, great rotation on the ball, and a perfect arc that gives him the benefit of the doubt with the rim. The problem is that he likes to pass more than score. Always has.

But he keeps at it, and an hour later the bagpipe player has thankfully moved on, and Arjun emerges from Sunwood ready to hoop. Kid is six-feet-four, five-feet-eight of which are legs. Just watching Arjun climb the fence is worth the price of admission. He doesn't climb it so much as swing one leg over and then the other. And when he jogs onto the blacktop he looks like that Italian tower Thomas has learned about in school, the one that is always leaning and swaying from side to side. Needless to say Arjun has absolutely no game, but he might be the single nicest guy Thomas has ever met. Or at least in the top three.

They don't say anything but pick up the game of one-on-one they've been playing for the better part of a year. Neither of them can guard the other. Arjun backs Thomas down for layup after layup until he misses one point blank and doesn't get to the rebound in time. Thomas then scores several times in a row by bringing Arjun out on the perimeter and then just blowing by him, Arjun like a Spanish matador the morning after a bender, his long legs like two skinny red capes that Thomas just darts past time after time for easy buckets.

"Damn Arjun," James says as he approaches the court. "No wonder John Wayne killed all your ancestors."

"I'm Indian," Arjun states for the hundredth time. "*Indian*. Not Native American."

"What's the difference?" James asks.

"The difference is that you're thinking Crazy Horse, and I'm thinking Gandhi," Arjun answers.

"Well," James says. "Gandhi couldn't play any defense either."

They begin to play 21, the three of them taking turns guarding each other. It's every man for himself, first to 21 wins. Of course James dominates. He hits a few long jumpers, buries the free throws that come after every make, and that's that. Game over. It feels like the whole thing lasts all of five minutes.

"Rematch," Arjun insists.

"You got it," James says.

The same thing happens again. And two more times after that. By the time they stop for a water break it's almost noon and there's a police helicopter circling high overhead.

"They're here for you, kid," James says to Thomas.

"I haven't done anything," Thomas says, actually believing James for a split second.

"This is America. Innocence and guilt have nothing to do with it."

Thomas, finally realizing James is messing with him, throws the ball at him. James catches it and promptly drains another deep jumper. But the ball, after coming through the hoop, is blown back in the direction of the fence when the helicopter begins to rapidly descend. After it lands in the middle of the street, four armed cops in uniform and a fifth one in a gray suit come barreling out, guns drawn. Almost immediately two guys emerge from the backseat of an old convertible that had been parked on the corner and start running.

Thomas, Arjun, and James stand there, awestruck. They couldn't be any more transfixed if a flying saucer had just landed in the middle of the street.

But it's over in thirty seconds. The first guy trips about twenty-five yards up the street and doesn't get up in time to keep himself from being tackled by two of the cops. The second one makes it another thirty yards before his lack of speed and overall lack of conditioning do him in. He bends over, puts his hands on his thighs, and attempts to catch his breath for a second or two before the cops are on him like leopards on a gazelle in one of those episodes of *Wild Kingdom* that Thomas so often watches.

"Damn," James says, watching the second guy get cuffed. "If you know the cops are after you, at least keep yourself in shape. Guy didn't even make it to the end of the block, never mind the Promised Land."

By this point black-and-whites are arriving from both directions, sirens blazing.

"I wonder what they did," Arjun says.

"It's Orange County," James answers. "They probably didn't pay their parking tickets."

"Then why the helicopter?" Arjun asks.

"They have to justify its expense somehow," James says.

"You're the smartest dumb guy I've ever met," Arjun says.

"Stop it," James says. "You're going to make me blush."

Within a minute the sidewalk is jammed with onlookers. Even the congregation for the 10:30 a.m. mass appears to have found the action on the street more interesting than the sermon inside. Thomas spots Arjun's father standing in a crowd of onlookers across the street. He doesn't look happy, but then again he never does.

"Arjun, why does your father always look like he's just stashed a body in the trunk of his car?" James asks.

"Screw you, Bianchi," Arjun responds.

"What?" James asks. "I'm just curious."

"I'll catch you guys later," Arjun says, heading towards Sunwood.

"Look at that," James marvels a few moments later. "Dude cleared the fence and crossed the street in four steps."

Thomas and James spend a few more minutes watching to see if anything else happens. Having been given a taste of excitement, the two of them want more.

"Seriously," Thomas says. "I wonder what they did."

"Who knows?" James says. "It could have been anything."

"Maybe they killed someone," Thomas says.

"That's too easy, kid. Let your imagination run a little more on this one."

"What do you mean?"

"The story I'm going with is that they were part of an international cartel that included drugs, prostitution, and gun running."

"I don't know," Thomas says. "You think they belonged to a cartel?"

"I'll tell you what they didn't belong to," James says.

"What?"

"A gym."

After another few minutes it becomes clear that nothing else of interest is going to happen. Instead the police try to keep the onlookers at a preferred distance, while a small group of detectives begin to search the convertible where the two men had hidden. The helicopter looks like the fossil of a dinosaur sleeping off the centuries in the middle of the street.

"You want to go to 7-Eleven?" James asks.

"Definitely," Thomas says.

Thomas begins to dribble the ball as they start walking in the direction of the liquor store. After leaving the blacktop, they move across the extended green of the soccer field. Fifty feet after reaching the sidewalk, the two of them turn left at Kathy's Massage Parlor and walk past Video Planet, Dodge Dental, and Princess Dry Cleaning before they arrive.

In front of the liquor store two skaters sit on the curb and smoke cigarettes. The older one wears a Sex Pistols t-shirt. James can't help himself. He never can.

"Johnny Rotten sucks," James says to him.

"Screw you, Bianchi," the skater responds.

Inside the temperature drops twenty degrees. The Slurpee machine glows like a junk food jukebox against the far wall. The old man behind the counter, who Thomas will learn a few years later flew B-52 bombers in WWII, is in the process of selling a handful of lottery tickets to an even older woman sporting two canes and a blue head of beehive hair.

"Why is she buying a lottery ticket?" James asks. "She'll be dead before the drawing."

"Not so loud," Thomas says.

"Why?" James asks. "She can't hear me."

James disappears into the back of the store to see about breaking his own in-house record on *Asteroids*, which leaves Thomas to aisle-hunt for some Big League Chew and Coca-Cola. Mission accomplished, he heads over to the magazine rack against the window that looks out onto the street. Through the glass he watches the two skaters, now having finished off their cigarettes, turn the half-empty parking lot into their own unofficial obstacle course. They jump curbs, they change directions while airborne, they spin pirouettes across the asphalt with such ease you'd think they were ice-skating. They're incredible, Thomas thinks to himself, these two guys who will likely never graduate, who are already so deep into drug habits that they look twice their age, and who were born a half-decade too early for Kurt Cobain to make grunge poetry of their lives.

Thomas scans the covers. Patrick Ewing is featured on the cover of *Sports Illustrated*. With his right arm extended and shoulders up near the rim, preparing as he is to drop some thunder down on the heads of the rival Orangemen, he looks less like a world-class athlete and more like a flying superhero. Meanwhile, on the cover of *Hoop*, Dr. J. is making a house call. He's in his road reds, his white number 6 shining beneath the house lights, the flecks of gray in the temples of his hair making the elevation he's getting as he leaps towards the basket all the more impressive. And on the cover of *The Sporting News* Dan Marino is preparing to throw one of his patented laser beams across the South Florida sky to an open receiver.

It's on an interior page of *Rolling Stone*, however, that Thomas pauses. Dressed in pirate shirt, purple coat, black go-go boots, Little Richard pompadour, and playing a white Telecaster guitar, Thomas studies the photograph. He notices that the performer's eyes are turned upwards, as if looking towards a God who drives a little red Corvette, a God who wants to party like it's 1999, a God who gets delirious every time the girl he loves is near.

At Thomas's school it's Michael Jackson territory. The girls wear

Thriller buttons and the boys blast "Billie Jean" while playing dodgeball on the blacktop. Entire recesses are taken up with contests where kids try to convince the assembled crowd that they've mastered the moonwalk. But Thomas doesn't partake. They don't know what they're missing, he thinks to himself. They don't seem to realize that there's a space alien from Minneapolis putting in real work, his voice possessed of a range that Michael doesn't have, his fingers doing things to a guitar that Michael needs Eddie Van Halen to match.

And it doesn't matter that whenever Thomas's father sees Prince on television all he can do is ask questions: Why is he wearing makeup? Where are his pants? What the hell is a raspberry beret? Though Thomas doesn't respond, he already knows the answer: because he's Prince and we're not.

It's become an obsession with Thomas, locating men who seem capable of the impossible. He pays attention at church on Sunday mornings not because he wants to worship Christ, but because he wants to know what the secret is. How it was that the reputed Son of God could step onto the sea and embark on a leisurely stroll. Thomas doesn't have doubts; he just has questions.

As he replaces the magazine and looks back up to see one of the skateboarders clear a parked Cutlass Sierra, he notices a flyer pasted onto the inside of the glass:

Independence Day Parade and Celebration, July 4th, Main Street, Huntington Beach

"Your mother would kill you," James says from behind him.

"No she won't."

"You're right. She'll kill me instead."

"You see? It's a win-win."

"Don't be a wise-guy, kid."

"I learned from the best."

"You can't teach what I've got."

As they leave the 7-Eleven Thomas continues to lobby James to let him go with him to Main Street.

"No way," James says. "I'm taking some girls with me. You'll cramp my style."

"I could be your wingman," Thomas insists.

"This isn't *Top Gun*, Goose. And you're too young to be a wingman."

"Goose? I'm Maverick."

"Are you out of your mind? You could be the Iceman. *Maybe.*"

"So it's settled?" Thomas says.

"I'm already regretting this."

"My father says you only regret the things you don't do in life."

"Yeah? Then let him take you to the parade."

James pauses, aware Thomas is not going to let this go.

"Alright. But try not to say anything."

"I won't."

"Nothing."

"Got it."

"At all."

"*Okay,*" Thomas says.

As they reenter the school grounds and walk towards the courts James begins to describe the wonders that await. Suddenly he's Scheherazade with a mullet, Marco Polo still a year away from a driver's license, telling tales of a world Thomas cannot believe is real. From the way James describes it, there will be women in bikinis small enough to fit inside a wallet, crowds large enough to be given favored nation trading status, bands loud enough to be heard from space. By the time James's monologue is over and they are back on the blacktop, Thomas no longer imagines an oversized beach party so much as an Old Testament bacchanal.

In other words, he can't wait.

"Looks like we've got ourselves a game," James says, as he nods towards the courts.

Thomas counts eight players, all of them looking between the ages of 16 and 18. A few of them stretch while several others get up shots. However, as he and James get closer, Thomas is struck by the fact that there appears to be none of the usual trash-talk. No one busts each others' balls, no one brags about the girls they're chasing at school, no one calls each another out over an imagined slight. Only here and there, he notices, the guys take turns motioning to one another with their hands, as if they were a fleet of baseball managers sending signs to a perpetual runner on first.

"Unreal," James says. "These mothers are deaf."

Years later Thomas will remember the way the players seemed to move as if they were on a string, everything eye contact, hand gestures, the occasional high-five. He'll remember that being on the court with them for the better part of two hours in silence made the game feel sacred, something not to be soiled with language. He'll remember that, unbelievably, even James was brought to silence, the presence of them inspiring a reverence for quiet that Thomas didn't know James possessed. And he will remember, after the games are over, the sight of those eight teenagers, none of whom would ever appear at the courts again, walking back in the direction of the parking lot like cowboys in a western only he and James would ever see.

"That was crazy," James says. "Like being in a silent movie."

"I've never seen one," Thomas says.

"For real?"

"Are they good?"

"You're not an American until you've seen a Charlie Chaplin movie," James says.

"Which one's your favorite?" Thomas asks.

"*City Lights*. The Little Tramp falls in love with a blind girl and tries to come up with the money to pay for an operation that will restore her sight."

"Sounds boring."

"Boring?" James says, almost offended.

"I don't like love stories," Thomas explains.

"It's not a love story. It's about a man finding his purpose in life."

"I already have one," he says.

"Yeah, what's that?"

"To be a better shooter than you."

"Keeping dreaming, kid."

They play several games of HORSE. James doesn't miss a single shot. After James heads home for the evening, Thomas continues to get shots up on his own for awhile before he sees his mother slip through the locked space in the chain-link fence and approach the court. Her arrival at the courts is a rare enough sight for him to know that something's going on.

"How were the games?" his mother asks, taking the ball from his hands and turning to shoot a set-shot from just beyond the lane.

"Everyone was deaf," Thomas says.

"James didn't say anything stupid, did he?"

"He didn't say anything at all."

"That's a first," his mother says, throwing the ball back to him. He dribbles the ball around his back and then makes a reverse layup with his off-hand.

"Nice," his mother says. "Did you learn that from Magic?"

"Yes. But it looks better when he does it."

"He's got fifteen years on you. Give it time."

For the next several minutes his mother rebounds his shots. After he has paused to catch his breath she says she wants to see how many free throws in a row he can make.

He gets to nineteen before one rolls out.

"Wow," she says. "Last time it was twelve."

"I want to get to one hundred."

"One hundred? That's an ambitious goal."

"I read that Larry Bird can make six hundred in a row."

"Well, then keep at it," his mother says, aware there's no point in trying to talk him out of whatever craziness he's gotten into his head.

After Thomas begins to shoot free throws again, his mother says, "Your father's mother died this morning. Or a few days ago. It wasn't clear on the phone. We didn't even know she'd been sick."

Thomas has never met his father's mother, only spoken to her a few times long-distance. No, that isn't true. He can't speak Farsi and his grandmother can't speak English. Instead he's listened to his grandmother tell him in Farsi how much she loves him, while his father listens in and translates for him, Thomas saying "thank you", and that he "loves her too", before handing the receiver back to his father.

Still. His grandmother. The woman in one of the many photographs that hangs in their apartment above the piano. She's still a young woman in the picture. Twenty-five, maybe thirty.

In the photograph she's wearing a blue scarf and a long black dress. She's standing in a large garden full of colorful flowers. She isn't smiling.

"That's at the Tomb of Hafez," his father has told him.

"Was Hafez her father?" Thomas asked.

"No," his father had laughed. "A famous poet."

"Was he any good?"

More laughter.

"Any good? He was the best there ever was."

His mother gestures for Thomas to throw her the ball. After she's caught it, she begins to dribble, challenging him to try to steal it.

"Your father's going back to Iran for the funeral," she says, moving fast enough to keep him from swiping at the ball.

"I thought they'd kill him if he went back," Thomas says, stopping. In truth, he doesn't know who "they" are. Only that there's a list, as he understands it, and his father's name is on it, and that there are men at the border who know he's on the list and have been waiting for him to try to come back. Or something like that.

"It won't be like that," his mother says, picking up the ball and looking at him. "It's different for funerals."

Thomas knows she's only saying this to make him feel better. His father is taking a risk. But even so. He loves his father for going back. And he loves his mother for lying to him about it. Love is a complicated thing, Thomas realizes. Especially between parents and children.

"How long will he be gone?" Thomas asks.

"A couple of weeks, probably. Maybe a month. Anyway there's nothing to worry about. But if your father seems sad tonight, I wanted you to know why."

They don't go straight home. Instead they stay on the blacktop for awhile longer. Thomas shows her a post move he saw Moses Malone use against the Supersonics. Then he tells her she's got to taste how cold the water is at the drinking fountain.

"You're right," his mother says after drinking from it.

"James used to tell me it was piped in from the Himalayas."

His mother laughs.

"James is quite the character."

"Do you think Grandma will still visit me in dreams sometimes?"

"Probably even more, I imagine," his mother says.

They take the long way back, walking across the grass that he and James had walked earlier in the afternoon while on their way to the 7-Eleven. They cross at the light, walking within the thick white lines of the crosswalk that shine like the lanes of an imaginary swimming pool.

"How old was Dad when he left Iran?" Thomas asks.

"18," his mother says, her eyes darting from left to right to make sure no car has decided to run the red.

"Rod is 17," he says.

"17 is too young to be so far from home," his mother says.

"Rod's father was tied to the railroad tracks," Thomas says, immediately feeling guilty for telling Rod's secret.

On the sidewalk now, his mother stops and looks at him.

"When was this?"

"I don't know. But that's why his mother sent him out here."

They begin walking again.

"There are some terrible people in this world," his mother says.

His father sits on the edge of the sofa and leans forward. A glass of water is on the table in front of him. On a second, smaller sofa to the right sits a man Thomas recognizes from his paper route. Building 36, Apartment 615. The man holds a can of Coca-Cola in his hand and raises it in greeting to Thomas.

"Here is the one who delivers the news!" the man says, his voice louder than Thomas is prepared for, his accent thick enough for it to take an extra second for Thomas to understand what he's said.

Thomas thinks the man looks like he could be related to his father. His hair is as thick as his father's, and his forearms are as full of the same dark, bushy hair. But where Thomas's father is casual, in khakis and white t-shirt, the man from 615 is in a full, freshly pressed suit, and his shoes are as shiny as the hood of a black limousine.

For the next few minutes Thomas is the center of the conversation. The man from 615 asks him about the NBA before peppering him with questions about his paper route. Thomas answers each question with enthusiasm, unaware that his arrival into the apartment has interrupted an important conversation. He will not find this out until years later, when Thomas's mother will tell him the man in 615 was the one with the contacts to get Thomas's father safely into Iran, and the one with two separate exit strategies prepared should things have gone badly once he'd crossed the border.

But for that night what Thomas will most remember is the smile on his father's face when his son begins to provide a play-by-play recap of Patrick Ewing blocking shots in the 1982 NCAA title game. He will remember his father clapping enthusiastically when he's finished his recap, even though his son is incapable of going more than a few hours at a time without mentioning Ewing's name, or wanting his parents to listen to the most recent amazing thing the Georgetown center has accomplished.

Hours later, after the man from 615 has gone, after Thomas's father has eaten a plate of spaghetti and several scoops of chocolate ice cream, and after his mother has completed a telephone conversation with her own parents, Thomas will reemerge from his room and relocate to the sofa. Thomas, his father, and mother will share a plate of sliced watermelon, and Thomas will ask his father what the death of his mother feels like.

His father will not know what to say. Not at first. Instead he'll look at Thomas's mother, then at the blank television screen, and then back at Thomas.

"The same as it did when I first boarded the plane for America."

"How did that feel?"

"Like I'd fallen down a well without a bottom."

"How long did the feeling last?"

"I don't know. I'll tell you when it's over."

"Is this the first person you've known that's died?" Thomas asks.

"No," his father says. "But it's different when it's your mother."

Thomas looks at his own mother and feels a wave of fear unlike anything he's ever experienced. The thought of living in a world where his mother no longer exists is something he can't even bring himself to imagine.

"I hope I die before you, Mom," he says.

"Don't say that," his mother responds. "That's not how it's supposed to work."

"Why not?"

"Because children are supposed to outlive their parents. Especially you."

"But I'd miss you every day."

"You'd better," his mother says, playfully pinching his nose. "But you'll still need to go on with your life, and enjoy it. That's why your father and I had you."

"To enjoy my life?"

"And to be a good person."

"Was your mother a good person?" Thomas asks his father.

His father nods, and begins to smile.

"The best."

With that Thomas's mother stands and crosses to the bookshelf, where the twenty or so LPs she owns are neatly stacked alongside several of her favorite books. After settling on the record she wants, she pulls it from its sleeve and places it onto the stereo. Seconds later the voice of Joni Mitchell fills the living room. It's the voice, Thomas thinks, of an angel too in love with the world to fly back to Heaven. He doesn't think he'll ever hear anything more beautiful.

"Who's this?" his father asks.

"Joni," his mother says, as if Thomas's father has simply forgotten the name of a mutual friend of theirs from college.

She returns to the sofa, and the three of them sit on the couch and listen to the record all the way through. Later on that night, after Thomas has fallen asleep on the sofa while his parents speak quietly, he'll dream that he has found the river Joni was singing about: the one magical enough for someone to have skated all the way across it. Only the one in his dream isn't a river that leads him away from where he is. It's a river that keeps leading him back to a place he never wants to leave.

The next morning Thomas will sleep through the sound of his parents saying their goodbyes in the living room. He won't remember his father coming into his room to kiss him on the cheek and to tell him to be a good boy. He won't see his mother stand at the window and watch her husband get into the passenger seat of a

Volvo sedan that belongs to a friend of the man from 615. He will not hear his mother crying on the sofa in the living room, aware that there are better than even odds she will never see her husband again, while Joni's record again plays on the turntable, her voice now like that of an older sister offering a younger sibling a warm shoulder to cry on.

3

THE DELI COUNTER IS LIKE A GLASS SUBMARINE. Thomas scans the meats and cheeses, the dressings and vegetables with a level of seriousness akin to an art historian trying to authenticate a painting believed to be by Rembrandt.

Coach Roth emerges from the back drying his hands with a white towel. He's wearing his usual outfit: long-sleeved, blue cotton shirt, black cargo pants dusted with flour, work boots he proudly boasts he's owned since the first week that he stepped foot onto American soil.

"Where's your father?" Coach Roth asks, the man with a full head of salt-and-pepper hair even though he's sixty-five, and with shoulders still broad from the one hundred pushups he does each night after closing, which are followed by a one-mile run in the small greenbelt a few blocks from his house.

"Don't you worry about having a heart attack?" Thomas often asks him.

"The heart attacks come when you stop doing your exercise," Coach Roth insists.

Thomas looks up at Coach Roth, who leans over the counter to perform their customary greeting, the two of them lightly bumping each other's fists, an old basketball greeting that Thomas never gets tired of engaging in.

"He went home," Thomas said.

Coach Roth seems to immediately understand the "home" to which Thomas refers. His eyebrows raise, and his eyes are suddenly filled with seriousness.

"Something has happened," Coach Roth says.

"His mother died," Thomas confirms.

With this news Mrs. Roth, a woman small enough to have been, during a particularly terrible storm a few years earlier, lifted by a strong gust of wind and carried halfway up the block with her umbrella acting as an accidental helicopter, appears from the back of the store. She comes to stand beside Coach Roth.

"The boy's grandmother," he says.

"I heard," Mrs. Roth says.

The deli is still twenty minutes away from its morning rush, when parishioners from the mosque at the end of the street, the Protestant church one block over, and the Quaker Friends gathering on Fairview Boulevard will all arrive more or less simultaneously, the desire for a good sandwich and a side of homemade potato salad doing, as Thomas's father often says, what religious faith is so often incapable of: getting everyone into the same room for long enough to make them realize they have too much in common to hate each other.

"How did she die?" Mrs. Roth asks, lifting the counter divider so that she is able to wrap her arms around Thomas before he's even able to answer.

Thomas doesn't know what to do except to respond in kind. However, every time he begins to soften his embrace, certain that she's about to pull away, Mrs. Roth only begins to squeeze him even tighter. It's not until, a good minute after the hug has begun, that Coach Roth breaks his wife's spell by saying, "The boy's going to die of hunger if you don't release him."

"The child needs to feel his feelings," she responds.

"As tightly as you're squeezing him," Coach Roth says, "he probably can't feel anything."

Around and around they go, this married couple who's the closest thing to an unintentional comedy duo Thomas has ever seen. Their constant two-way teasing the only way they seem capable of showing one another the abiding depths of their love.

She pulls away. Thomas notices there are tears in Mrs. Roth's eyes. She smiles at him and waves off her husband. She recites something from memory in Hebrew. Upon finishing, she says, "For good luck," she tells Thomas.

"This boy has a Catholic mother and a Muslim father," Coach Roth says. "He's already confused enough."

"Don't listen to him," she says to Thomas. "The man knows nothing about the mysteries of the Almighty."

As Mrs. Roth returns back behind the counter, Coach Roth points his knife at Thomas and says, "A special sandwich for you today. It'll make you a better defender."

"I averaged three steals a game last season. Remember?" Thomas says.

"Yes, but you gambled too much for them. What about all the times you were out of position and your man scored because you'd didn't get the steal you'd gone for?"

"No risk, no reward."

"Keep talking like that and I just might eat the sandwich myself."

"You wouldn't."

"Who's to say?" Coach Roth responds, winking at him. "Anything's possible."

Over the next few minutes Thomas watches Coach Roth work his magic. Tomatoes are cut, carrots and cucumbers sliced, cheese sprinkled. At the end of this impromptu show there's meat packed so tightly between two pieces of freshly made bread that Thomas will skip lunch altogether. After the sandwich is placed on a sheet of paper and then settled into the small boat of the plastic receptacle, Coach Roth looks at him and says, "Full stomach, full heart."

As Thomas eats he thinks about his father, and wonders whether he has safely arrived. He finds himself imagining what the clouds look like in the world his father has traveled to, whether the sunlight looks different, and whether, when it rains, the streets flood as easily as they do here. It's almost as if he were not picturing another country, but another planet entirely.

There are so many questions Thomas has never asked his father about Iran. He spends the majority of his lunch attempting to visualize his father's homeland from the handful of details his father has provided over the years. He imagines a place full of wells, soccer fields, graveyards, and shrines. He imagines households with no television sets, policemen who don't wear uniforms, and women who are never allowed to show their hair. He imagines gardens stretching out as far as the eye can see, old men tending flocks of sheep in rolling hillsides rising beyond the towns, and young girls picking apples on their way home from school. He imagines soldiers pointing guns at one another in the middle of ancient deserts, tombstones being destroyed by bombs that have missed their intended targets, and children no older than himself being forced to walk across fields full of land-mines.

The sight of Coach Roth standing in front of him with his hands on his hips, and with his apron and pants smudged with mustard and relish, pulls him out of his thoughts. Thomas looks towards the counter to see Mrs. Roth and two of her newly arrived adult cousins attending to the customers. Before Coach Roth even says a word Thomas thinks of the first time he met this man that he now loves like a second grandfather: the old man introducing himself to Thomas's team as their new coach on the first day of that season's practice. It didn't take more than ten minutes into that practice for Thomas to realize he'd met a man every bit as obsessed with hoops as he was.

"How is the sandwich?" Coach Roth asks.

"It's the best sandwich I've ever had," Thomas says.

"Right answer," Coach Roth says, sitting down.

As Coach Roth wipes a bit of mustard from his wrist, Thomas sees, for the briefest of seconds, a series of numbers tattooed onto Coach Roth's skin peek out from beneath his shirt-sleeve. He's never noticed them before.

"My mother won't let me get a tattoo," Thomas says.

"Good for her. A tattoo is a crime against the Lord."

"She won't let me get a mohawk either."

"A mohawk?"

"A haircut. Like Mr. T."

Coach Roth puts his face in his hands and emits a groan of frustration.

"I've never met anyone with more bad ideas than you."

"When did you get your tattoo?" Thomas asks.

"A long time ago. Before you were born."

"What are the numbers for?"

"It's a long story," Coach Roth answers, looking back towards the counter, clearly not wanting to talk about them.

Thomas worries he's hurt his coach's feelings.

"Sometimes I ask too many questions."

"There's no such thing. But sometimes people don't want to answer," Coach Roth says and pauses, as if considering whether to go on. Instead he changes the subject.

"How's your mother?"

"Good," Thomas says. "She sang this morning."

"I didn't know she was a singer."

"She sings in the choir every Sunday."

"Good for her," Coach Roth says. "A beautiful voice is a special thing."

"My father says it's his second favorite thing about her."

"What's his favorite thing about her?"

"That she thinks he's handsome."

"Your father has never lacked for confidence."

"He says his confidence is his second favorite thing about himself."

"What's his first?" Coach Roth asks, clearly amused.

"His humility."

The two of them laugh.

"When will your father return?"

"My mother says a few weeks. But she said there isn't anything to worry about."

"Of course there isn't. Your father has Allah with him."

"He says you don't call him that."

"He's right. We call him Adonai. Or Yahweh."

"God sure has a lot of names," Thomas says, taking a drink of his lemonade.

"A rose by any other name is still a rose."

"Did Yahweh say that?"

"No. Shakespeare."

"Who's Shakespeare?"

"A great poet."

"What does it mean?"

"That it doesn't matter what you call the Lord, so long as you believe in him."

"I'm not sure that I do," Thomas says.

"Why not?" Coach Roth asks, as the deli begins to fill up.

"I've never seen him."

"What does that matter?"

"How can I believe in something I've never seen?"

"You pass the ball to teammates you don't see all the time. I've watched you do it."

"That's different. I know they're there."

Coach Roth leans back and looks up at the sky in exasperation.

"Exactly. It's the same with Yahweh."

"Do you ever pray to Yahweh when you're coaching our team?"

"Of course."

"What do you pray to him about?"

"That my star player will work harder on defense."

"Does he ever answer?"

"Yes."

"What does he say?"

"That there are certain things even he cannot control."

An hour later Thomas is back at Matsuya. The teams are unequally divided. Three on one side, four on the other. But Mississippi Rod counts as two, especially on a day like this when he's feeling it, seemingly unable to miss. By 1 p.m. it's nearly 100 degrees, so the players regularly stop mid-game to run to the water fountain, or to swig from the glass Gatorade bottles many of them have brought to the courts.

Other than Rod, Thomas has never seen the rest of these guys before, which means he often goes several possessions without anyone passing him the ball. This always happens when he's playing with people he doesn't know. They look at his youth and diminutive size and are immediately convinced he's a weak link, a charity case who likely isn't strong enough to get the ball to the basket. The few times Thomas does touch the ball he passes it almost as quickly, worrying that to make even a single move might turn his teammates against him completely.

Still, he couldn't be happier. The weather is great, Rod is making everybody look stupid with the moves he's putting on them, and Thomas is loving the new high-tops his mother's purchased for him. They make him feel like he isn't running so much as gliding.

During the next water break, after his team has lost its third game in a row as a result of Rod doing his best World B. Free impression by filling it up from all over the court, Rod pulls Thomas aside.

"Listen, shorty. Next time you touch the ball, shoot it."

"But what if they don't pass it to me anymore?"

"Who cares? You've got more game than the three of them combined. This is a good test for you. You can't let bad teammates scare you out of playing your game. Remember, you're either a player or your not."

Thomas follows Rod's advice a minute or so after play resumes. There's a long rebound, and one of Thomas's teammates can't get to it in time. Thomas darts in, scoops up the ball and heads the other way, at one point putting it behind his back to keep one of his opponents from stealing it. Although a few of his teammates keep calling for the ball and wildly waving their hands for him to give it up, certain he's in way over his head and is seconds away from turning it over, he looks them off and heads towards the basket. After he gives a little hesitation move that freezes the defender in front of him, he pulls up from just inside the top of the key.

As the ball's in mid-air one of the teammates who'd been yelling for Thomas to pass registers his frustration by shouting in disgust, "No!"

Nothing but net.

Thomas turns and heads back down the court. He makes eye contact with Rod, who gives him a knowing smile. Even though there are no high-fives from his teammates, Thomas doesn't care.

"Forget them," he thinks to himself, remembering Rod's advice. "*You're either a player or you're not.*"

Each time Thomas lucks into the ball for the rest of the afternoon he doesn't even think about passing. By game's end he's hit three more shots: two jumpers and a layup he makes in traffic that gets a friendly bounce off the back rim. By the third make, the guys on his team have begun to high-five him, marveling at the fact that the kid appears to have game after all. But Thomas isn't having any of it. He doesn't smile, doesn't engage, doesn't speak. Instead he stays focused and waits for the next opportunity to make things happen.

Forty-five minutes later, as everyone's begun to slowly head off in the direction of their cars, their homes, or the nearest bus stop, Thomas finds himself wishing Earl had been here to see how he'd kept the defense honest by shooting from the outside.

"That's what I'm talking about," Rod says, hanging back to talk to Thomas for a few minutes before leaving himself. He palms Thomas's skull with his hand and affectionately gives it a shake. "You made those guys look bad, shorty."

As Thomas smiles, Rod snatches the ball from his hands and swoops towards the opposite basket for a dunk. Thomas would give anything to be able to do what Rod does with such ease just once in his life. In fact, he dreams about it more often than he does anything else. The only thing that varies in his dreams are the kinds of dunks that he performs. Sometimes he does a 360 degree spin before cramming the ball home, a la Gerald Wilkins in the open court. Other times he does a classic double-pump, just like the one Michael Jordan did last year on that fast-break against the Knicks, where it seemed like he'd grown wings and begun to fly straight out of Madison Square Garden entirely. When Rod is preparing to return back down the court for another dunk, Thomas calls out, "Do the double-clutch reverse."

Rod begins beyond the half court stripe, making a wide arc upon approach. As he leaps he turns his back to the rim, his tongue wagging in an homage to Jordan, and holds the ball down beside his ankles before bringing it up and over his head just in time to cram it through the rim. After he lands, Thomas says, "You're going to do that for the Lakers someday."

"Just as long as it's not the Celtics," Rod responds.

"Or you could play for the Knicks."

"I'd be down with that. Ewing and I'd make a good one-two punch," Rod says, before adding, "but it'd be great to play for one of the less famous franchises. The Bucks or the Cavs. Maybe the Mavericks. Go somewhere and build a legacy instead of trying to live up to one already in place."

"Just don't go to the Clippers," Thomas says

"I'm a dreamer, kid. But I ain't crazy."

The two of them play a game of HORSE before heading home. Thomas hangs in for a little while, but Rod puts him away with a few shots from well beyond the corner sideline.

"Don't feel bad, shorty," Rod says, putting his arm around him. "There wasn't a man in Mississippi who could keep up with me either."

Rod places the ball back into Thomas's hands.

"Have a good 4th. Be careful around the fireworks."

"You too, Rod."

They exchange high fives before Rod jogs off towards the apartment he shares with his uncle, a man Thomas will never meet.

Thomas thinks about getting up some more shots before calling it a day, but instead he climbs the fence and crosses the street. Rather than heading home, he detours and takes the first walkway into the complex instead of the second. After ascending the stairs to James's apartment, he knocks on the door.

James's mother answers. She's wearing a denim cowboy shirt, faded blue jeans, and an unholy amount of heavy makeup. She squints at Thomas as she inhales on her cigarette, as if he were a door-to-door salesman come to sell her a set of encyclopedias, or on the assurance of an afterlife if she were only willing to join the Jehovah's Witness. From inside the apartment, Thomas can make out the unmistakable sounds of "The Gambler" playing on the stereo. He wonders if the woman owns any other records.

"Is James here?" Thomas asks.

"Maybe," she says, blowing a smoke ring above his head. When Thomas realizes an invite is not forthcoming, he says, "Can I come in and see him?"

At that she neither nods nor speaks, but simply disappears back into the house, leaving the door open so that he can enter. Thomas does so, closing the door behind him as he steps inside.

The walls of James's bedroom are covered with Black Sabbath and Led Zeppelin posters, and his tape-deck is playing Van Halen's

"Beautiful Girls", one of Thomas's favorites. The song always makes him think of the woman in Apartment 226, the one who lays out at the pool in a black bikini that her breasts always seem on the verge of spilling from.

"I don't think your mother likes me," Thomas says.

"Don't take it personally," James says. "She doesn't like anybody."

"How come?"

"She's always been that way."

"She sure loves Kenny Rogers though," Thomas says.

"Tell me about it."

Thomas looks around the room, taking in the photograph of Ozzy Osbourne appearing to bite the head off what looks like a live bird.

"Ozzy's scary," Thomas says.

"It's just theater, kid. He doesn't mean it."

"Tell that to the bird."

"The bird isn't real."

"It looks real."

"It isn't. It's as fake as pro wrestling."

"What're you talking about?"

"Nothing."

"Can I still go with you tomorrow to the pier?"

"Depends."

"On what?"

"You've got to ask your mother."

"Why?"

"Because my mother already wants to kill me. My girlfriend's mother too. There's too many prices on my head."

"Okay, I'll ask her," Thomas says, already ninety-three percent certain his mother will say no.

"If she says yes," James answers, "I'll meet you in front of the Electric Chair at 10:30 tomorrow morning. Now beat it. Sherry's coming over tonight, and I've got to finish making this mix tape before she gets here."

"Are you putting any other Van Halen songs on it?" Thomas asks.

"Maybe. I haven't decided."

"Put 'Jump' on it. And 'Dance the Night Away.' I love that one."

"I'm making it for her, kid. Not for you."

"Can you make one for me after you've finished?"

"You don't seem to get the point of a mixtape," James says, carefully writing down the next song title.

"What'd you mean?"

"Never mind."

"You say that to me a lot. How come?"

"Because I don't have time to explain all the things in the world that you don't understand."

"Then who will?"

"Santa Claus."

"Very funny."

A minute later Thomas is bounding down the stairs, headed for home. Turning right at the walkway, he moves back out onto the sidewalk. He passes the parked cars, most of them long past their expiration dates, an assortment of Buicks, Chevys, and Fords that all look like metallic fossils from a bygone age when the American automobile was still king, a time as long ago and far away as the Pleistocene Era that he's learning about in school. At the end of the street the green light at the intersection of Slater and Ward shines like a symbol in a great American novel Thomas won't read for another several years, while across the street a couple of kids are kicking a soccer ball around with their father in the field closest to the basketball courts.

As he reenters the complex he's greeted by the sounds of Buddhist chanting coming from Apartment 110, and by the sight of the people in 412 having a barbecue on their balcony. One of the men, a heavyset guy in his early 50s, sways as he holds a bottle of beer in his hand, as if he were one false step away from falling over the railing. Thomas doesn't pay it much mind. It wouldn't be the first time that had happened.

Further on, in the doorway to Apartment 416, a woman in a waitressing uniform fumbles with her keys while trying not to drop her groceries, and at the pool, an old man in wrinkled blue pants, his trouser bottoms cuffed to keep them from getting wet, dips his toes into the water several times before putting his shoes back on and heading for home.

Years later, when Thomas is introduced to the poems of Walt Whitman, he'll come to think that these evenings were his own version of Whitman's "Crossing Brooklyn Ferry", the Sunwood Apartments standing in for the East River. But at the moment he has more pressing concerns than to locate the poetry in his surroundings. As he climbs the stairs, he hopes his mother is enough of a patriot to let her ten-year-old son spend the Fourth of July at the Main Street Pier with James Bianchi and what's certain to be a guaranteed cast of drunken thousands.

When he enters, his mother is sitting on the sofa watching a documentary about something called Woodstock. On the screen a man in a blue bandana and with just about the coolest facial hair he's ever seen is playing a guitar solo that makes Thomas feel as if he's witnessing a miracle.

"Who's that?"

"Carlos Santana," his mother says, gesturing for him to join her on the sofa.

"When did this happen?"

"A long time ago."

"He's good," Thomas says, nodding towards the guitarist.

"Yes, he is," his mother says.

The camera pans out to show an audience full of young men and women wearing beads and paisley, many of them with flowers and mud in their hair. Most of them are dancing. All of them look happy. Almost too happy, he thinks. Like the kind of happiness you have when deep down you know sad times are just around the corner.

"There's a lot of people there."

"There were," his mother says. "But not enough."

He doesn't know what his mother means by this but is in too much of a hurry to change the subject to ask for clarification.

"Can I go with James to the beach tomorrow?"

His mother looks at him, then back at the television set. She picks the remote up from the coffee table and mutes the program.

"It's the 4th of July parade tomorrow, isn't it?"

"James said I could go if you said it was alright."

"I don't know if that's such a good idea," she says. "It's gong to be crowded, and things might get out of control."

"It won't be just James and me. There will be some girls with him too," Thomas adds, immediately realizing this additional informa-tion might hurt, rather than help, his cause.

"What do you think your father would say?"

"He'd say my first mistake was asking you."

"He would say that, wouldn't he?" his mother says, laughing. Then she adds, "Do you know that when you were a baby your father threw out your crib?"

"Why'd he do that?"

"Because he said it was too much like putting you in jail."

"I'll be with James," Thomas emphasizes.

"That's what I'm worried about."

His mother turns the volume back on. The man named Carlos Santana has transitioned into another solo. This one is slower, each note held long enough for the audience to name it, describe it, and fall in love with it. Thomas wonders if Prince has heard this man play. He figures Prince would love his music, and that it might even inspire some of his own.

"I wanted to go to Woodstock," his mother says.

"Why didn't you?" Thomas asks.

"My parents wouldn't let me."

He doesn't say anything. He realizes he might be home free if he doesn't blow it by over-talking.

"Tell James I'll kill him if something happens," she says.

"He knows that. He said it already."

"Of course, his mother might beat me to it."

"He said that too."

"Wear a hat," his mother says. "And lots of sunscreen."

"I will. I promise."

"And if anyone offers you anything to drink or smoke, you say no."

"Cross my heart," Thomas says.

That's that. They spend the next hour watching the documentary together. Thomas doesn't recognize any of the performers but likes the music anyway. Loves it, even. Especially when someone named Creedence Clearwater starts to play. His voice sounds like what Thomas imagines Jesus might have sounded like after a few nights of riverboat gambling.

"Maybe you can go to the next Woodstock, Mom."

"There won't be a next one. That world didn't last as long as it should have."

"Why not?"

"Because too many people would rather drop bombs than dance."

"You think that'll ever change?"

"I hope so."

"I hope so too," he says.

Thomas thinks of the images of dead bodies in the streets that he saw on the news last Sunday, when he and his father had sat in front of the television together. He wonders whether his father thinks the world will ever change. But a few moments later he puts the thought out of his mind and focuses on the concert. Creedence is asking the audience if they have ever seen the rain, and a few moments later Thomas's mother begins to softly sing along, her voice pretty enough for him to wish she had not only been able to go to Woodstock, but to perform at it. The crowd would have loved her. Maybe she and Joni Mitchell could have even sung a duet together.

"THERE HE IS," HE SAYS, LOCATING JAMES AMONG THE CROWD THAT HAS ALREADY OVERTAKEN MAIN STREET. James is standing a few feet from the entrance to the Electric Chair, a clothing shop whose window mannequins are wearing an assortment of leather outfits, platform shoes, and sheer miniskirts. On the roof of the store is a sign featuring a man strapped into a neon-colored chair, his hair standing on end, his face contorted into something resembling deranged joy. James is dressed as he always is when he isn't shooting hoops, in stone-washed blue jeans, a white t-shirt, and black high-tops. But it's the three girls James is with that Thomas cannot stop staring at: two of them are dressed in bikini tops and cutoff denim shorts, while the third, a brunette with a deep tan and a broad smile, wears a red-white-and-blue print bikini, white low-top sneakers, and what appears to be a red-white-and-blue beaded chain around her waist.

"Well, they love their country," his mother says as she pulls the car to the curb. "I'll give them that."

His mother's already given him the speech three times on the drive over: don't ingest anything other than hamburgers and fries; don't go off on your own; don't handle any fireworks; and, most importantly, don't wander away from James.

"And if you get separated," she begins to repeat.

"Go to the payphone in front of the Shake Shack and call you,"

Thomas answers.

"That's right. Don't forget," his mother says. "Now go have fun."

He's out the door and across the street before his mother can tell him, for the fourth time that morning, that she loves him.

"For future reference," James says as he approaches. "Always have your mom drop you off at least two blocks away."

"Leave him alone," the girl in the American Flag bikini says.

"Thomas," James says. "Meet Sherry." And then, nodding at the other two girls, both of whom are distracted by the sight of a man riding a unicycle down the middle of the street while playing a trumpet, adds, "Jennifer, Karen, meet Thomas."

Sherry extends her hand for a shake. Jennifer and Karen don't appear to be interested in what James has said, nor do they, when their attention drifts back to the group, seem interested in Thomas at all. As the five of them begin to walk in the direction of the pier, they notice a fight has broken out several feet ahead of them. A surfer in flower-print board shorts seems to have taken issue with a bald-headed guy who's got a skull-and-crossbones tattooed onto the side of his face. Moments later, when the inevitable punch is thrown and the bald man is lying on his back, James leads them across the street and says, "That's not a good sign."

"What'd you mean?" Thomas asks.

"I mean a guy just got his nose broken and it's not even 11 a.m. Wait until people start drinking for real."

"What kind of drinking are they doing now?"

"Warmup drinking."

"What's that?"

"You know when you stretch before playing a game?"

"Yes."

"Same thing."

As they head south on Main Street there's so much happening around them that it's impossible for Thomas to take everything in. From the young man sitting on a pristine Harley-Davidson motorcycle; to the group of women in red-white-and-blue face-paint with t-shirts reading "Ronnie's Girls" on the front; to the band performing on a small riser in front of the Brewery dressed like punks but playing note-perfect covers of KISS and AC/DC; to the women in bathing suits so awe-inspiring that he can't believe they're even legal, Thomas marvels at the world he's surrounded by. If anything, he thinks, it's even better than James said it would be, broken noses or not.

Closer to Pacific Coast Highway Thomas spots a few of the board-walk regulars he often sees when he comes to the beach: the old man with the parrot on his shoulder; the shirtless man with a boa constrictor draped around his neck; the group of placard-carrying born-agains walking up and down the street telling everyone that Jesus Died For Their Sins. Summer or winter, rain or shine, the latter group especially is always out here, incapable of seeing the beach as existing for anything other than to remind people that they are most likely going to hell.

When Thomas pauses to stare at a man on a ladder decorating the side of Jack's Surf Shop with an almost-finished mural—featuring a group of Mexican men marching through what appears to be a field of grapes—he's pulled forward by a sudden hand.

"Come on," Sherry says, with the same kindness in her voice that it had when she told James not to make fun of him. "We don't want to lose you."

They cross PCH against the light, and on the other side it appears that Jennifer and Karen want ice cream from a stand located just to the right of the pier.

"Have you seen the line?" James asks in disbelief. "It starts in San Francisco."

The girls appear unmoved by his protestations.

"Fine," James says. "Sherry?"

"Nothing for me, thank you. Thomas and I'll meet you at the contest."

Thomas is about to ask what contest when his attention is captured by the sight of a basketball game in full swing at the court a few hundred yards south of the pier.

"You want to go and watch?" Sherry asks, sensing his interest.

"Yes," he says, nodding.

"Me too. Come on."

As they approach Thomas is surprised at the crowd that's congregated to watch the game. There are so many onlookers, in fact, that it takes him and Sherry a solid minute before they find a good spot along the southern sideline from which to watch.

"Can you see?" Sherry asks.

Thomas nods, and then looks out at the court to watch the game.

He sees Earl immediately. He's wearing a white jersey with the word *Nets* stitched across the chest, a pair of baggy blue shorts, and two knee braces large enough to resemble pieces of heavy artillery. Even among this group of big men, Earl stands a few inches taller than everyone else. It's possible, Thomas now realizes, Earl might indeed stand 7 feet in his sneakers.

It's an intense game, given that the players know a loss, considering how many men are waiting to play, means they won't see the court again for the better part of an hour. And within thirty seconds Thomas realizes there's some serious talent assembled. In fact, he's seen several of the players on the Pac-10 telecasts on Sunday afternoons, lacing it up for Division I schools like UCLA, USC, Oregon,

Washington, Stanford, and Cal-Berkeley during the season. A few others are fringe NBA players, including a journeyman Thomas recognizes as Maurice Johnson, a veteran enforcer who currently comes off the bench for the Warriors. Johnson is all shoulders and biceps, mustache and elbows, and he crashes the offensive boards like he's just discovered his wife's been cheating on him. Thomas can't believe his good luck. He's never been to an NBA or college game in person, and he's somehow just stumbled onto a pickup game stacked with nearly as many top-level players as he would find at any of those.

It's Johnson who's matched up with Earl. Though Earl has a few inches on him, Johnson tries to use his significant weight advantage to muscle Earl out of the lane every time he tries to post on the block. He's successful at it, more or less, as Earl typically winds up receiving the ball a foot or so outside of the lane. But time and again it makes no difference. Earl scores at will on an array of post moves so beautiful Thomas wishes his father were here to see it with him.

Earl's footwork is so good it doesn't matter that it often looks like he's moving in quicksand. Even though he must be carrying an extra twenty pounds on account of those braces, he gets to whatever spot on the floor he wants, and once he's arrived, he settles down to the business of taking it to his opponents with an array of jump-hooks, finger-rolls, and tomahawk-dunks that Thomas thinks are works of art.

He's so dialed in on Earl's mastery of the game that it takes Thomas several minutes to realize Sherry's still holding his hand, and an additional few to become aware of the surrounding conversation that's slowly moving through the assembled crowd like an unofficial game of telephone.

"That's Earl Lewis, ain't it?"

"None other."

"Didn't he run with the Doctor in '75?"

"Won a couple of titles with him too."

"There was no one like him before he blew out his knee."

"How'd it happen?"

"Came down on Artis Gilmore's foot."

"No, it was Zelmo Beatty's."

"It was neither. He blew it out diving into the stands for a loose ball."

"Don't think so. Slipped on a wet spot. Freak thing."

"You're both wrong. He banged it against the stanchion after being fouled by Mel Daniels."

"Nah, a jealous girlfriend hit him with a crowbar."

"For real?"

"Don't you remember? Car accident. He broke three ribs too."

"I'd forgotten."

"Time flies, don't it?"

"It's undefeated."

"You're right about that."

Thomas absorbs everything he's hearing and, not for the first time in his young life, he wishes he'd been born a decade earlier so he could've followed the ABA. He's heard the stories, and even seen what little highlights there are from some of the games, but mostly that league is something he can't access, a hardwood Atlantis buried too far beneath the surface of a time before national television to call back up. It's as he finds himself daydreaming about Earl running the high pick-and-roll with Charlie Scott that Earl, a few seconds after spinning baseline for the game-winning layup, jogs up the sideline, points at Thomas, and gives him a high-five before being congratulated by his teammates for his stellar play.

"Do you know him?" Sherry asks, surprised at Earl's acknowledgment of Thomas.

"He lives in Sunwood. I met him a few days ago. He was really nice."

"James is going to be impressed."

A moment later a garbled voice on the loudspeaker from back in the direction of the pier makes an announcement that Thomas can't quite make out.

"Come on," Sherry says, hurriedly pulling him away from the court. "The contest's starting."

He looks back one more time to see Earl drop in a jump-hook over the outstretched hands of two defenders to start the next game before he and Sherry are swallowed into the thick of the crowd.

There are, Thomas discovers, actually two contests happening simultaneously: one on the water and one on the stage. The former consists of surfers riding what seem to him to be unimaginably large waves, the type that look capable of killing anyone who loses their balance and goes under. James seems to agree as, looking out at one particular surfer who's staying barely ahead of the collapsing wave he's riding, he says, "That's some Jonah-and-the-Whale madness right there."

"I didn't know Jonah surfed."

"Course he surfed. They all did. Jesus won the O.P. Invitational three years running."

"What happened the fourth year?" Thomas asks, laughing.

"He decided he didn't need a board anymore. Just walked out onto the waves and started showing off. They disqualified him."

Sherry playfully rolls her eyes at Thomas while the other two girls talk to a couple of tanned surfers.

The latter contest, which begins a minute later, consists of a parade of women in a variety of bathing suits walking across the stage to roars of applause from the audience. To the right of the stage, a group of men and women sit at a large table holding up placards with numbers written on them. The participants all appear to be between the ages of twenty and thirty, and possessed of varying degrees of boldness in their choice of bikinis. When a dark-haired girl in a small red number and high white heels struts out onto the makeshift catwalk, Sherry, Jennifer, and Karen all begin to cheer excitedly. Thomas looks towards James for an explanation.

"That's Sherry's older sister," James says. "Vivian."

It occurs to Thomas that Sherry and Vivian's mother must be the greatest-looking woman on Planet Earth, a cross between Kim Basinger and Wonder Woman.

As he watches Vivian walk to the edge of the stage, place one hand on her hip, and wave to the audience, he finds himself momentarily wondering if he's chosen the wrong pastime. After all, you don't see women like Sherry and Vivian hanging around the basketball courts. Surfers, Thomas suspects, may be onto something he hasn't previously considered.

"Does Vivian have a boyfriend?" Thomas asks.

"What'd you think?" James says. "Look at her. She'll have a boyfriend for the next thirty years. Even when she gets married, she'll have a boyfriend. Probably a few of them."

As Thomas tries to make sense of what James has said, three men in the audience suddenly jump onto the stage and begin attempting to forcibly remove the bathing suit tops of a number of the contestants. Suddenly a collective, atonal roar rises up from the crowd that's unlike anything Thomas has ever heard. It sounds like an angry lion's been plugged into an amplifier. The women on the stage begin to scatter. A few of the judges leap onto the stage in an attempt to restore order. The man who was emceeing the show hits one of the attackers on the head with his microphone before being pushed off the stage entirely.

In the years ahead it will be impossible for Thomas to figure out just how long the five of them stood there, watching in disbelief at the seemingly simultaneous outbreak of an assortment of sights—security members vainly attempting to clear the stage, a man smashing a beer bottle across the face of a police officer and then shouting unintelligibly into the microphone, several people in the crowd pushing towards the front of the stage like a series of sunburned dominos—but he'll never forget Sherry grabbing his hand for the second time that afternoon and saying, "Come on, Thomas!"

The five of them head in the direction of the boardwalk, though their flight is consistently interrupted by swarms of people moving in several directions at once. Several fights seem to have simultaneously broken out around them, and it takes them a few minutes to make it to the boardwalk. Once there, Thomas sights a middle-aged man on the sidewalk several feet above where they stand, raise a trashcan over his head, Atlas-style, and heave it down onto the sand below. It strikes a man attempting to unlock his bicycle from the rack where he's parked it, immediately sending him to the ground, blood trickling from a cut above his eye.

They make their way up the stairs and onto the sidewalk, only to find the chaos has already spread there as well. People throw beer cans at the cars on PCH, while a few have even begun to take to the hoods of a few of the stopped cars in what seems to Thomas either rage or celebration. It seems impossible that the craziness of a few men has infected so many others in such a short amount of time, yet there's no denying that it has.

As they begin to weave through the stopped cars, Thomas sights a shirtless man charge headfirst into the torso of a police officer several feet away. The two men grapple on the ground in the middle of the crosswalk, like WWF wrestlers who have continued their grudge match outside of the ring. A few seconds later the sound of a gunshot so startles Thomas that he stops short to see what's happened. As he watches the shirtless man place his hands to his newly wounded shoulder, Thomas realizes he's lost hold of Sherry's hand.

All he can do for the next several moments is to allow himself to be carried along by the energy of the mob. The crowd is like an angry elephant, or a wave that has continued to gather force even after reaching dry land. Either way, for the first time since the riot began a few minutes earlier, Thomas is afraid.

He tries to go against the momentum of the crowd, and to do what he's seen Eric Dickerson and Walter Payton, his two favorite NFL running backs, accomplish on the football field: cut back and see if he can reach daylight in a place no one else has thought to look. Remaining low, he makes his move, his face at times banging into the waists, stomachs, and hands of those moving wildly around him. But after enduring a solid ten seconds of this he finds himself on the other side of the street, in front of a liquor store whose owner is wielding a shotgun to scare off potential looters.

He moves further down Main Street, in the direction of the phone booth his mother had told him to use if he got separated from his friends. But he's forced to pause when two men carrying the largest surfboard he's ever seen decide to throw it through the window of a tattoo parlor just ahead of him, making it temporarily impossible for him to continue on his way. To avoid the shattered glass, he circles out into the street, passing a girl, sixteen or so, who's down on her knees on the pavement, looking around in apparent surprise that no one's thought to ask if she's alright.

Finally he makes it to the Shake Shack, only to find the phone booth is no longer a phone booth. Instead it's a glass canoe, laid out horizontally on the ground, its yellow pages like the vestiges of an exposed, jaundiced heart. He stops and looks back in the direction of PCH, wondering if he has perhaps outpaced James and Sherry, and might be able to find them if he moves back towards the pier. As he starts to do this, he's stopped almost immediately by what appears to be a mass of fog into which people are disappearing for seconds at a time before reappearing, their eyes burning, their breath short, their language filled with obscenities. The police have arrived, he realizes, and they've brought their tear gas with them.

He cuts through the alley behind the Penny Lane record store, its windows smashed, its aisles and aisles of LPs in the process of being turned over by a handful of individuals. Yet at the end of the alley he comes upon a young couple, a woman in blue jeans and a pink polo shirt, a man in green Army fatigue pants and a black tank-top, who are making out against a mural. The scene reminds him of the photograph his grandparents have in the den of their house, where a sailor kisses a woman on the black-and-white streets of New York City.

When he again reaches the intersection at PCH and Main, he stops and surveys the landscape. Across the street several men are in the process of toppling the statue of the Original Surfer, as if he were not merely a symbol of man's elemental communion with the sea, but the bust of an authoritarian leader the proletariat has finally decided to overthrow. The craziness of the hour is such that only a few people even seem to turn from their own machinations to register awe at the sight. It's a maelstrom of chaos, and Thomas worries that he's running out of moves. He stops. Considers his surroundings. Tries to spot another phone booth. Nothing doing.

It's another several moments before he happens to turn his gaze southward to the basketball court. At first he can't believe it, as if what he were witnessing were a time-lapsed mirage: ten men still moving up and down the court in unison with one another, either oblivious or, more likely, entirely disinterested in the madness occurring so close to where they're playing. He feels a rush of elation at his discovery, as if he's stumbled onto the gate-key for the Garden of Eden at the exact moment the world from which he's fleeing is going up in flames.

He pauses to make certain that Earl is one of the remaining players. He is. With this knowledge in hand Thomas looks up and down PCH, sees he's got a little daylight, and books it. Upon reaching the other side he slows into a jog, at first keeping his eyes on the court, but then letting them drift to the sea itself, where there not only remain several surfers in the water, but plenty of bathers still laying out at the shore. In the years ahead he'll think this is the moment where he learned the secret to a good life is to never stop doing what it is you love, no matter what's happening around you. People are throwing bottles at one another? Just keep working on your jumper. Everyone is destroying the very neighborhoods they call home? Focus on the rim as you stand at the free-throw line preparing to shoot. Be in the world but not of it. Love your fellow man but don't do as he does. Or something like that.

Upon arriving at the courts he slows to a walk and goes to stand on the sidelines. It's on the next change of possession, as Earl's team heads back to play defense, when Earl notices Thomas has returned. The level of surprise on Earl's face is such that Thomas worries he might no longer be a welcome sight at the courts. But a few moments later, at the next dead ball, Earl jogs over to where Thomas is standing.

"Where's your friend?"

"I can't find her."

"You call your parents?"

"The phone booth's broken."

"You're not hurt, are you kid?"

Thomas shakes his head.

"No, but I'm not sure what to do, Earl. I need to find another pay phone."

Earl looks back at the court, aware the other players are ready to resume.

"Hang out for a few more minutes, kid. This is the last game. I'll drive you home afterwards."

"You sure?"

"Absolutely, kid. I'm running out of gas anyways. These knees need a little rest."

"Ok. Thanks, Earl."

Thomas is amazed at how different the world seems here, only a few hundred yards from the chaos. When, a minute or so later, he hears a large boom that's rapidly followed by several staccato bursts he's certain are more gunshots, it feels far enough away for him to return his attention to the game in time to see Earl annihilate his defender with a baseline drop-step and reverse-layup combo that wins the game for his team.

"Damn, Earl," one of his opponents says. "You should be doing that in the NBA, not on chumps like us."

A few of the other guys laugh, nod in agreement, and trade high-fives and half-hugs as they begin to change their shirts, drink from thermoses full of cold water and soda, and unlace their high tops.

"It ain't too late yet," another player says. "You're old but you're not *ancient.*"

At this all of them break into laughter, Earl included, as he pretends to raise his fists and challenge the guy, a high-flyer Thomas recognizes as a small forward for Arizona State, to a boxing match.

For another few minutes the players talk as they begin to pack up their duffels and wind down from the hard hours of competition. To Thomas's surprise the talk doesn't concern the craziness occurring just up the street. Instead the conversation centers around the state of the Lakers, the dominance of the Big East Conference in college hoops, and the relative merits of Grandmaster Flash, LL Cool J, and the Treacherous Three, before a few of the elder statesmen of the group, Earl included, engage in a brief debate over two musicians Thomas has never heard of. Decades later, Thomas would come to understand that dedicated athletes shared the same ability to block out any and all surrounding distractions as completely as the most committed Buddhist monk.

"Teddy Pendergrass, all day."

"You crazy? 'Love T.K.O.'s' got nothing on 'Mercy Mercy Me.'"

"Listen, I love Marvin as much as the next guy, but that Motown production had too much money on it. Made a man tryin' to sing about what was happenin' in the streets sound like he was sittin' in a limousine and just passin' through."

"Besides, I've got no love for a man who let the Jackson Five walk."

"Berry Gordy?"

"They should've taken the company from him right then and there."

"That wasn't Marvin's fault. Gordy didn't even want to release *What's Going On*. Marvin had to fight to make that happen."

"Besides, ease up on Berry."

"The man *did* discover Stevie Wonder."

"You think somebody else wouldn't have instead?"

"I'm just sayin'."

"Teddy P. All day. The Spinners too."

"You all are forgetting Eddie Floyd."

"And what about Johnny Taylor?"

"I don't care what any of you say. It's Otis and James and then it's everyone else."

There's more playful banter and handshakes before the inevitable splintering that comes when it's time for everyone to vanish back into the lives that are waiting for them away from the court. Thomas never likes these moments. They always seem like little funerals, memorials for a few hours of basketball that will never happen again. In the back of his head, he's always worried that the next day at the courts will be the one when no one besides himself shows up to play.

"Crazy afternoon," Earl says to Thomas as the two of them look up at the continuing chaos at PCH and Main.

"But you kept playing," he answers.

"What else was there to do? Start throwing bottles? No point in that."

"I don't know why people do that."

"Don't think on it too much, kid. It'll never make any sense. And they'll never stop doing it."

"That's sad."

"It is what it is."

"People in the crowd said you played with Dr. J."

"A long time ago."

"In the ABA?"

Earl nods, drapes his duffel bag across his shoulder as he and Thomas begin walking further south.

"With the Nets," Earl says.

"Did you win any titles?"

"Two. In '74 and '75. But I was just a kid then. Didn't know how special it was. Figured every year was going to be like that. And then you realize years later that the good times never last as long as you think they're going to."

"When did you hurt your knee?"

Before he can answer, Earl nods and says hello to an old man sitting in the back of a pickup truck, eating a sandwich and listening to music on a handheld transistor radio.

"How'd you get your separated from your friend?" Earl asks, changing the subject.

"We were trying to cross PCH. I got distracted when someone got shot."

Thomas is embarrassed. He feels he's fallen short of what a man should be capable of in moments of danger.

"Your parents are probably worried about you."

"My mother's always worried. She's probably got a SWAT team out looking for me already."

"Mothers tend to be that way, kid."

"Yours too?"

Earl laughs.

"Are you kidding? My mother still calls me when it's raining outside to remind me to wear a sweater."

As they get into Earl's car, a blue jeep in need of a paint job and a wash, Earl adds, "Put your seatbelt on, kid. We don't want you surviving a riot and then getting thrown through a windshield."

After Earl has turned the ignition, released the parking brake, and put the car into drive, he turns on the radio. A moment later Prince's "Delirious" slips through the speakers.

"I love this song," Thomas says.

Earl looks at him in surprise.

"How do you know about Prince?"

"A friend of mine's older brother lets us listen to his records when he's not home. He's got a bunch of Prince's stuff."

Earl smiles as he turns the car south onto Pacific Coast Highway, avoiding the logjam still occurring in the other direction. A few blocks later he turns left and begins to cut across the backstreets that will lead them back towards Fountain Valley.

They drive in silence for the duration of the song. Through the windows Thomas takes in the surroundings, looking at the old one-story homes that were originally built twenty years earlier, when land was so plentiful people were gifted plots in exchange for purchasing a set of encyclopedias. When they pass the City Gym, a concrete structure that looks like a smaller version of City Hall, Thomas says, "There are some good games in there."

"Oh yeah?" Earl asks, interested.

"My mother takes me there sometimes to watch on weekends. Pistol Pete Maravich was there one time. It was crazy."

"I bet he put on quite a show."

"He did. Even though he had gray hair and everything."

After a few moments of silence, Thomas asks, "Did you come out here from New York?"

"You bet," Earl says, nodding. "Greatest city on earth."

"I want to go there someday."

"Just be aware, kid, that once you do, you'll never want to come back."

"I hear it's cold though."

"That's part of its charm."

As they pause at a stop sign, Thomas asks, "Are you out here on vacation, Earl?"

"No, I'm looking for an old friend."

"What friend?"

"Buddy of mine I haven't seen since back in the day. Through the grapevine I heard he lives out here now. Thought I'd try to look him up."

"When was the last time you saw him?"

Earl pauses, grows thoughtful.

"Ten years ago."

"How come it's been so long?"

Earl pauses, taps his fingers lightly on the steering wheel.

"Because he feels guilty about something that happened. And I've let him carry that guilt."

"What're you going to tell him when you see him?"

"That it's time for him to put that guilt down."

Earl begins to search the dial to find another song worth listening to. He settles on one about a shining star that Thomas immediately loves.

"Who's this?"

"Earth, Wind, and Fire. Not bad, right?"

"They're awesome."

"You got that right."

The rest of their drive home is soundtracked by the song, its bass line like an aural password to the funkiest planet in the solar system. Thomas spends the rest of the drive peppering Earl with questions about music: what are his favorite bands? Who's the best singer alive? What does he think of Bruce Springsteen?

"The Boss is something else."

"Something else?"

"He's as good as they come."

"I like him too," Thomas says. "It seems like he cares more than everybody else."

"That's a good point. The man never mails it in."

When they arrive back at Sunwood Earl pulls the car into his parking space in the carport. After they've exited the car Earl says, "Don't get mad if your mother is a little out of sorts. She's probably been pretty worried about you. Cut her some slack."

"Ok, Earl. I will. I promise."

"Good man," Earl says.

The two of them bump fists and say goodbye. Thomas winds his way back through the complex to his own apartment. After all of the day's craziness, it's still only a little after 5 p.m., which means the local celebration is in full swing. The pool's packed with partiers. Kids play Marco Polo in the water, while the adults drink beers and grill hot dogs. Mario, one of Thomas's favorite neighbors, is doing what he does best: doubling as DJ and Master of Ceremonies, his black boombox blasting Michael Jackson's "Wanna Be Startin' Somethin'" as his girlfriend dances with some of her cousins nearby. In fact, one of Mario's cousins is doing a better-than-average moonwalk that has everyone cheering.

The door to his apartment is wide open, and Thomas takes the steps two at a time, imagining he's Rocky Balboa climbing the stairs in downtown Philly after finishing his triumphant morning run. He even pauses to do a little shadow-boxing on the landing before going inside.

"Hello?" he says.

"Hello?" his mother says as he steps into the living room and sees her standing at the window and holding the telephone to her ear.

At the sight of him her eyes light up, a smile appears on her face, and she says into the receiver, "He just walked in. Yes, yes, officer. I will. Thank you," followed by a quick laugh that Thomas knows is meant to signify his mother's relief.

When she hangs up she walks over to him and asks, "Are you okay?"

"Yes. It was wild. People were fighting everywhere. Breaking windows. They tipped over the phone booth in front of the Shake Shack and the glass all cracked."

"The police called about an hour ago," his mother says as she hugs him. "James went to the local station. He said he'd lost you in all of the commotion."

"It wasn't his fault. There was a shooting, and we got separated."

"I'm just glad you're safe."

And then, after a moment's pause, she asks, "How'd you get home?"

"Earl drove me."

"Earl?"

"He's staying here for ten days in a temporary. Apartment 237. Where Clara Bowers used to live."

"How do you know him?"

"I met him on my paper route. And he was at the beach today, playing hoops. He's really cool, Mom. He likes Prince, and we listened to Earth, Wind, and Fire on the way home. Do you know them?"

His mother appears to be attempting to process so much new information simultaneously that he thinks the best thing to do is add as many clarifying details as possible.

"He played in the ABA."

"The ABA?"

"It was a professional basketball league in the '70s. Like a second NBA. They used this red-white-and-blue-colored ball. Most of their games weren't on TV. He and Dr. J. were on the same team though. They won two titles together. But then he hurt his knee. Both of them, actually. He wears these big knee braces that must weigh ten pounds each. Maybe twenty. He's playing again now. You should see his drop-step, mom. It's unguardable. Anyway have you heard of them?"

"Heard of who?"

"Earth, Wind, and Fire."

"Oh, yes, of course."

"We don't have any of their albums though."

"Well," she says, changing the subject. "It was very nice of Earl to drive you home. I'd like to thank him. Can you show me where he lives?"

"Yes," Thomas says, but then adds. "Just don't ask him how he got hurt."

"You mean his knee?"

"Knees. He hurt them both, remember?"

"I won't."

Thomas nods.

"Because I already asked him. But I could tell he didn't really want to talk about it."

The two of them walk back through the complex, stopping to say hello to a few of the neighbors who wave to them from the pool, including Mario, who offers to grill them some hot dogs. There are so many barbecues operating on the patio balconies that the entire place is covered in a thick haze of smoke.

"You should have seen it there, Mom," Thomas says. "The police shot a guy right in the shoulder. Blood was coming out of his arm and everything."

His mother tries not to betray the nervousness she's still feeling.

"That's awful," she says. "Did the man live?"

Thomas shrugs his shoulders.

"I don't know. He had blood all over his hands. But the same thing happened to Sylvester Stallone in *Rambo II*, and he was alright."

It will be several years before Thomas realizes that his mother's default setting was one of a constant awareness of everything that could potentially go wrong in any given situation, and that a day like this afternoon, where she has gone against her instincts and let her son go to the parade with no adult supervision, is the type of disaster that justifies all of her anxieties.

Thomas will later come to feel as if his mother's true calling wasn't as a singer in a folk-rock band, but as an analyst for the CIA. She wasn't meant to be Joni Mitchell; she was meant to be Jack Ryan. And this July 4th has become her personal Red October.

"It's this one," he says, pointing to the door.

As they walk up the stairs they can hear music coming from inside Earl's apartment. A few moments later Earl opens the door, dressed in his go-to look of dark khakis, dark t-shirt, and white high-tops. Thomas wonders whether he might be able to find those items in his size.

"You must be Thomas's mother," Earl asks.

"I am," she says, as the two of them shake hands.

"Please come in."

What first catches Thomas's attention upon entering is that Clara

Bowers possessed the most impressive stereo system he has ever seen. It looks like something on loan from NASA, with a main console that could double as a flight simulator, and standing speakers that sound like they'd be more than capable of piping sounds into deep space. It occurs to Thomas that Clara probably didn't go to Miami to look for her boyfriend. Something more serious must have happened for her to leave so much cool stuff behind.

They stand in the middle of the living room as Earl turns down the volume.

Thomas knows that his mother has come here to do two things: to thank Earl for delivering her son safely from the beach, and to run an unannounced home visit on Thomas's newfound friend. As she covertly scans the entirety of the living room, she makes sure there are no signs of an over-reliance on alcohol, and no lingering scent of cigarettes that she knows will trigger her son's mild asthma.

It's clear even ten seconds in that everything checks out for her.

"I wanted to thank you for taking care of Thomas today," she says.

"The kid was doing fine on his own. He was hot-wiring a car when I found him."

"I wouldn't be surprised," she says, laughing. "Thomas mentioned you played for the Knicks."

"The Nets, Mom."

"I did. Back in the '70s."

"He's making a comeback," Thomas says to his mother.

"That's wonderful," his mother says. "Well, we didn't mean to intrude."

"Not at all. I'm glad you came by. My mother would have done the same thing."

"Really?" Thomas asks.

"Yes, really," Earl says. "The time to get worried is when your mother *doesn't* want to know who you're hanging with. That's when you know she thinks you're a lost cause."

"That's true," Thomas's mother says.

"Well, I bet your mother never showed up at your school to bring you lunch after you forgot it at home," Thomas says.

"I've only done that twice," she says.

"That's nothing," Earl says. "My mother used to sit in the front row at my games wearing a t-shirt that read *Earl's Mother* on it. Every time I scored she'd shout, 'That's My Son!'"

"Ok, that's pretty bad too," Thomas admits.

"You see?" his mother says to him. "It isn't just me."

It's not until Thomas and his mother turn towards the door a few minutes later that Thomas notices the photograph on the countertop. He approaches to take a closer look. It's of two men, both wearing their dark, road-colored uniforms, holding their index fingers up and smiling for the camera. The recently cut-down nets dangle like homemade necklaces from their necks, while a large crowd celebrates behind them. It's not, however, the fact that it appears to be a photograph taken moments after the New York Nets had won the title that most interests Thomas. Instead it's that he realizes he knows the man who's celebrating with Earl in the photograph. His name (or at least the name that everyone calls him at the courts) is Wings. He's something of an area playground legend, a man who periodically appears at courts all over the county to dominate the competition for two or three hours at a time before vanishing back into that white Trans Am of his, the one with the *Jesse Jackson For President* sticker on its bumper, and whose speakers are always playing Stevie Wonder at high volumes whenever he drives away. As Thomas studies the photograph, it occurs to him that he hasn't seen Wings in a year or so.

"You played with Wings?" Thomas asks.

"Wings?" Earl asks.

"Wings," Thomas says, picking up the photograph. "At least that's what we call him."

"You know him?" Earl asks, surprised.

Thomas nods.

"I haven't seen him in awhile though. I saw him score all eleven points in a game out at Morris Park last summer. He was incredible. The last two shots he hit were from thirty feet out, and he called bank on the second one."

"When were you at Morris Park?" his mother asks, concerned that her son might have traveled one city and fifteen miles over without parental supervision to play at courts known to attract a rougher, more serious crowd than Matsuya, or even Mile Square.

"Dad took me," he says, unaware of his mother's concern. "He was with me when I saw him at the Garden Grove Reservoir too."

"The Reservoir?" his mother asks.

"It's not really a reservoir. I mean it is, but there's also a court there," Thomas says.

"When was the last time you saw him?" Earl asks, trying to steer the conversation back onto the subject of Wings.

"About a year ago, I guess. It was down at Laguna Beach. There's these two courts right on the boardwalk, like fifty feet from the water. He was one court over, killing everybody. Some guy got so frustrated at trying to stop him that he finally tried to punch him."

"What did Wings do?"

"He just ducked, took a few steps to the side, and let a few guys break it up. He was cool as cool can be."

"Does he look the same as he does in this photograph?" Earl asks.

"Pretty much," Thomas says. "I mean, his hair is a little shorter. A lot shorter, actually. He doesn't have an afro anymore. But he's got more muscle."

Thomas's mother, silent throughout this exchange, says to Earl, "When was the last time you saw your friend?"

"About a decade back," Earl responds.

"That's a long time," Thomas's mother says, as she registers the sense of sadness on Earl's face. "How did you two lose touch?"

Earl looks back at Thomas's mother and pauses, as if he's trying to decide whether he should tell her the whole story. But after a few moments, he begins to speak.

"We were driving home from the arena after a game against the Colonels," Earl begins. "We'd lost in triple OT, and by the time we left the arena it was after 1 a.m. It'd been snowing for hours. Between that and the darkness you couldn't see more than five feet ahead of you, if that. I remember Jackson saying it felt like we were driving on the moon."

"Jackson?" Thomas cuts in, but his mother looks at him and shakes her head, letting him know now is not the time to say anything.

"A few minutes later we're spinning out on the highway, and by the time it's over the car's flipped six or seven times, slid down an embankment, and slammed into a tree. The cops said Jackson—that's Wings' real name, kid—was going too fast for the conditions. Of course had I been driving I would have been doing the same thing. Anyway, the next thing I know I wake up in the hospital with the doctor telling me I'd torn both my ACLs, fractured my right kneecap and cracked my left one, broken both my ankles, damaged some nerves in my left elbow, blew out an Achilles, and ruptured my spleen. They said I was lucky to be alive, because the passenger side of the car, when it crashed against the tree, just kind of gave in, which meant my body had basically slammed into a tree at top speed.

"The next day Jackson came to visit me, all broken up. He had a concussion, had broken his nose and wrist, but other than that he was fine. He said it should have been him lying there, and that he wouldn't ever be able to forgive himself. And I was so full of anger at that moment I let him say it. All of it. I didn't try to make him feel better, didn't even acknowledge I'd heard him, let alone accept his apologies. He came back a few more times later on in the week to see how I was doing, but I told the nurses not to let him in. And that was that. By the time I'd been released from the hospital, Jackson had packed up his stuff, told the team he was done, and vanished. It was radio silence for years after that. Every now and then I'd get it in my head to try to find him, but I didn't even know where to start. He didn't have any living family, and besides, I was still carrying around more rage than I should have been. I just wasn't ready, I guess."

Outside the afternoon has slipped into the early minutes of twilight. The magic hour, Thomas so often hears his father call it. That space when past is present, present is future, and time proves itself to be less of a straight line than you had thought it to be.

Thomas is expecting Earl to continue, but he doesn't. At least not right away. It's a minute or so before Earl begins again, as if he'd needed to gather his thoughts before continuing.

"But a couple months back a friend of mine said a buddy of his had run into Jackson out here, playing hoops at a court in the area. I figured it was time to do what I should have done a long time ago: try to make things right."

After a few seconds of silence, Thomas's mother looks at Thomas and says, "Can you remember each of the courts where you've seen Wings before?"

"Yes."

"Then I want you to show Earl where they are, okay?"

"Okay," he says, nodding his head and trying to hide his excitement at this prospect of an adventure. He feels as if he's just been knighted, or given a private detective's license.

"He doesn't have to do that," Earl says to Thomas's mother.

"It'll be fun, Earl," Thomas interjects, worried as he is that his mother might change her mind. "We can drive around in your car and listen to Earth, Wind, and Fire some more while we're looking for him."

Thomas's mother laughs.

"That's good," his mother says to Earl. "It'll force him to listen to something other than Prince and Bruce Springsteen."

"Mom," Thomas says. "We're going to listen to them too. Aren't we, Earl?"

"You know it, kid," Earl says, laughing.

"Should we go tomorrow, Earl?" Thomas asks.

"Tomorrow it is," Earl says.

After a few more minutes of conversation, Thomas and his mother get up to leave. As Thomas is about to open the door Earl says, "Hey, kid, how come you call him Wings?"

"Some of the guys say it's because he used to tell people every time he made a jumper, an angel got his wings."

"Is that right?" Earl says.

"But other people say it's because he grew up next to an airport."

"Not in a million years," Earl says. "Jackson was a country kid."

"I finally asked him though," Thomas says. "After he'd just won a game with a long jumper."

"What'd he say?"

"He said a bunch of women gave him that name because they figured anyone as handsome as him must have been sent straight down from Heaven."

"Good lord," Earl says, shaking his head. "He always did talk a good game."

Later on that night Thomas and his mother sit on the sofa and listen to The Beatles' *Abbey Road*. It will be years before he will appreciate The Beatles' music, which means on this night, like on so many others, he will ruin his mother's listening experience by asking her who Mean Mr. Mustard is, and why anyone would climb through a bathroom window instead of walking in the front door. But in between all of that, Thomas will ask his mother another, simpler question.

"Why do you think something as bad as a car accident would happen to guys as good as Earl and Wings?"

"I've been wanting an answer to that question ever since I was your age," his mother says.

"It doesn't make sense."

"No, it doesn't."

"Do you think Father O'Connor would know?"

"You could ask him. Although he'd probably just say it was all part of God's plan."

"God needs a new one, then."

"I'll second that."

"I guess we could blame Nixon," Thomas says, as the opening melody of "Here Comes the Sun" begins to fill up the room.

"What?" his mother asks, surprised.

"That's what Dad says whenever something bad happens. Blame Nixon."

"He does?"

"He says everything bad that's happened in America can be tied back to Nixon. Last week he said 'Blame Nixon' when there was that landslide up in Malibu, and a couple of weeks before that he said it when that man walked into a McDonald's and started shooting people for no reason. Blame Nixon. He says it all the time. Don't you remember the night Reagan was re-elected? Dan Rather said it was Mondale's fault for running such a bad campaign and Dad shook his head at the television and said, 'No, Dan. This is Nixon's fault. It always is.'"

"I never noticed that. Your father has an interesting way of seeing the world."

Thomas is silent for a moment, his mind making connections that his mother often finds difficult to expect or understand.

"Dad said it made him sad to watch Wings play."

"How come?"

"Because he said a man that talented shouldn't be wasting his time playing with a bunch of weekend warriors in Orange County."

"All the more reason for you and Earl to find him then," his mother says, standing up to go and flip the record over.

"Can we listen to Prince instead?" Thomas asks. "I think you'd like him if you gave him more of a chance."

"Thomas, you've given Prince enough of a chance for both of us."

MILE SQUARE IS ALREADY CROWDED BY THE TIME THE TWO OF THEM CIRCLE THE PARKING LOT NEXT TO THE BASEBALL FIELDS THE FOLLOWING MORNING, SEARCHING FOR AN EMPTY SPOT. It's Little League season, which means each of the several diamonds are filled with kids wearing cheaply produced versions of Major League uniforms. On the diamond closest to where Earl parks the car the Dodgers and the Expos are facing off, the pitcher throwing sidearm to a southpaw whose stance suggests he'd rather be anywhere other than the batter's box.

"You play baseball?" Earl asks, as they exit the car and walk in the direction of the courts.

"No, but I like watching it," Thomas says. "My dad doesn't though. He says he's watched a hundred baseball games in his life and has never seen anyone score."

"I feel him," Earl says. "I don't even think it's a sport."

"Why not?"

"Because if you can play it at the highest level and still have a beer gut, that disqualifies it from being called a sport."

They walk past the entrance to the model plane airport, where fifty or so middle-aged men fly remote-controlled planes over the airspace of the park.

"You're lucky," Thomas says to Earl.

"What'd you mean?" Earl asks, still getting used to Thomas's unparalleled ability to change subjects on a dime.

"That you get to dunk."

"You will too someday."

"You think so?"

"Absolutely. You've still got a lot of growing to do."

"That's not what the doctor said. He told me that I was never going to be taller than 5′2″."

"What did your mom say when he said that?"

"That the only reason she didn't break his nose was because she didn't want her son to think violence was ever the answer."

"Good for her. Besides, doctors don't know anything. They told me I'd never play again."

"They did?"

"Absolutely. They said just running up and down the court would be too much for my knees to take. And I made the mistake of believing them for too many years."

"What changed your mind?" Thomas asks as the courts come into view. Ahead of him he can see the familiar sight of men in t-shirts and tank tops running up and down the ten full courts, calling out screens, switches, and the score with an intensity that would make one think there was money hanging in the balance instead of simple pride.

"I got tired of letting other people say what my body could and couldn't do."

"How do your legs feel now?"

"They hurt. But you know what?"

"What?"

"It's worth it."

A few moments later Earl nods towards the courts and asks, "Anyone here know Wings?"

"Bomber. He knows everybody."

"Bomber?"

"You know, like the B-52 Bomber?"

"Why do they call him that?"

"Because they say he's as deadly from outside as a B-52 Bomber."

"Which one is he?"

They're at the edge of the courts now, standing on the grass a few feet from the concrete. There are roughly one hundred and fifty men scattered around the courts, in addition to thirty or forty people who've come to watch, mostly wives and girlfriends, many of whom are holding babies, or who keep one eye on their children playing in the grass while they cheer on their men.

Thomas scans the courts in search of Bomber, a brash gunner forever sporting a necklace that spells out his nickname in gold letters.

"There he is," he says, pointing towards a man standing with a few other guys underneath one of the hoops. As they walk in his direction, Thomas figures Bomber is likely in the middle of yet another story where he's either hit the game-winning shot or gone home with the most beautiful woman in the bar. Thomas is no regular, but he's been here enough times to know Bomber's act. Bomber who's never seen a shot he didn't like. Bomber who's the unofficial Mayor of Mile Square. Bomber who Thomas's father says hasn't played defense since Gerald Ford was President.

Heads have begun to turn at their approach. It's clear to Thomas that a lot of the players here recognize Earl from back in the day, while others are simply curious who the slender giant is that has stepped onto their turf.

"I knew it was you!" Bomber calls out as they approach, as he turns to one of his fellow players and says, "Didn't I say that cat looked like Earl Lewis?"

"You did," the second man affirms.

Bomber gives Earl a handshake and a semi-hug, as if the two of them were old friends. And yet Thomas's reservations about Bomber and his outsized ego aside, it's one of his favorite things about basketball: it's a fraternity you belong to wherever your are, no questions asked. Doesn't matter if you're black, white, tall, short, smart, dumb, serious, funny, rich, or poor. If you can play, you're in. Simple as that. As the years go by he will discover there's no group, institution, or organization he'll belong to as unconditionally all-embracing as that. Not the Democratic Party, not the world of academia. Both of them will, in one way or another, define themselves as much by who they keep out as by who they let in.

"When did you switch coasts?" Bomber asks Earl, Thomas suddenly invisible, the men crowding around to eavesdrop on the impromptu summit between their local Prime Minister and the visiting hoops dignitary.

"A few days ago," Earl says, clearly aware that he's going to have to accept a few minutes of small talk before down-shifting into asking about Jackson's whereabouts.

"You going to show some of these young guys how it's done?"

"Not today."

"You sure? We've got some players out here this morning."

"You definitely do," Earl says, as if he were not looking out at some part-time pickup players but at the assembled military of a dictatorial junta the autocrat has rolled out to show off for his guest.

"No doubt. Got a couple of ex-DI guys playing right now," Bomber boasts.

"The guy in the red high-tops looks familiar," Earl says, nodding towards a man in his late 20s, 6'4", maybe 6'5", with a lightning-quick first step and a feathery touch from outside.

"That's Jarvis. Played for UNLV. Had a cup of coffee in the CBA before heading overseas. Reminds me of the guy you played with your first year with the Nets, Bad News Bromley."

Earl laughs, shaking his head at the mention of a name he's clearly not heard in years.

"Bad News," Earl says. "Brother was good for twenty-five a night."

"And the man he was guarding was good enough for thirty," Bomber adds.

Everyone breaks up laughing at this, and Thomas looks at Bomber and tries to imagine what Bomber does when he's not at the courts. It's an almost impossible task. The thought of Bomber teaching the sixth grade, or helping people file their taxes, or performing arthroscopic surgery on someone's knees, or working construction all seem equally impossible. Men like Bomber Wilson, Thomas thinks to himself, were born to spend the entirety of their lives near a hoop. Whether they can make a living at it is immaterial. He suddenly sees in Bomber a kindred spirit, a fellow hoops samurai for whom no other way of life is possible.

"How'd you get hooked up with Wonder Boy?" Bomber asks.

"Wonder Boy?" Earl says.

"Wonder Boy," Bomber repeats, putting his arm around Thomas's shoulder.

Thomas is equally surprised. He's never heard this nickname before.

"That's what we call him," Bomber says, good-naturedly palming Thomas's head for a moment with his hand. "Because he's too young to be Batman and too skinny to be Superman."

"Wonder Boy was on my team out at the Pier a few days back," Earl lies. "He kept dropping so many dimes that I told him I didn't want anyone else throwing the ball to me in the post."

At this moment two players in the game occurring in front of them have gone from shouting in each other's general direction to squaring up chest-to-chest near the top of the key, their fists cocked, neither willing to keep their disagreement over a perceived foul from becoming the catalyst for a fight. Bomber turns his attention from Earl and Thomas and walks out onto the court, stepping between the men. He says a few things to them that Thomas cannot hear, but that the two men appear to grudgingly accept. A few moments later there are handshakes. Order's been restored. The ball is checked up top and the game resumes.

"I knew that was going to happen at some point today," Bomber says after walking back to the sidelines. "Cedric showed up this morning wanting to hit somebody."

A few moments later, after the three of them watch a beautifully run pick-and-roll between a middle-aged man and a kid just out of high school, Bomber lowers his voice and says, "I haven't seen him in over a year, brother."

Earl pauses before responding.

"How'd he look?"

"Same as always. Like he'd been created in Hoops Heaven and sent down to show the rest of us how it's done."

"Know where I can find him?"

"He used to run quite a bit out at the Reservoir. But I don't think anyone's seen him there for awhile either."

"That close to here?"

Bomber nods.

"Wonder Boy'll take you there. Kid's like one of those sherpas they have on Kilimanjaro, except for roundball instead of mountain climbing. There isn't an outdoor court in all of Orange County he doesn't know how to find."

While Thomas basks in Bomber's approval for the second time this morning, the smile quickly vanishes from Bomber's face. Instead he looks towards the court and says to Earl, "I'm surprised you care though."

"Why's that?"

"Because if Jackson'd been a better driver, you'd still be playing."

"He's been living with that around his neck for long enough. It's time that changes."

"So this is a mission of mercy?"

"For me, maybe. I can't speak for him."

"Took you long enough," Bomber says. "There's a reason they call those things accidents."

With that Bomber and Earl shake hands and then embrace with a sincerity that surprises Thomas. He watches as the two of them speak for another few moments about the pointlessness of living in the past before Bomber says, "God is good."

"I'm hoping you're right," Earl says.

Bomber starts to laugh.

"Course I'm right. Look around you. It ain't even 10 a.m. and it's already 80 degrees out here. There's kids playing in the grass, there's women still in love with their men, there's ten games going on where guys who don't even know each other are working together. You don't need any more proof than that."

"You should've been a preacher."

"What're you talking about, Earl Lewis?" Bomber asks. "I *am* a preacher. And this here is my cathedral *and* my congregation."

Back in the car, Thomas gives Earl the first set of directions to the Reservoir. Then he asks, "Were there a lot of courts where you grew up?"

Earl nods as they turn onto Brookhurst, which is already crowded with parents ferrying their kids to soccer games, baseball contests, and tennis matches.

"Too many to count," Earl says. "We had De Witt, Great Lawn, Riverbank, Columbus, St. Nicholas, the Roosevelt, G.W., the Cage. All of them were something else. But of course the crown jewel was Rucker Park."

"Rucker Park? How come?"

"Because it's the Madison Square Garden of playground hoops," Earl says, in reference to the New York Knicks' home court. Some weekends you'd get three, four hundred people lining up to watch. And in the summers? Forget it. There'd be tournaments where guys would show up from all across the Eastern seaboard to play. Big names too. Tiny Archibald. Clyde Frazier. Connie Hawkins. Black Jesus."

"Black Jesus?"

"Earl Monroe."

"You mean Earl the Pearl?"

"The one and only."

"My dad used to watch him, Walt Frazier, and Willis Reed when he was still living in Iran. He says those Knicks teams were the ones that made him fall in love with basketball."

"What was your father doing in Iran?"

"He was born there."

"That right?"

"He came out here in 1973 to San Francisco. That's where he met my mother."

"That must've been quite a shock."

"Meeting my mother?"

"No, going from Iran to San Francisco."

"He says anyone who went from Tehran to Frisco shouldn't be called an immigrant."

"No? What should they be called?"

"An astronaut."

"I hear that," Earl says, laughing.

After they've turned onto McFadden, they drive in silence for the rest of the way to the Reservoir. Thomas keeps hoping Earl will turn on the radio, but he never does. He recognizes the look in Earl's eyes; it's the same one his father gets when he's thinking about home. Thomas spends the rest of the drive wondering if there's a grown man in the entire world who doesn't wish he was somewhere other than where he is.

"Turn here," Thomas says, as they hit Centennial Boulevard. They follow that up with a few more quick turns before arriving on a residential street that leads into a neighborhood populated with mean-looking dogs in small front yards, aging muscle cars parked in tight-fitting driveways, and bars on the windows of one-story houses that look like run-down fortresses aware their perimeters are in danger of being breached.

They park at the curb in front of a wall bearing so much graffiti that geologists could mark time by studying the layers of braggadocio sprayed onto its surface. But what most jumps out at Thomas is not a word or a phrase but a painted silhouette of a flying man, basketball held aloft, floating towards an invisible basket the viewer is asked to imagine for himself. The Number 23 has been sprayed onto the flying man's sneakers. It's just about the greatest image

Thomas has ever seen. An American Icarus, had Icarus, instead of falling to earth, dunked a basketball right through the hoop of the sun.

"I don't see it," Earl says, looking out at an untended park featuring a few wooden benches that look less like places to sit and more like medieval torture devices no longer in operation.

"It's on the other side of those trees," Thomas says, pointing to a thick strand of cypresses standing in formation.

After moving through the thicket of trees, they emerge to see a single full basketball court featuring two iron backboards and a pair of chain nets hanging on for dear life. Beyond the court is an iron fence topped by barbed wire that marks the beginning of the Reservoir.

"Last time I was here there were a bunch of people swimming in the water. Fishing too," Thomas says.

"That's reassuring."

"My dad said it was the best advertisement for bottled water he'd ever seen."

"Your dad's a funny guy, isn't he?"

"He's the funniest man in America, according to him."

"What do you think?"

"I think he's the second funniest man in America."

"Who's the first?"

"Steve Martin."

"Can't fault your father for falling short of that."

"I always tell him that if he wants the top spot he's going to have to be funnier than a roller-skating King Tut."

"I don't think it can be done."

"Neither do I," Thomas says.

Ahead of them two men idly shoot hoops at one of the baskets, while a small dog sleeps just inside the half-court line. As Earl and Thomas approach, the older of the two takes notice of the new arrivals and waves, as if he were greeting a couple of friends.

"What'd you say, Earl?" the man asks, as if he'd been expecting the arrival of this ex-New York Nets star all along.

"How you doing?" Earl asks, shaking the man's hand.

"Ruben Fernandez," he says. The man is nearing fifty, his thinning gray hair offset by a thick black beard and hands dirtied from what looks like engine grease. He's dressed in black work boots and blue jumper pants. Not the usual pickup hoops attire.

"You must be the last Nets fan in America," Earl says.

The man laughs and says to his friend, "You should have seen this guy play, Hector. He was better than Kareem."

"I don't know about that," Earl says. "But I'll take it."

"What're you doing out this way?" Ruben asks.

"My buddy and I here," Earl says, nodding towards Thomas, "are looking for a friend of mine. Goes by the name of Wings."

"Yeah, I heard Jackson used to play here once in awhile," Ruben says.

"So you *are* the last Nets fan in America," Earl says.

"That was quite a team. Especially the '75 one. I always thought you guys could have hung with the Celtics."

"I feel the same way," Earl says. "Especially with Havlicek on the far side of thirty by then."

"Definitely," Ruben says, before adding, "Maybe some of the regulars can give you more information. I don't get out here as much as I used to. Most days, by the time I get off work, the games are already over."

Earl takes a look at the quiet surroundings and asks, "Going to fill up later on today?"

"Definitely. Another hour and there'll be twenty-five or thirty guys."

Thomas listens as the three men continue to talk for the better part of ten minutes. Where the conversation Earl had engaged in with Bomber had begun as a kind of glorified masculinity contest, this is different. Ruben and Hector both seem incapable of putting on a front. Instead they talk about the neighborhood, about the shuttered furniture factory they'd passed on the drive over, and about where to find the best Mexican food in the area.

"Depends," Ruben says.

"On what?" Earl asks.

"On whether you're willing to risk hepatitis," Hector jokes.

"For a good enchilada, I'm willing to risk more than that," Earl says.

"Then it's Ortiz's," Ruben says. "I doubt he's cleaned the grills in thirty years, but rumor is that's why the tortillas taste so good."

"It's close to here?"

"Head back out the way you came in," Hector says. "Then two blocks over. It's a hole-in-the-wall next to Luis's Stockade."

"Stockade?" Earl asks.

"Luis is under the impression we're going to retake America one of these days, and he wants everyone to be ready when it happens," Ruben says.

"It never hurts to dream," Earl says.

"Course it does," Ruben responds. "But you gotta do it anyway."

Earl nods and looks at Thomas and says, "You hungry?"

"Yes," Thomas says, aware that somewhere his mother's telepathic maternal radar had begun sounding alarms the minute the words "hole-in-the-wall" and "hepatitis" had been mentioned. So as they drive back out onto Centennial in search of Ortiz's, Thomas imagines his mother's already on the phone with their doctor, alerting the old man to the fact that she'll be bringing her son in later on this evening with a possibly fatal case of food poisoning.

They return to the Reservoir an hour later, after Thomas and Earl have devoured chicken-and-steak enchiladas so good that Thomas had found himself wondering, for the first time in his life, whether a McDonald's Quarter Pounder was, in fact, the single greatest meal the world had to offer. Probably, he finally decided. But it was good to know it had some competition.

There's a full-court game in progress, and there are four other guys waiting to run. But the overall quality of competition isn't great, Thomas notices. The best player's a guy pushing fifty. He's 6′2″ or so, and the assortment of tapes, bandages, pads, and goggles he wears gives Thomas the impression that the man's body is being held together with duct tape and, if the gold crucifix dangling from his neck is any indication, Catholic prayer. Nevertheless, the guy has one of those awkwardly unstoppable games that Thomas has always marveled at. Even though half the time he looks like he's about to lose his balance and fall, the other half he's destroying the opposite team with a series of fadeaway jumpers that hit nothing but net. Earl notices too.

"Brother looks like he's moving in quicksand and yet no one can stay in front of him," he says.

"How's he doing it?" Thomas asks.

"Don't know. But there's a guy like him on every playground in America. It's the law. They don't let you build a court unless you can prove you've got a guy like that already on site."

"Wings isn't here though."

"Maybe somebody's seen him. We'll ask at the break."

The two of them spend the next several minutes watching the game. Though the talent isn't even second-tier, it doesn't make any difference to Thomas. Any game of hoops is gold.

Indeed, it doesn't matter to Thomas if the players are old, out of shape, and so slow that even a man with a walker could stay in front of them. A perfectly executed back-cut is still a thing of beauty, as is a jumper that ends with the ball arcing through the sky before settling into the basket. It's why Thomas is convinced that hoops is the greatest invention of the 20th Century. Forget the Wright Brothers. Forget Alexander Graham Bell and his telephone. As far as Thomas is concerned, James Naismith was where it's at. End of story.

It's game point, 10-10, straight to eleven, and one of the men waiting for the next game, a hard-looking guy with sleeve tattoos on his arms and a neck tat of a viper slithering its way up—strangely— a telephone pole, approaches Earl.

"You the guy looking for the shooter?"

It takes Thomas a moment to realize he's referring to Wings.

"That's right," Earl says.

There's an aspect of latent violence in the exchange, as if both men are cautiously circling each other, trying to figure out how civil they can be without losing face. After several more seconds of the man seeming to size Earl up, he says, "He used to live off 106th. Second to last house on the right."

"How do you know that?"

"He was living with a girl there. A friend of my cousin's."

"He don't live there now?"

"Not for at least a year. Maybe more."

"You know where he's gone?"

The man shrugs his shoulders.

"No idea. But Denise is still there. Tell her Flaco sent you."

"You Flaco?"

The man nods. The tension is lifted.

"Ruben said you were pretty good back in the day," Flaco says.

"*Way* back in the day," Earl responds. "Like in another life altogether."

"I hear that. One day you're a young man and the next day you're telling the kids to turn the music down."

"You got that right," Earl says, as he and Flaco share a laugh.

A moment later the man in goggles drains a turn-around fifteen footer to win the game.

"He's like a Mexican Bernard King," Earl says, nodding towards the court.

"Believe me, Jorge reminds us of that himself a couple times a week."

The two of them talk a bit more about Jorge and his bag of hoops tricks before Earl thanks the man and he and Thomas head back towards the car.

The neighborhood has come alive in the past hour. In one driveway a pony's been outfitted with a sombrero and saddle while a line of young kids take turns being photographed sitting on him. The last thing Thomas thinks as they pull out is that, were his father here, there'd be a better than fifty-fifty chance he'd steal that horse and give him his freedom. It's this thought that explains why, as they head up Centennial in the direction of 106th Street, Thomas asks, "Do you like cowboy movies, Earl?"

"What? You mean like Clint Eastwood?"

"Yes."

"They're alright."

"My dad loves them. He says the only things he needs in a movie are one good man and ten bad ones on horses. The rest will take care of itself."

"I've always been more of an action movie guy myself," Earl says.

"Like Burt Reynolds?"

"Burt's cool," Earl says, nodding his head. "Steve McQueen. Richard Roundtree too."

"I don't know Steve McQueen."

"One of these days you're going to have to watch *Bullitt*, kid."

"Ok," Thomas says, filing the title away. "I will."

They park in front of the small, adobe-style bungalow that Flaco described. A two-door Toyota Celica sits in the driveway. It has a small sticker of the Virgin Mary on its rusted bumper, and a rosary dangling from its rearview mirror. A large retaining wall divides the street from the 22 Freeway on the other side, but the constant hum of engines makes it seem as if the world's forever speeding away from this neighborhood. As they approach the door, Thomas wonders if the people who live on this street are ever able to get a good night's sleep.

The door is answered by a woman in her late twenties with dark hair and a beauty mark on her left cheek. Although she's dressed simply, in blue jeans and a white blouse, there is, from Thomas's point of view, simply no question: Wings must've gone crazy. You don't leave a woman as beautiful as this even if it's just to go out for food. You order takeout and keep her as close to you as humanly possible.

"Earl Lewis," the woman says, with a nonchalance that clearly surprises him.

"That's right," Earl says.

"And who's this?" she says, looking at Thomas.

"This is Thomas," Earl says.

"It's nice to meet you, Thomas."

Thomas attempts a response, but the entirety of his body seems to have slipped into a temporary state of paralysis. Earl looks at Thomas and starts to smile, aware of what is happening.

"You Denise?" Earl asks.

She nods and leans against the doorframe for another few seconds before stepping back and inviting them into the house.

"You two want some water?"

"Love some," Earl says.

"What about you, Thomas?" Denise asks.

"Yes, please," Thomas says, thankful he's regained the use of his vocal chords.

The dining room table is located in the middle of the kitchen, and there's a window over the sink that looks out onto a yard featuring a second, smaller house. A clothesline is stretched between the two roofs, and a handful of dresses wave like small flags in the breeze.

"I told Jackson for years he should look you up," Denise says, pouring water into three medium-sized glass jars.

"Wouldn't have done much good," Earl says, his voice thick with regret.

"He said the same thing. Jackson insisted you'd hate him until the day you died."

"I never hated him. But I didn't have the courage to admit that. To him or myself."

"I don't blame you," Denise says. "It was his fault, after all."

As she leans against the sink and takes a long drink from her glass, Thomas is relatively certain he's never seen anything more singularly exciting in his entire life.

"Maybe," Earl says. "But he didn't mean to do it. And I shouldn't have let him carry the burden for as long as I have. It ain't right."

Denise refills Thomas's water glass, smiling at him as she does so. Thomas smiles back, and considers proposing marriage.

"So how do you fit into all this, Thomas?" Denise asks him.

"I know Wings too," he says, worried that she knows what he's thinking.

"Oh, that's right. Jackson's nickname. Which one did you hear, kid? That he used to fly crop-dusters over his father's farmland? Or that he'd once dated an American Airlines stewardess who liked to make it when they were at 30,000 feet?"

"I've never heard those before," Thomas says. "There are a lot of them though." As he wonders whether he should tell her the real story behind Wings's nickname, Denise's eyes suddenly widen a bit, and a look of recognition appears on her face.

"Wait a minute. You the boy who lives over by the Matsuya courts?"

"Yes," Thomas says.

"Jackson used to talk about you," Denise says, a broad smile appearing on her face. "He said you could see things on the court that hadn't happened yet."

"Look at that, shorty. You're famous."

"He said you were like a miniature Magic Johnson," Denise adds. "Although you're quieter than Magic is."

"Not usually," Earl says. "But right now he's trying to gather up the courage to ask you to elope."

"That's not true," Thomas responds, even though he has no idea what "elope" means.

As Earl laughs, Denise walks over to Thomas, leans down, and kisses him on the cheek.

"I accept," Denise says, before turning back to Earl and adding, "Either way, I'm glad you're looking for him. It's time for both of you to make your peace. It's been too long already."

"Flaco said he's not living here anymore."

Denise nods.

"He moved out about ten months ago."

"What happened?" Earl asks.

"I wanted a family. Jackson wanted a maid."

"The man never did know a good thing when he had it."

"I don't see a ring on your finger either, Earl Lewis. What's your excuse?" Denise asks.

"Haven't met the right woman yet."

The woman folds her arms at her chest and nods knowingly before looking at Thomas and sarcastically rolling her eyes.

"You know what that is?" she says to Thomas. "It's the excuse men use when they don't have the courage to settle down and commit. Don't fall into that trap when you grow up. There are men who spend their entire lives thinking there's a better woman out there than the one they've already got. And you know what happens to them?"

"No," Thomas says, as if she were about to reveal to him the location of the Holy Grail. "What?"

"They die alone in their living rooms eating TV dinners with plastic silverware."

"She's exaggerating, kid," Earl says, laughing. "Don't let her scare you."

"I'm not scaring him. I'm just trying to save him from a lifetime of unhappiness."

"You know where I can find him?" Earl asks, trying to change the subject.

Denise bites her lower lip and considers.

"Don't you dare tell him I said hello if I do," Denise emphasizes. "Either of you."

"I promise," Earl says, placing his hand to his heart. Thomas does the same.

"Suddenly everyone's a Boy Scout," Denise says, shaking her head as she walks to the counter to refill Thomas's glass.

"YOU GOT A GIRLFRIEND, KID?" Earl asks, as they turn back onto Centennial Boulevard and head in the direction of the 405 Freeway.

"No," Thomas answers.

"Yeah, I could tell."

"You could? How?"

"You weren't exactly light on your feet back there. The way you went silent when she tried to talk to you made you look like a serial killer."

"She was one good-looking woman, Earl," Thomas says by way of explanation. "I got nervous."

"I know. I don't blame you. But all the more reason to be cool."

"You think she could tell?"

"Every woman in America could tell. Probably overseas too. There were women in Paris saying to themselves, 'Shorty needs to work on his charm.'"

"Sorry, Earl."

"Don't worry about it, kid. The next woman we meet, I'll show you how it's done. You'll be Valentino in no time."

"Who's Valentino?"

"He was a famous ladies-man."

"Like Wilt Chamberlain?"

"Exactly. He was the Wilt of silent films."

"My friend James likes silent films."

"Not you?"

"I don't think I would."

"Why not?"

"They're silent."

Earl laughs.

"You've got to give something a chance before you decide whether to like it or not."

"I tried that with avocados."

"Yeah? How'd it go?"

"Not well, Earl. Not well at all."

Before they left, Denise told the two of them that Wings had moved to Los Angeles. She showed them a postcard Wings had sent her about six months prior that read *Greetings From Venice Beach*, and its cover featured a photograph of a shirtless, muscle-bound man holding a woman dressed as the Statue of Liberty above his head. On the back of the card Wings had signed his name alongside his old jersey number with the Nets, 21.

"Brother loved signing autographs," Earl had said to Thomas and Denise. "There was one night in St. Louis, the middle of winter. Twelve degrees plus windchill. We'd lost by twenty-five or something. And there we were, sitting on the bus, waiting for Jackson to finish signing everything the fans put in front of him. Must have been close to a hundred people there, and he didn't get on the bus until every last one of them had gotten a signature."

"Don't tell me these kinds of things," Denise had said.

"Why not?"

"Because I don't want to fall in love with him again."

Thomas rolls through almost the entirety of the radio dial before settling on one of his favorite songs, though he doesn't know the name of the singer. It's about a man waking to the sound of thunder as autumn closes in. At least that's what it seems to be about, Thomas thinks. But more than that, he thinks the singer has the greatest voice he's ever heard, as if all the joy and sadness, all the hope and loss that the world possesses have somehow found their way into it. The singer's voice doesn't tell a story so much as cast a spell. Whenever Thomas hears it he stops what he's doing to listen. Right now is no different. He turns the volume up so it sounds like the singer is in the car with them.

"Bob Seger," Earl says approvingly. "Good choice."

"That's his name?" Thomas asks.

"You're kidding?"

"He's famous?"

"Kid, don't say these kinds of things out loud to anyone else, okay?"

"Why not?"

"Because you just asked if the greatest vocalist since Sam Cooke is famous."

"Who's Sam Cooke?"

Earl removes his hands from the steering wheel for a moment to signify his disbelief.

"I thought you knew your music."

"I do," Thomas says. "I mean, I know Prince. And Bruce. The Beatles. Run-DMC too. A few others."

"What others?"

"Joni Mitchell."

"Joni works. Anyone else?"

"Tom Petty."

"Who's coming off the bench?"

Thomas shrugs his shoulders.

"Kenny Rogers, I guess."

"Kenny Rogers?"

"He sings 'The Gambler.'"

"I know what he sings."

Earl looks askance at Thomas and then, on impulse, gazes over his shoulder before piloting the car across three lanes.

"We're going to take a little detour," Earl says.

"To where?"

"The mothership. Then you won't have any reason to mention Kenny Rogers in public ever again."

What Thomas will later remember about Sunset Boulevard will be enough material to last several lifetimes. He'll remember the shortness of the women's skirts, and the way they wore them with a confidence that made him feel as if they were a race of superheroes, ten thousand Wonder Women keeping the area safe from harm. He'll remember the grown man dressed in a pirate outfit crouching on top of an *LA Times* newspaper kiosk like there couldn't have been anything more natural in the world for him to do. He'll remember the old man waiting for the bus, his battered cane propped against the bench. And he'll remember the way the sunlight reflected off the hoods of passing cars in such a way that they looked as if they'd all been touched by the healing hand of God.

They park at the curb in front of a Safeway and walk up the street. A few blocks later they stop in front of an enormous, warehouse-sized building whose sign reads, in big red letters against a yellow background: Tower Records.

"Like I said, the Mothership," Earl says to Thomas as they enter.

Thomas has never seen anything like it. As he surveys the aisles upon aisles of albums, cassettes, and eight-tracks, he is reminded of the scene at the end of *Close Encounters of the Third Kind*, when the spaceship lowers its drawbridge and invites Roy Neary on board.

"Have at it, kid," Earl says. "Just one rule."

"What's that?"

"No Kenny Rogers."

They separate, Earl leaving Thomas to discover the wonders of the store by himself. Immediately Thomas finds himself almost as entranced by his fellow shoppers as by the records themselves. The man wearing a Talking Heads t-shirt with several earrings dangling from his left ear; the two college-aged girls with purple hair and pink lipstick who are singing along to the Blondie song playing on the in-house sound system; the woman with gray hair down to her waist and wearing a floor-length tie-dye dress who is walking up and down the aisles offering to tell people their fortunes.

After a few minutes of aimless wandering, Thomas, overwhelmed at the amount of options, realizes he needs a goal, some specific destination to shoot for. He decides to locate the Bob Seger section. As he's about to set out on this miniature quest, he hears a woman's voice behind him ask, "Would you like to know your future, young man?"

He turns to see the gypsy woman smiling at him, her eyes the kind of blue he would later see every time he looked at a painting by Van Gogh. It occurs to Thomas that, if the woman is capable of feats as awe-inspiring as being able to see into the future, then it's also likely she can point him in the direction of where to find the record that "Night Moves" is on.

"Actually, I'm just trying to find Bob Seger."

"The actual Bob Seger, honey, or just his records?"

"Just his records."

"That I can do. Come on."

She leads him several aisles over. As he follows her Thomas spots Earl standing in another section of the store, talking to a fellow customer about an album Earl appears to be considering purchasing.

"Here you are, sweetheart. Bob Seger."

"Thank you."

"You're welcome. You're sure you don't want your fortune told?"

Thomas pauses to consider, weighing the possible pros and cons.

"You're not going to tell me how I die, are you?"

"Of course not, honey," she says, winking at him. "Because you're going to live forever."

"You think so?"

"I know it."

"I hope you do too, miss."

"You've got a good aura, honey," she answers, smiling as she turns away, her long dress trailing behind her like the extra material from a magic carpet.

The first cover Thomas spots is of a long-haired man with a beard thick enough to hide contraband in, and whose brown leather jacket is something Jesus might have worn had he hailed from the Motor City instead of Nazareth. In the years ahead the cover will make Thomas think about rainmakers, about medicine men, about rock-and-roll singers like Seger and Springsteen being modern-day Tom Joads, but at this moment all he thinks is that he's looking at the single coolest man he's ever seen in his life. He pulls the record from the shelf and stares at it, flipping it over and back, studying its surface the way an archaeologist might upon unearthing an unexpected treasure from underground.

He scans the back cover to see if "Night Moves" is on there. No dice. He replaces the album and flips through the LPs until he finds what he's looking for. The cover of *Night Moves* is relatively similar to *Stranger in Town*, except in this one a spotlight shines above Seger like a full moon. Thomas doesn't know his mythology yet, and he's years away from hearing the word "archetype", but still: he knows an explorer when he sees one. He can tell the singer's a man who's traveled highways, forded rivers, climbed mountains, raced cars, hunted wild game. Some of these things he's probably done alone, others with friends and lovers. Always he's done them with courage. The man on the cover of *Night Moves* is a grown Huck Finn, Thomas will later realize, an urban Ishmael, and rock and roll is the floating coffin that will save his life on the open seas as many times as he needs it to.

Armed with *Night Moves*, Thomas begins to move up and down the aisles with more confidence, acting as if he's now old hat at this, and that, if this is indeed the mothership, then he's now its Captain Kirk, all instinct and swagger. As he explores, Thomas tries to catalogue as many artist and band names as possible, aware that it'll at least be months, if not years, before he has the opportunity to be here again. After several minutes, worried that he's going to run out of time before they will have to get back on the road, he makes his way to the Prince section, excited to see whether the Purple One has recorded any albums in addition to those he's already familiar with. Upon finding the section, he's immediately greeted by the sight of Prince looking back at him while outfitted in an unbuttoned trench coat, a neck bandana, skimpy black underwear, and nothing else. If years later Thomas will feel Bob Seger to be a character out of 19th Century American Literature plugged into an amplifier, he'll come to see Prince as electric funk's version of a Romantic Poet: Keats with a drum machine, Lord Byron raised on *Soul Train* and soft-core pornography.

"Hell no," Earl says, approaching from Thomas's left. "You come home with that and your mother'll kill me."

"He's got courage," Thomas says.

"It's a great album too. But you're not old enough for *Dirty Mind* yet, kid. I'm not sure *I'm* old enough for *Dirty Mind* yet. Pick another one."

Thomas flips through several other Prince records before becoming transfixed by a psychedelic cover featuring a blue sky that several white doves appear to be gliding through. The scene is populated by a young, bohemian-looking woman sitting on the steps of an outdoor park and playing the violin, a man wearing a flashy, blue-and-white jumpsuit playing a white electric guitar, and a man with an impossibly white, mime-like face dressed all in black and holding what looks like a tambourine. Another man is dressed like a surgeon about to operate, and a scantily clad woman wears a cheetah-print bikini and matching wrap, while a trio of individuals, their genders impossible to decipher with any certainty, are wrapped in purple robes. And at the very bottom right corner of the cover an old, balding man, his chin leaning on his cane, appears lost in apparent thought or reflection. The image also contains a gold ladder rising up out of what may or may not be a swimming pool, an uneven, multi-colored wall, and the title: *Around the World in a Day.*

"I want this one," Thomas says.

"Good choice. It's got 'Paisley Park' on it."

"I don't know that one."

"Then you're in for a treat, kid. It's the happiest song he's ever written."

"Even better than 'Let's Go Crazy'?"

"I said happiest, kid. Not best."

Thomas, buoyed by Earl's support of his album selection, says, "This is the best place I've ever been to, Earl. Better than Disneyland, even."

"I'm not going to disagree with you there. Especially since they're not playing 'It's a Small World' on the in-house stereo round-the-clock."

At the register Earl and Thomas are greeted by a woman in her early 30s with cropped black hair and dark black eyeliner. She's wearing a t-shirt of John Lennon that says *I Love New York* on its front. As she scans the records she pauses at *Around the World in a Day* and says, "Which one of you is the Prince fan?"

"That would be him," Earl says.

"I'm off in six hours," the woman says. "Where are you buying me dinner?"

Thomas, for the second time this afternoon, is left speechless by the fact that an older woman has talked to him. As he's attempting to formulate a response, Earl says, "I'm a Prince fan too."

"That true?" the girl asks, playfully looking at Thomas for corroboration.

Thomas smiles and shakes his head from side to side.

"You kidding me?" Earl says. "This is the moment you choose to throw me under the bus?"

Thomas and the woman both begin to laugh.

"Don't let him bully you, sweetheart. He's just jealous that I like you more than him."

"Unreal. No good deed..."

She rings them up, places their records into two bags and says to Earl, "You should have passed the ball to Dr. J. more often when you played with him."

Earl, surprised, starts to laugh.

"Doc should have passed the ball more to *me*. I was unstoppable in the post."

"Dr. J. shouldn't have to pass to anybody," she says.

"Yeah, that was his opinion too," Earl responds.

On an impulse, Thomas asks her, "Do you remember Jackson Curtis?"

It's the girl's turn to be surprised.

"Of course. He was good too. Earl didn't pass to him either."

"My God," Earl says.

"We're looking for him," Thomas says.

"Well," she says, looking from Thomas to Earl, suddenly aware that the afternoon is a more serious one than she'd realized. "I hope you guys find him. If you need any help, I'm off tonight at 8 p.m.."

"I don't know," Earl says. "I can't take any more criticism."

"I'm just kidding you," the girl says. "You were my brother's favorite player."

"What about yours?"

"You were my second favorite."

"Who was your favorite?" Earl asks.

"George Gervin, all day," she says, mimicking the motion of Gervin's patented finger-roll as she speaks.

"Oh yeah? The Iceman? Okay. I can respect that."

"Are you planning on making a comeback?" she asks him.

"It's crossed my mind."

"Well, if you do, make sure to call me so I can come and cheer you on," she says, opening up Earl's palm and writing her name and phone number inside of it.

Earl looks at what she's written and says, "It's good to meet you, Vivian Nguyen."

"Right back at you, Earl Lewis."

Back out on the sidewalk Thomas says, "I thought you were going to teach me how it's done, Earl."

"What are you talking about? She gave me her phone number."

"You just got lucky."

"Lucky? Well, I needed some with you trying to sabotage me. You're the worst wingman I've ever seen."

As the two of them walk towards the car, Thomas says, "Thanks for the records, Earl. I can't wait to listen to them."

"You got it, kid. Anytime."

Minutes later, as they drive north on Sunset, heading for the freeway, Thomas asks Earl something he's been wanting to ask him all day.

"Why did Wings stop playing for the Nets?"

Earl looks at him for a moment before putting his eyes back on the road.

"I guess he felt like it was the right thing to do."

"I don't understand."

"He blamed himself for the accident. And I imagine he figured that if I couldn't play anymore, then he shouldn't either."

Thomas attempts to process what Earl has said. He can't decide what to make of Wings's decision, whether it was heroic or unnecessary. Or maybe both.

"Are you going to tell him he should start playing again, now that you're better?"

"I haven't thought that far ahead."

They slip into silence for the rest of the drive. Twenty minutes later, as they exit the freeway and begin to move towards the water, Thomas is still thinking about Earl and Wings and the directions that their lives took after the accident. As they look for a parking spot a few blocks from the shore, Thomas finds himself depressed at all the ways men can lose the things they love the most: youth, health, friendship, purpose. Until this point in time, he'd always thought of life as being one long series of gifts until the big loss arrives at the end. But he realizes this isn't true. Life is nothing but loss. Small things, big things. Death isn't an exception to the rule. It is the rule. Thomas looks at Earl and wishes he could stop Earl from having to lose any more than he already has. But Thomas knows that he can't. And that he's going to lose his share of things in his own life as well. If those losses haven't already begun.

Out on the Venice Beach boardwalk Earl and Thomas pass an outdoor weight-room that features an assortment of bench presses, squat racks, barbells, and sit-up machines. It's populated by several men who look like the physical prototypes for the characters Thomas so often reads about in comic books, their bald heads offset by thick beards, dark tattoos and, in a few cases, neon-colored workout gear that makes them look radioactive. It occurs to Thomas that even the Incredible Hulk wouldn't look so incredible here; he'd just be one more chemically-enhanced bodybuilder no longer in possession of a neck.

The courts come into view a little further on. They're busy enough to make Thomas wonder if the city should start charging viewers admission in order to watch. But the crowd is even more intense than the one that had gathered to watch the pickup games at the pier on the Fourth of July. These people, by any definition, are clearly hoops diehards. They haven't come to the beach for the waves or the women; they have come only to be close to the game that they love. This group knows good basketball when it sees it, and it's obvious from the way they watch that they function as an unofficial chorus: fail to hit the open man, or force up a bad shot instead of swinging the ball, and you're going to hear from them.

"Is this like Rucker Park?" Thomas asks.

"A little bit," Earl says. "Except the courts are nicer."

"You running?" a voice asks Earl.

They turn to see a man, 6'3", maybe 6'4", with shoulders broad enough to make Thomas figure that he spends considerable time lifting weights at the outdoor gym they've just passed. His tank top is so tight it looks like the man has stolen it off a small child, and each of his legs appear to be roughly the width of a fire hydrant. Thomas has seen eighteen-wheeler trucks that look less intimidating.

"No," Earl says. "Just looking for a friend."

"Yeah, who's that?"

"Jackson Curtis."

"Wings? Haven't seen him around for a minute. Hey Terry!" the man shouts, turning towards another baller idly stretching down near the other end of the court.

"What?" Terry asks.

"You seen Wings lately?"

"Nah," Terry responds. "Heard he moved."

Earl begins to move in Terry's direction. Thomas follows him. Terry continues to stretch, his long limbs contorted into shapes that seem borderline impossible, as if he were an acrobat preparing for a turn on the trapeze.

Earl extends his hand to Terry and introduces himself.

"Hell," Terry says, laughing. "I know who you are. And I'm glad you and Jackson are still friends."

"Any idea where he might have moved to?"

"I'm not sure he did," Terry says. "Just what I heard."

"You know where he was living around here?"

Terry stops stretching, stands up, and points south.

"Down that block. Turn right just past the ice cream shack. It's the second building on the right. Upstairs."

"Appreciate it," Earl says.

"No problem. You sure you don't want to stay and run?"

"No, I'm good."

"What about you, kid?" Terry asks, surprising Thomas.

"Me?"

"Yeah, you. Anyone Earl Lewis brings to the courts must have a little game in him. Earl never ran with no scrubs."

"No, that's okay," Thomas says, unable to hide just how much this moment means to him. "I'll stick with Earl."

"Sounds good, kid. But you two come back and run some other time."

Earl and Thomas head back in the direction they've come, turning left off the boardwalk at the point Terry had instructed them to. Almost immediately the Frozen Circus Ice Cream Shack comes into view. Its roof is done up like a wooden carnival tent, and the front door is painted to resemble a couple of heavy velvet curtains waiting to be pulled back by a hidden Master of Ceremonies. At the outdoor tables a few families sit together enjoying their cones, while a flock of kids Thomas's age idle out front on an assortment of skateboards and roller skates, eating their ice creams while balancing on their wheels.

"It must be this one," Earl says, stopping in front of a two-story fourplex in dire need of a paint job. They climb the stairs and knock on a door whose wood is so thin it makes Thomas wonder whether Earl could put his fist through it if he accidentally knocked too hard. Actually, Thomas thinks, he could probably do that himself.

A moment later the door is answered by an old woman in a long, blue dress with frizzy gray hair. She holds an enormous cat in her arms who appears to be asleep, and each of her nails are painted a different color.

"Yes?" the woman asks, the word struggling from between her lips as if the energy it took for her to speak will leave her exhausted for the rest of the day.

"We're sorry to bother you," Earl says. "But we're looking for a friend of ours."

"Oh?" the woman asks, her eyes glazing over at the recognition, Thomas realizes, that they're not who she'd hoped they'd be.

"Yes, ma'am. His name's Jackson Curtis. I think he used to live in this building."

"Jackson died in the war," the woman says, with an air of melancholy that saddens Thomas.

"The war?" Earl asks, with a sensitivity that Thomas picks up on immediately. "Which war was that, ma'am?"

"The big one," the woman says, squeezing the sleeping cat like an infant to her chest. "He wrote for the first few years, and then nothing. You two here from the service?" she asks, looking from Earl to Thomas and back again. Thomas wonders if she's drunk. Or maybe just crazy.

"No, we aren't. But would you like us to take a message back to them?"

"Oh yes, that would be nice of you. Just tell them that I'm proud of the boys, and that we're all waiting for them to come home." She smiles warmly after saying this, and touches Earl on the arm with genuine affection.

"Will do, ma'am. Will do. We're sorry to have bothered you."

"Nonsense. I'm always happy to speak with our fighting boys."

After they've descended the stairs and are back out on the sidewalk, Thomas asks, "What's wrong with her, Earl?"

"Nothing, kid," Earl says, as they head back past the Frozen Circus. "She's an old woman. Sometimes the memory starts to go."

"That's sad."

"It is. But it's beautiful too."

"Beautiful?"

"You saw how friendly she was? That she still had a goodness about her even though she was struggling to keep things straight?"

"Yes," Thomas says, as they step back onto the boardwalk.

"That means she was always a good person. That even with her memory shot, and her body breaking down, all that kindness hasn't gone anywhere. And that's a beautiful thing."

"I hadn't thought of it like that."

Earl pauses a few hundred feet from the courts and Thomas asks, "What now, Earl?"

Earl looks out at the waves and says, "You know how to swim?"

"I'm half-dolphin. Three quarters, actually."

"That right? Then come on, Aquaman."

They walk onto the sand, high-tops and all. They weave in between hundreds of sunbathers, all of whom seem to share the unspoken knowledge that the real Eden was never really a garden, but instead a Southern California beach in the middle of summer, the lifeguards sitting in their towers like shirtless Adams silently naming the waves.

"Coney Island was never like this," Earl says.

"What's Coney Island?" Thomas asks, as the two of them take a seat on the sand and begin to unlace their shoes.

"A beach in New York I used to go to when I was a kid."

"Was it fun?"

"It depends."

"On what?"

"On whether you don't mind swimming in raw sewage or not."

"For real?"

"Pretty much."

"My father used to try to make me believe there are mermaids out there this time of year," Thomas says, looking out at the sea.

"Maybe we'll get lucky today," Earl says as he removes his shirt and begins to walk toward the water.

By the time Thomas has finished untying the double-knots in his sneakers and makes it into the water himself, Earl's already out near the break, his arms like windmill-blades scissoring through the sea. Thomas dives down beneath the first wave and then opens his eyes when he reemerges from the water, and then swims out towards where Earl is floating on his back.

"Can your feet still touch the bottom?" Thomas asks as he reaches Earl.

"They can."

"Man, you're lucky."

"Luck is relative, kid. I think you're lucky with those two healthy knees you got."

"Do you ever wonder what you're going to do when you can't play any more?"

"Youth counseling," Earl says, splashing water on his face. "You know, try to help keep kids out of trouble. And try to keep the ones who've already gotten into trouble from getting into any more."

"What about coaching?"

"It's possible. Maybe some day."

"If you do that, can I be your assistant coach?"

"I'll keep a space open on the bench for you."

"We'll have to wear suits like Pat Riley."

"Those suits may be a little out of our budget, kid. But it's not a bad goal to set. Riles definitely knows how to dress."

After Earl dives down into the sea for a few seconds, he reemerges with a strand of seaweed wrapped around his shoulders. As he removes it he says, "What about you, kid? What're you going to do with your life?"

"I don't know. All I want to do is play basketball. Nothing else is half as much fun."

"I feel you, but there'll come a time in your life when you're not going to be able to play anymore," Earl says, as the two of them are lifted by the current. "And you don't want to wait until then to start thinking about what to do next. I learned that the hard way."

"What did you do during the years when you weren't able to play?"

"Everything you can imagine. Worked security at Yankee Stadium. Drove for UPS. Tended bar. Did construction. Finally went to night school and got my degree. After that I started working as a counselor for the city. Juvenile Services. It was hard, but I liked it. It's always easier to get up for work in the morning when you feel like you're making a difference."

Thomas thinks about what Earl has said.

"Maybe I'll be a guitar player then."

"Oh yeah? You play the guitar?"

"No, but I think I might want to learn. I could be like Eddie Van Halen."

"Now you're talking. Everyone needs a fallback plan. Maybe save up some of that paper route money and get yourself an axe."

"An axe?"

"It's slang for 'guitar.'"

"I like that. That'd make me the axe-man."

"Most definitely," Earl says, laughing.

Thomas, treading water, says, "I'm sorry we didn't find Wings today."

"That's alright. This is the way things go sometimes."

Earl grows quiet and, looking in the direction of Catalina, says, "Mermaids, huh?"

"That's what he says."

"I'm not sure I believe him."

"You shouldn't. When I was little he told me there were sharks in our apartment complex swimming pool. I believed him for two or three months before my mom told him to tell me the truth."

The two of them share a laugh before Thomas swims into a wave that's just begun to break. During the span of time when he's within the rolling tunnel of the water, he feels as if his body is weightless, a ghost of itself, as elemental and intangible as sunlight, or love. He catches a few more waves before swimming back to where Earl remains, floating on his back and looking up at the sky.

They stay in the water for the better part of an hour, sometimes bodysurfing, other times watching the seemingly endless parade of beautiful women who walk along the shoreline. It occurs to Thomas that, even if he never makes the NBA or becomes the second coming of Eddie Van Halen, a job as a beach lifeguard might not be such a bad way to make a living. There are worse fallback plans, he figures.

"Do you ever wonder what your life would have been like if you'd never been in that accident?" Thomas asks Earl as a seagull settles onto the water a few feet from them.

"Not as often as I used to."

"How often was that?"

"About every five minutes."

"How often do you think about it now?"

"Only every ten minutes or so."

The two of them laugh.

"Does it make you sad when you think about it?"

"Sad isn't the right word for it. More like disappointment. Like you still can't believe things didn't turn out the way you thought they would."

Earl stretches his arms out as if he were trying to touch the shore-line and the horizon at the same time. As he does so, Thomas notices a small tattoo on the inside of Earl's right bicep.

"What do the initials stand for?"

"Cazzie Lewis."

"Who's he?"

"Cazzie Lewis was my father."

Thomas picks up on Earl's use of the past-tense.

"Your father's dead?"

"Twelve years ago next month."

"What happened to him?"

"He got sick. The kind of sick you don't recover from."

"I'm really sorry, Earl."

"Thanks, kid. But he's still with me. I can feel it."

"What do you mean?"

"I mean his spirit. There'll be days when I'm not feeling too good about things, and I'll hear his voice in my head. Or I'll see an old movie that he used to like and suddenly I'll feel him next to me, watching it with me."

"What kinds of movies did he like?"

"All kinds. Funny movies. Action movies. War movies. 'So long as the good guys win in the end,' he used to say."

Above them a flock of seagulls fly in formation. Thomas looks back at Earl's tattoo and says, "Coach Roth has a tattoo also. But it's not initials. It's numbers."

"Coach Roth?"

"He's my rec league coach. He makes the best sandwiches in the world. I go to his deli every weekend, and sometimes after school too."

"What type of numbers?"

"It's a bunch of them right here," Thomas says, pointing at his forearm, still treading water. "There's like six or seven of them in a row. There aren't any designs around them or anything."

Earl's face grows thoughtful. He squints and tilts his head back to look up at the sky before returning his gaze to the shore. Thomas watches and waits, expecting Earl to say something about what he's told him. But instead Earl shakes his head from side to side for a moment, as if thinking about something too sad for him to want to talk about, and then says, "You ready to head back in, kid?"

"Yes."

"I'll race you," Earl says, taking off before Thomas even realizes he's been challenged. Once Thomas makes it back to their place on the sand, Earl is already lying on his back, his forearm shielding his eyes from the sun. Thomas decides not to bother him by talking. Instead he takes in the sights around him. He watches the slow progression of a sand castle being built by two little girls about twenty yards away from him, and listens to the music emanating from the speakers of a small boombox belonging to a group of college-aged women a few feet over from where he sits. And he looks back out to sea just in time to marvel at a pod of dolphins leaping in and out of the water as they swim. For whatever reason, Thomas finds himself wondering what his father might be doing at this very moment. Perhaps, he thinks, he's sitting beside his mother's grave, singing an off-key version of those ancient songs he loves to sing around the apartment. Or maybe he's secretly visiting old friends, moving through the streets without making eye contact, careful not to draw attention to himself. But Thomas finally settles on something simpler: he pictures his father sitting on a large carpet in an otherwise empty room, reciting his prayers. Whether or not there's actually a God listening to what his father is saying, he's always found his father's certainty that somebody is listening comforting enough.

Or, as his father has told him, "The miracle of prayer is not whether it gets answered, but the fact that you have the imagination to believe that it might be."

For the first time Thomas feels like he knows what his father means. He closes his eyes and, for the next several minutes, prays that Wings will turn up soon.

Twenty minutes later Earl awakens and says, "What do you say we head for home?"

"Shouldn't we keep looking?"

"We've put the word out, kid. Maybe it'll somehow get back to him. There's nothing more to be done today."

"Are you going to look for him again tomorrow?"

"Maybe. But I've got to be in Philly on Friday."

Thomas looks at Earl and tries not to hide his sadness at the quick turnaround of Earl's trip to Southern California.

"I thought you were going to be here for another week, Earl."

"I was. But I found out late last night that I've got a tryout with the Sixers first thing Saturday morning."

"You do?" Thomas asks excitedly, stunned at the news. "That's awesome!"

"It's just a tryout. Let's see what happens before we start celebrating."

"You're going to make the team for sure. This is going to be great!"

"I'm not sure it'll feel that way when I'm banging with Moses Malone down low."

"Are you kidding? Moses should be worried about losing his starting spot."

"You're never short on optimism, kid."

As they begin to walk back across the sand in the direction of the boardwalk, Thomas asks Earl how he got the tryout.

"I called my ex-agent about a month ago. Told him to see if anyone might be willing to give an old, washed-up center a shot."

"I bet he was surprised to hear from you."

"You're right about that. At first he thought it was a prank call, and then when he realized it was actually me, he asked me if I'd been drinking."

"Will Dr. J. be there?"

"Maybe."

"Remember to pass him the ball."

"Very funny, kid. Very funny."

Suddenly the two of them can make out the sounds of a big band playing a slow song. For a few moments Thomas isn't sure where the music's coming from, but then he sees them. There are perhaps as many as thirty people, all of them walking down the middle of the street, their brass instruments catching the sunlight and sending it back out in all directions. They're dressed in dark suits, pressed white shirts, and polished black shoes, and most of them wear hats like the one Thomas's grandfather wears on Sundays to church. Earl and Thomas pause at the edge of the street and watch the procession move towards them. Several other passersby do the same.

"What is it?" Thomas asks.

"A second line," Earl whispers.

"What's that?"

"It means a funeral's about to begin."

It's the saddest music Thomas has ever heard, its tempo somehow even slower than the pace at which the men walk. The song's melody is less a series of notes than what he imagines a soul might sound like as it's leaving a person's body for the afterlife. It's unlike any other type of music Thomas is familiar with. It feels older, more rooted in history, and its lack of vocals provides him with the opportunity to let his own imagination help to picture the story it's telling.

Thomas looks in the direction the musicians are heading and sees, two blocks further south, a small wooden church, its facade in need of paint, its slim steeple in need of reinforcement. Already several people stand on the steps that lead to the open doors of the chapel, watching as the band approaches.

It's the first time in his life that Thomas has thought of music as a truly collective endeavor, and that the audience is as much a part of the music as the players themselves. Indeed, Thomas realizes, it sounds less like a song written by a particular individual, and more like something an entire people, or country, even, has written together. And as the trumpets sway, and the saxophones bear witness, and the large drums that a handful of men have strapped to their chests keep time, Thomas feels like the music is doing everything it can to, if not defeat death, then to at least refuse to give it the final word. He feels sad and happy at the same time.

The coffin's held aloft by a group of men at the front of the line, the white handkerchiefs in each of their breast pockets looking like the sails of small boats drifting a long ways from shore. Thomas wonders if the dead can hear music, and whether the spirit is still able to tap its imaginary feet along to a beautiful rhythm. He hopes so. It'd be a shame for whoever's in the coffin to miss what his friends are playing in his memory.

A few minutes later the music stops. The band silences their instruments, climbs the steps to the church, and slowly, in twos and threes, enters the church. Thomas cannot imagine a sermon capable of matching the power of the performance he's just heard.

"I thought they only did that in New Orleans," Earl says, after he and Thomas have returned to the car and are putting on their seat-belts.

"Did what?"

"The second line. It's a New Orleans thing. They play melancholy music on their way into the church, and joyful music on their way out."

"I'm glad they do it in L.A. too."

Earl laughs softly.

"Me too, kid."

"One thing though."

"What's that?"

"At my funeral I hope the second line plays Prince. Or Bob Seger. Maybe they could play both."

Earl laughs more loudly now.

"I'm sure that can be arranged. But you've got a long time before you've got to worry about anything like that."

"What do you want them to play at your funeral?"

"Don't let the knee braces fool you, kid. I'm still a young man too."

An hour later, as they pull up to the curb in front of Sunwood, they see a full-court game in progress. The ten players comprising the two squads don't have any familiar faces, but James, Rod, and Arjun are standing on the sidelines waiting for the next game.

"Well, we've gone from court to court all day today and haven't played once," Earl says, looking across the street. "Why don't we change that?"

"Let's just make sure we're on the same team," Thomas answers, unable to contain his excitement.

Thomas doesn't even have a chance to make introductions before James does what he does best: insult the new guy. It's clear to Thomas that James would make fun of the Pope if he showed up at the courts and wanted to run.

"My dad says you cost him 500 bucks in the '75 Finals," James says.

"That's what he gets for betting on the Squires," Earl responds.

"I told him the same thing," James says. "But what could I do? The man voted for Mondale."

"So he was the other one," Earl says.

Introductions follow. Rod, especially, is in awe of Earl, hanging on his every word as if Earl were Moses recently returned from the top of Mount Sinai. Earl, sensing this, says to Rod, "The Kid tells me you're the king of this court."

"Kid, how could you?" James asks. "After all I've done for you."

"Like leaving him alone in the middle of a riot?" Arjun responds.

"Nah," Rod responds to Earl, ignoring James. "I was just holdin' down the fort until you arrived."

The two of them shake hands while Thomas looks out at the guys playing, all of whom appear to be a collection of standard weekend warriors. They're in their mid-to-late 30s, and several of them are clearly angry at the fact that they're no longer the high school heroes they once were, or at least believe themselves to have been. Though they're obviously friends, not a play seems to go by without at least two of the players trading elbows, arguing over a foul call, or yelling in frustration at being overlooked by a teammate when they felt they were open. They are the exact kind of guys Thomas promises himself on a daily basis he's never going to become when he gets older.

"These guys don't seem very happy," Thomas says.

"Imagine how their wives must feel," James says.

"You think they're all married?" Arjun asks.

"It's the only explanation for this kind of misery," James says.

"Don't you want to get married some day?" Rod asks.

"No," James says.

"Why not?" Thomas asks.

"Because I want to remain sexually active," James says.

"The hand doesn't count," Arjun says.

"No, but your sister does," James counters.

Earl begins the next game by blocking a shot. His swat kickstarts a fast break that ends with James draining a jumper off a pass from

Thomas. Over the next several minutes it seems to Thomas like their squad is the playground equivalent of the Showtime Lakers, Rod swooping in for layups, Arjun crashing the offensive boards, and Earl drop-stepping and dream-shaking his defenders so consistently that they don't even have time to foul him before he scores. When, on game point, Thomas throws an alley-hoop to Earl for a one-handed dunk, Thomas exclaims, "Earl, tell the second line I'm ready to go!"

Earl laughs, while James says, "Wait until you've lost your virginity until you say something like that."

"How do you know I haven't?" Thomas asks.

Rod, Arjun, and James all break up at this, as Thomas flashes a wide smile.

Over the next hour the courts fill up with so many players that three full court games are going simultaneously. But even with the increased and improved competition—some of the neighborhood's best have shown up after the word has spread that a former professional is at the Matsuya courts—Earl's all-around dominance keeps their squad on the first court for the entirety of the evening. Around 8 p.m. Thomas sees his mom step out onto the sidewalk for what he thinks means it's time to come home, but instead she only smiles and waves at him before heading back inside.

It's not until around 9 p.m., when it's grown so dark that the ball looks less like a tangible object than a floating silhouette unsure of whom to haunt next, that the players begin to reluctantly scatter for home. As Earl, James, and Thomas walk back towards Sunwood, James says, "I'm beginning to think the fast break is proof that God exists."

"I'm not going to disagree with that," Earl says.

"Then what does the slam dunk prove?" Thomas asks.

"That God had one hell of a vertical leap back in the day," James says.

The three of them share a laugh before James says goodnight and disappears into his building. A minute later Earl and Thomas stand at the bottom of the steps that lead to Thomas's front door.

"You're a good one to run the streets with, kid. You earned your gold detective's shield."

"That's the one they gave to Frank Serpico."

"It is. But you didn't have to get shot to get yours."

"I'm glad about that," Thomas says, and then, wanting to say something to inspire Earl the same way Earl has just inspired him, says, "Don't give up hope. Wings is out there somewhere."

"I know he is, kid," Earl answers, as the two of them bump fists. "I know it."

7

"WHEN'S YOUR DAD COMING BACK?"

James asks as he and Thomas walk up Harbor Boulevard. The late morning sun spreads its fingers wide enough to palm the entire city with its light, as if the sun were Meadowlark Lemon and the city an oversized basketball.

"I don't know," Thomas says.

"You're lucky. I wish my father would go away for a few months. Longer, actually."

"You'd miss him, wouldn't you?"

"Miss what? Him yelling at the TV in frustration because he bet on the wrong team again? Or the entire apartment smelling like a tire-fire because he's the last guy in America who still believes smoking is good for you?"

"It could be worse."

"How so?"

"Your dad could be Kenny Rogers."

The two of them laugh at this, pausing as they do in front of an automobile dealership, the cars lined up like multi-colored dominoes waiting to be tipped over.

"I need one of those," James says, pointing towards a red Mercedes convertible, the same make and model as the one Eddie Murphy drove in *Beverly Hills Cop*.

"They don't get good gas mileage," Thomas says.

"Gas mileage?" James asks. "You think girls care about gas mileage?"

"I'm just saying. A car like this isn't very cost-effective. The tune-ups alone will be a lot of money."

"Cost effective? Tune-ups? Jesus, kid."

"Besides," Thomas says, unable to let it go. "You should buy American anyway."

"Thanks for the advice, Lee Iacocca."

They take their time as they walk, pausing at each successive dealership to imagine the kinds of cars they might buy. James loves the luxury models: the BMWs, the Jaguars, the Range Rovers. Thomas likes the simpler, sturdier makes. He tells James that if money were no object, he'd buy a convertible black Ford Thunderbird.

"And then I'd take Pacific Coast Highway all the way to Alaska."

"PCH doesn't go to Alaska, kid," James says.

"Really?

"Really."

"Well, then I'll drive to Seattle."

"Why Seattle?"

"My dad climbed Mt. Rainier once. I'd like to do that too."

"There aren't any hoops on Mt. Rainier. And I can't imagine you being able to go more than ten or twelve hours at a time without playing."

As Thomas prepares to respond, James stops walking. After a few seconds he shakes his head and says, "I don't believe it."

"What?"

"Listen."

Thomas tries to ignore the traffic and focus on whatever it is James has noticed. It takes him a handful of seconds before he hears it too: bagpipes. Someone is playing "Take Me Out to the Ballgame" in the middle of a Sunday afternoon. On bagpipes. In Orange County.

"Do you think it's the same guy?" Thomas asks.

"Who else could it be?"

"I don't know. A lot of people play them, don't they?"

"In Scotland, maybe. Not in Southern California."

Deciding that they must confirm whether it is indeed the same man they saw a few days ago at Matsuya, they cut through the lot of a Datsun dealership and walk down a long side street that dead-ends in a park Thomas didn't know existed. It's amazing, Thomas thinks to himself. The only area he's ever known continues to offer up new discoveries on an almost daily basis.

Upon entering the park, there's a main trail that immediately breaks off into three directions. They follow the music down the trail to the right, winding their way through foliage and bush so thick that at times the trail seems to disappear entirely. As the grass and leaves brush against his skin, and the pollen from the flowers begins to irritate his nose, it occurs to Thomas that nature is, like the junk food sold at the fair every summer, better in the abstract. For many years, in fact, this walk through a relatively well-kept park an hour south of Los Angeles will be the closest Thomas will ever come to camping.

"I told you," James says, as the two of them emerge around the final bend in the trail and see him.

"Crazy," Thomas admits.

Just like the week before, the man is dressed in full Scottish regalia: plaid kilt, knee-length socks, and a hat that looks vaguely like a graduation cap. He is, Thomas figures, somewhere between fifty and sixty.

They stand for a time and watch him. When he finishes playing, the man removes his mouth from his instrument and says to the two of them, "You two get around."

"We were going to say the same thing about you," James responds.

"How far away could you hear me playing?"

"Chicago," James answers.

The man laughs and says, "My wife's always said this instrument is a better home security system than a guard dog."

"It sounds good though, mister," Thomas says.

"Thank you, young man," he says, before abruptly shutting his eyes and drawing out a long, slow note on the pipes. Thomas recognizes it almost immediately: "Amazing Grace."

"This is my grandfather's favorite song," he says to James.

"Shhh," James says, suddenly transfixed.

Thomas is reminded, for what seems like the hundredth time, that James Bianchi is one of the more complicated individuals he has ever met.

The two of them stand and listen to the song until its final note, after which the man opens his eyes and smiles at the two of them.

"How hard was that to learn?" James asks.

"The song? Or the instrument itself?"

"The instrument."

"It's difficult to say. I can't remember a time in my life when I didn't know how to play it."

"Who taught you?" James asks.

"My father. And his father taught him."

"Does every guy in Scotland know how to play it?"

"I don't know. I was born in San Diego."

As James and the old man continue to speak, Thomas's attention is drawn to the basketball court about two hundred yards away, where two men shoot hoops at a rim that no longer appears to possess a net.

"I'll be right back," Thomas says, though neither the bagpipe player nor James seem to take notice of his announcement.

As he moves across the greenbelt, from the corner of his eye he senses the silhouette of a large fan moving towards him. A moment later a peacock, its blue neck and multi-colored feathers like something designed by a psychedelic artist doing ad copy for the Grateful Dead, crosses his path. The peacock seems as equally fascinated by Thomas as Thomas is by him, and the two of them have their own unofficial standoff for several seconds, an inter-species *High Noon* without six-shooters or cowboy hats. And then, just as quickly as he has appeared, the bird disappears back into the bushes. Thomas is in disbelief at what he's just seen.

Upon reaching the court, Thomas recognizes the two men as regulars from Coach Roth's deli, though he doesn't know either one of them by name. For a minute or so Thomas stands on the sideline watching them play HORSE. Then, after one of the men badly misses a three-pointer and has to chase down the ball as it bounces across the concrete, the other one, a forty-something man with a beer belly and a beard that looks like he's stolen it from Gandalf, says, "What's up, kid?"

"Who's winning?"

"You saw that last shot," the man responds, as his buddy comes back with the ball. "I'm taking it to him."

"Hey kid," the other one says, recognizing Thomas. "Rough news about Mr. Roth, huh?"

"What do you mean?" Thomas asks.

The two men look at each other and trade frowns before the former says, "He had a heart attack on the Huntington Pier two days ago."

"Is he ok?" Thomas asks.

This time the two men don't make eye contact at all.

"He didn't make it, kid. The funeral was this morning, I think."

For some reason Thomas finds himself turning to look off into the bushes, as if a second glimpse of the peacock might somehow undo the news he's just been given. When it's clear, after several seconds of waiting, that the bird won't be making an encore appearance, Thomas turns back to the two men and says, "Was he hurt?"

"Hurt?" one of the men asks.

"I think it was pretty sudden," the other one says. "I don't think he suffered."

"No," Thomas says, "I mean…" He's not sure what he means, actually. But he continues. "I mean, did it hurt him? Was he in pain?"

The one with the beard takes a step towards Thomas and softens his voice.

"I don't know, kid. But he lived a long life. Nobody lives forever."

"He should have," Thomas says.

"I'm not going to disagree with you there," the other one says. "He was as good as they come."

Thomas doesn't say anything for a few moments, but instead focuses on trying not to begin crying.

"It's my fault," Thomas says.

"Your fault?" the bearded one asks. "How'd you figure that?"

"I told Coach last week he shouldn't work out as hard as he does. That it was going to give him a heart attack. Maybe I cursed him."

"That's not how things work, kid," the bearded one says. "Mr. Roth just had some bad luck. These things happen."

Thomas nods and tries to gather his feelings.

"I have to go," Thomas says, with as much calmness as he can muster.

Before the men can respond he turns and sprints back across the greenbelt to James, who's still speaking to the bagpipe player. When he arrives Thomas points back towards the men shooting hoops and says, "James."

"Hold on."

"*James.*"

"What?"

"Coach Roth died."

"What do you mean?" James asks, turning to look at Thomas.

"On the pier. The Huntington Beach Pier. They said he died."

It's James's turn to be disoriented. He steps closer to Thomas and repeats, "What are you talking about?"

"He was on the pier."

"The pier. Ok."

"And I guess he had a heart attack. They couldn't save him."

"Was anyone with him?"

"Mrs. Roth, I think."

"You think?"

"I'm not sure. Probably."

Thomas will never be able to remember what he and James say to the bagpipe player before leaving, only that the old man offers his condolences before the two of them turn and head back in the direction of the park's entrance. But he will remember that, thirty or so seconds after they've left, the opening notes of "Ave Maria" begin carrying out across the park. Years later Thomas will still wish he knew the bagpipe player's name so he could thank him for playing that song at this particular moment.

It's not until they're back out on Harbor and walking in the direction of Coach Roth's deli when the two of them begin to speak again.

"I wonder who's running the deli," James says.

"Probably no one."

"We should do something."

"Like what?"

"Do you know where he lives?"

"Yes."

"Where?"

"It's that way," Thomas says, pointing past the Exxon Station.

"How much money you got on you?" James asks.

Thomas kneels down and pulls a crumpled five-dollar-bill from his sock. When he stands back up he notices James is removing a ten, three singles, and a few quarters from his own wallet.

"Come on," James says. "We can't show up empty-handed."

The supermarket is nearly as busy as the floor of a Vegas casino. Mothers push shopping carts through the aisles as their infants perch like koalas on their backs, while the slightly older children crouch in the bodies of the carts among the apples, cold cuts, and soda cans as if they were oceanographers preparing to descend into the sea to get an up close and personal view of the hammerhead shark.

"Over here," James says, walking towards the flower section.

"What kind should we get?" Thomas asks as he looks at the roses, daffodils, carnations, lilies, orchids, and sunflowers that surround them.

"Whatever we can afford," James says.

After a few minutes of assiduous price checking, Thomas pulls a large bouquet of red and white flowers from a vat of water and says, "What about these?"

"How much are they?"

"Ten dollars."

"Perfect", James says. "Let's get them."

Back out on the street, the two of them pause at the corner and wait for the light to change. The streets are even busier than normal; two lanes have been blocked off because a fire hydrant has burst, spraying its water up into the air. Local kids, some of them having removed their shoes, play beneath the impromptu waterfall, while a few parents take photographs.

"Have you ever seen a dead body?" Thomas asks.

James continues to look at the scene across the street, where a young girl darts beneath the water, laughing in exhilaration.

"Of course."

"Who?" Thomas asks.

"My father. Every time he comes home from the bar."

"I'm serious."

James pauses.

"My sister."

"You had a sister?"

"For three days."

"What was her name?"

"She didn't have one."

"How could she not have one?" Thomas asks, as they cross the street and head in the direction opposite of where the waterworks are taking place.

"My parents said they were waiting to see what her personality was."

None of this makes any sense to Thomas.

"What'd they put on her birth certificate?"

"I don't know."

"What'd they put on her tombstone?"

"She doesn't have one. We scattered her ashes at sea."

"They did that for one of the Beach Boys."

"Which one?"

"I don't know. The surfer."

"They were all surfers."

"Then I don't know."

"They do it for soldiers too," James says.

"I wonder where she is now," Thomas says as they pass, in succession, two pawnshops, a Guns-n-Ammo store, and an Adult Book Mart that features a window mannequin of a scantily clad woman conspicuously absent a head.

"Hopefully eating one of Coach's turkey sandwiches," James says.

"You think they eat in Heaven?"

"If there's actually a Heaven, I don't see why not."

"You think there might not be a Heaven?"

"Any world where a good guy like Coach Roth has such terrible things happen to him means there's a better than 50/50 chance that

God doesn't exist."

"Terrible things? You mean his heart attack?"

James looks at Thomas in consternation.

"No, not his heart attack."

"Then what?"

"You've seen his tattoo."

"What about it?"

James realizes Thomas doesn't understand the awful significance of the numbers.

"It means he was in a concentration camp."

Thomas stops walking and looks at James, as if hoping James will take back what he's said. Thomas has seen stories about the camps on television. And he's heard about Auschwitz from his own grandfather, who helped liberate the camps at the end of the war.

"I didn't know that's what the numbers were for," Thomas says.

"Mrs. Roth is Coach's second wife. His first one died in the camps. A daughter too, I think."

They've turned onto Coach's street as James tells him this, and Thomas has difficulty reconciling this information with the simple beauty of the surrounding cul-de-sac, which is full of modest homes, many of them featuring an assortment of children's toys and tree swings in the front yards.

"Do you ever hate the world we live in, James?"

"At least once a day. But usually more than that."

Neither one of them speak for several seconds as they continue to walk, before Thomas, sighting Coach Roth's house, says, "It's this one."

They weave in and out of the cars that are double and triple-parked out in front of the driveway and, after pausing in front of the open door for a moment, step inside. The first room is crowded with people dressed in dark colors, most of them standing in groups and speaking to one another in quiet, but not overly hushed, tones. Many eat from small plates and look at the assortment of photographs that have been pasted onto several large white boards for viewing. Thomas scans the room and looks for familiar faces, but other than a few people he's seen in passing at the deli from time to time and a handful of other tall men he figures are former players of Coach Roth's, he doesn't recognize anyone.

"I don't see Mrs. Roth," Thomas says.

"Maybe she's in the living room," James responds.

The living room is even more full of people than the previous room, and at the far end of it, standing in the middle of a small semi-circle of people, all of whom are taller than her by several inches, is Mrs. Roth. She sees James first, and then Thomas, and it's clear that her surprise at their appearance is equalled by her happiness at their arrival. She motions them over.

As they approach, Thomas thinks Mrs. Roth looks both like the oldest woman in the world and like someone who has moved beyond time entirely. She makes him think of the Lady of the Lake, if the Lady of the Lake had moved to America and lived a long, long life. As Mrs. Roth reaches out to embrace both of them in a hug, Thomas notices that she smells of perfume and strawberries and rosewater soap.

"These are for you," Thomas says, holding up the flowers.

"Oh, how lovely," Mrs. Roth says, giving both of them kisses on the cheek. "Thank you so much for these," she says, even though Thomas will learn a few years later that it's not the tradition in Jewish culture to bring flowers to a memorial.

After Mrs. Roth introduces the two of them to some of the people in her immediate orbit, including a daughter who's flown down from Portland and a niece who works at a hospital in L.A., she says, "Joseph loved you boys."

"We loved him too, Mrs. Roth," James says, his voice possessed of the same surprising conviction he'd showed when speaking to Thomas about whether or not God existed. "He was a great man."

Thomas, not knowing what to say, asks, "Did you bury Coach at sea?"

"At sea?" Mrs. Roth asks, confused.

"That's where they buried James's sister."

From the look on James's face, Thomas realizes it isn't the moment for such a question. However, Mrs. Roth acts as if it's the most natural thing in the world for Thomas to wonder.

"No, we buried him in the Veteran's Cemetery in Los Angeles."

"I didn't know Coach Roth was a veteran," James says.

"He fought in Korea. He thought it was his duty to serve the country that had helped to save his life."

"We miss him already, Mrs. Roth," Thomas says.

"I miss him already too, Thomas," she answers, squeezing his hand.

Mrs. Roth embraces both James and Thomas again. A few moments later, as other people wait to pay their respects to her, they say goodbye and find their way into the dining room, where a table as long as a canoe is covered with food.

James scans the table full of breads, cold cuts, vegetables, and dressings, and says, "These sandwiches are never going to be as good as if Coach was making them."

"He was a magician," Thomas agrees.

But the two of them fill their plates nevertheless, and then wander through the house to look at the photographs that seem to cover nearly every inch of the walls. After a time, Thomas, having lost

James in the crowd, returns to the main room to look more closely at the photo collages he noticed upon first entering the house.

What jumps out to Thomas is how simple, and how full, a life Coach Roth seemed to have led. In just about every photo, he's either with his family, behind the counter at the deli, or on a basketball court somewhere, instructing kids, teenagers, and sometimes college players on the fundamentals of the game he knew so well. Thomas even locates himself in a handful of the pictures, including one where he and Coach Roth smile just minutes after Thomas had hit the game-winning shot to win their team the city championship.

Thomas moves back and forth between the picture boards, gazing at a few of the photos before moving onto another collage, and then returning after a little while to look at the rest. This scatter-shot process is why it takes him several minutes to stumble upon a photograph of Wings, in blue tank top and matching blue shorts, rising up for a jumper on an outdoor court, all five defenders looking on helplessly as he releases the ball.

Surprised and excited at his discovery, Thomas looks around for James, only to notice that James is talking to three girls his own age, all of whom are dressed in conservative black dresses, and all of whom appear to be hanging on to James's every word.

Thomas turns back to further study the photograph. He focuses on the banner draped above the makeshift bleachers and against the rising backstop that appears to separate the courts from the soccer fields beyond. It reads:

An Afternoon of Shooting Stars: Arden Park's 17th Invitational Tournament

"Arden Park", Thomas repeats to himself, as if it's a prayer he's attempting to memorize, or a spell he's trying to cast. He considers asking Mrs. Roth about it but decides against it. Instead he commits everything in the photograph to memory, from the large trees rising south of the park to the silhouette of the downtown Los Angeles skyline towering behind it, the skyscrapers rising like steel turrets above a smog-filled kingdom.

Thomas goes back through the collages again, searching for Wings in any of the other pictures. Shortly thereafter Thomas spots a second one. In it, Wings and Coach Roth are sharing a laugh. It's clear from the backdrop that the photograph was also taken in Arden Park, although given that Wings is wearing a different outfit, most likely on a different afternoon. Thomas's excitement at the discovery of a new lead is offset by one particularly inconvenient fact: he has no idea where Arden Park is. But that's alright, he figures. Someone will know. He can start asking around when he gets home.

"Can you get home on your own?" James asks as he suddenly appears at Thomas's side.

"Yes."

"Good. Because even if you'd said no it wouldn't have mattered."

Thomas looks past James's shoulder to see the girls looking in their direction.

"How do you do it?"

"That's like asking Michael Jordan how he jumps so high. Some things just aren't meant to be explained."

"You're no Michael Jordan."

"You're right," James answers. "Michael can't shoot like me."

Thomas's mom is still on shift at the library for another two hours, so when he gets home he's got the apartment all to himself. A lot of his friends, especially the ones who live in the big houses in Green Valley, often complain of boredom as they sit in their living rooms eating fast food with only the family dog for company. But Thomas loves that he's alone as often as he is. It makes him feel like a spy, or a superhero, hanging out in his very own Fortress of Solitude, preparing himself for whatever his next adventure might be.

After he's warmed up the plate of chicken, rice, and tater tots that his mother has prepared for him before heading to work, he turns on the television. He finds a rerun of *Magnum P.I.*, where the titular detective's kayak has been wrecked by a passing boat, and he's now stranded alone at sea with no way back to shore. As the hours pass, Magnum treads water and begins to hallucinate, increasingly haunted by flashbacks to his childhood when he was at the beach with his father. At first Thomas is entertained, absorbed even, by Magnum's dilemma. However, as Magnum's hallucinations become more and more intense—to the point where he's even begun to have a dialogue with his long-dead father—Thomas suddenly finds himself, to his surprise, starting to cry. Initially it's a few tears, mild stuff. But soon, as Magnum's longing for his father escalates into outright despair, Thomas's sadness transforms into something else entirely. He begins to sob. He's angry at Magnum's father for getting killed in the Korean War. Angry at Coach Roth for dying without saying goodbye. Angry at his own father for flying off to a country that he might not be able to make it back from. Thomas tries to focus on the screen through the thick film of his tears, but he can't. A few minutes later, he turns the television off and stands in the middle of the living room, trying to will himself to stop crying. His Fortress of Solitude has suddenly become more like a prison, and he wants out.

Years later Thomas will not remember making the decision to leave the apartment, but he will remember the speed with which he sprinted down the stairs and through the complex, past the pool where a few of his neighbors are sitting on their deck chairs and drinking, and through the carport that links one section of buildings to the next. Not even the Flash, he would later think, could've matched the time he made getting to Earl's front door.

When Earl opens the door, Thomas is still trying to knock, as if it's a tick that he can't keep himself from exercising. Earl, immediately seeing that Thomas is near full hysterics, doesn't ask what's wrong, but instead takes Thomas by the shoulder and brings him inside.

Earl leads Thomas to the sofa, and then sits on the coffee table in front of him. Thomas has begun to shake so hard that Earl wonders if he's about to go into shock.

"What happened, kid?"

There are so many tears in Thomas's eyes that it feels as if he were trying to swim underwater with his eyes wide open. As he tries to speak he finds that he can't catch his breath. Instead he hiccups, and tries again. Nothing doing. He thinks he might throw up.

"Take your time, kid," Earl says, standing up. "I'll get you some water."

Earl returns and puts the glass on the counter. He sits across from him, puts one hand behind Thomas's neck and says, "It's alright, kid. It's alright. Just get it out. Take your time."

Thomas does just that, crying so hard that he's almost silent, his body feeling as if it's had the wind knocked out of it. He thinks of Coach Roth at the pier and wonders if he felt shock, fear, or peace in those final moments, and if there was anything he regretted or wished he'd had the chance to do differently. Thomas thinks of his own father and wonders if his father misses him, or if he's happy to be so far away from here, to be instead with his own brother and sisters, speaking the language Thomas has never learned to speak. He thinks of Mrs. Roth and of how empty the house is going to feel for her after everyone leaves. He thinks of his own mother and wonders what she misses most about his father, and about what fears she has that she doesn't share with him because she worries he's too young to understand. But when he finally speaks he says none of these things. Instead he says, "I'm sorry you and Wings were in that car accident, Earl."

Earl can't hide his surprise. So much so, in fact, that he almost laughs.

"Is that why you've been crying? Hell, that's life, kid. Those kinds of things happen. You can't sweat that. Besides, everything worked out."

"But it isn't fair. You should be playing in the NBA right now."

"That still might happen. Don't lose hope in me yet."

Thomas rubs his eyes and says, "I could never lose hope in you, Earl."

Earl lightly taps Thomas's shoulder and says, "Come on, kid. Tell me the truth. Something else must've happened. There's no way that car accident is making you feel like this."

Thomas tries to answer as simply as possible but almost immediately his words get away from him. He knows he's rambling but is unable to stop it. He tells Earl about the episode of *Magnum*, about the shattered kayak, the empty sea, the hot sun, Magnum's dead father, all of it. He tells him about Coach Roth, the deli, and all those years Coach would work with him on his game. He tells Earl that he doesn't think his own father misses him, that he's worried he's never coming home, that he might be dead already, and that, even if he isn't, the government will never let him leave a second time. He tells Earl all of this, and he tells Earl that he wishes Earl had two good knees, that Earl was playing for the Lakers, and that he didn't have to leave on Friday for Philadelphia.

When he finally finishes Earl remains silent for a few moments, and then says, "That's a lot to carry. Too much, in fact."

Thomas wipes a few more stray tears from his eyes as Earl continues, "You're going to have to put some of that down, kid."

"What'd you mean?"

"I mean you're too skinny to be Hercules."

"Who's Atlas?"

"It doesn't matter. Bad example. But you've got to find a way not to keep all that pain inside. Otherwise it's gonna eat you up."

"How do I get rid of it?"

"I can't tell you that. You'll have to figure that out for yourself."

"I feel like it's my fault."

"Your fault? Why?"

"I never told Coach Roth thank you."

"For what?"

Thomas shrugs his shoulders.

"Everything."

"How often did you go by his shop for sandwiches?"

"Two or three times a week. And every Sunday. He'd always give me a bag of chips for free. A large Pepsi too."

Earl starts to laugh.

"Believe me, kid. He knew you loved him."

"You think so?"

"No doubt."

"I wish I'd told my father the same thing."

"You don't have to do that. Not even when he comes back."

"Why not?"

"Because he's your father. A son never needs to say thank you to his father. Everything a father does for his boy is what he's supposed to do."

"I wish I'd said it anyway."

"Well, tell him tonight."

"How do I do that?"

"When you go home, turn on some of that music we bought yesterday, and just tell him."

"You mean like prayer?"

"Call it whatever you want. Just put it out there, and wherever your father is, it'll find its way to him."

Thomas takes a deep breath, relieved that the tears seem to have stopped. He looks out the window at a few of Clara's plants that are still sitting on the ledge of the balcony.

"You know you're the coolest guy I've ever met, Earl?"

"That's just because I took you to Tower Records," Earl says, laughing.

"No, it isn't," Thomas says, and then begins to smile through his sniffles. "Well, only partly."

A few minutes later, after Thomas has finished his glass of water and fully caught his breath, Earl orders a pizza and turns on the stereo. Once it arrives, they spend the next hour eating and listening to music, while Thomas peppers Earl with questions about what it was like to play in the ABA.

"Who was the best player you ever played against?"

"Artis Gilmore. Hands down."

"How come?"

"Because Artis was strong enough to bench-press a bus. He'd put his body on you and lift you right off your feet. There was nothing you could do about it."

"What was the hardest thing about playing in the ABA?"

"The travel. I don't want to ride another bus for as long as I live. And I mean *ever*."

"I like riding buses."

"That's because you're four feet tall, kid. And riding a bus a few blocks to go to the movies is one thing. Riding a bus in a snowstorm through northern Massachusetts after a back-to-back is something else entirely. One night we had to share a bus with the team we'd just beaten. It was six straight hours of wondering if a brawl was about to start."

"What was your favorite thing about playing in the ABA?"

"Other than the women, you mean?"

Thomas starts to laugh.

"I'm only kidding you. Just being able to *play*. Know what I mean? That two, three nights a week, you're out there for forty-eight minutes running up and down the floor, doing your thing, just like you used to do when you were a kid on the blacktop. It's the only gig in America where you get paid for not growing up. Truth is I'd play until I was a hundred years old if I could."

"Tell me more about the women," Thomas says.

"When you're older, kid."

"Come on, Earl."

"I'll just say this: you know those women in the James Bond movies?"

"Yes."

"Like that. Except without the British accents."

Thomas gets so swept up in Earl's answers that it isn't until he's back climbing the stairs to his own house later on that evening that he realizes he's forgotten to tell Earl about the new lead he has on Wings. He's about to turn back to go and tell him when his mother opens the front door to greet him and ask about his day.

Later on that night he lies awake in bed, playing his new records at low volume so as not to wake his mother. He listens over and over again to "Night Moves" and tries to picture what exactly the world that the singer inhabits might look like. He imagines an old convertible, a sky full of stars, and a lake that the singer used to swim in when both he and his girlfriend were younger. It doesn't make sense to Thomas, this simultaneous feeling of sadness and joy that the song creates in him. It was the same feeling he'd experienced the day prior upon hearing the Second Line. He thinks it should be one or the other. But the music says otherwise.

Listen, the singer's voice seems to say, *and I'll tell you the secret to learning to live in the world. The key is to embrace and lament, to celebrate and eulogize, to laugh and shed tears about the very same things. That's the only way to survive on this crazy planet.*

It's true, Thomas thinks, nodding along to the music's rhythm. He pictures Coach Roth cheering him on after making a three-pointer; he pictures his father gathering his mother into his arms and sprinting up the stairs as she laughs and tells him to put her down. Thomas wants to smile and cry at the very same time. Except he's already cried. Now it's time just to smile. He's got to even the scales.

After an hour or so of repeated listens he finally slips out of bed and turns the record player off. As he settles back into bed while still quietly humming the song's melody, he makes two decisions:

1. He's going to save up his paper route money and buy himself a guitar.

2. He's going to find Jackson Curtis.

WHEN THOMAS ARRIVES AT THE CARPORT TO ASSEMBLE THE NEWSPA-
PERS FOR HIS ROUTE THE FOLLOWING MORNING, HE FINDS THEY HAVE
YET TO BE DROPPED OFF. At 4 a.m., it's too early for him to ride
over to Earl's to tell him about Arden Park, so he heads to the
7-Eleven instead. After carefully running his bike chain through the
front tire, around the frame, and then through his back tire before
snapping the combination lock, he walks inside.

Other than Dustin, the graveyard shift cashier, who sits on a
large stool with his arms crossed, his eyes shut, and an unlit joint
dangling from his lips, the store is empty. A Paul McCartney song
that Thomas's mother likes is playing on the in-store stereo. He
weaves his way through the store's closely packed aisles before
turning the corner to where a quartet of video game machines are
forever poised like electric sphinxes, guarding the tombs of wine
crates and surplus candy bars that are stacked in the storage closet
beyond them. He's been planning to take a run at *Pac-Man*, but to
his surprise, there's a police officer outfitted in his uniform, replete
with gun, mace, nightstick, and flashlight on his belt, already
playing the game. The officer appears to be in his early 40s, and
while short, his broad shoulders and large biceps make Thomas
figure the man probably played football in high school, most likely
free safety or outside linebacker. At first Thomas keeps a respectful
distance, but after a few minutes, when it's become clear the officer

is an absolute savant at the game, the *Pac-Man* equivalent of The Who's mythical pinball wizard, he approaches the console to take up a position to the officer's right. Several more levels pass before the officer, without removing his eyes from the screen, says, "You want to play, kid?"

"No, thank you, Officer. I'll just watch."

What the officer is doing to the ghosts isn't victory, Thomas thinks, it's a straight-up war crime. After twenty minutes and God knows how many dead goblins, Thomas figures the game's low-fi electronica soundtrack should be replaced by a lone trumpeter playing "Taps." Or maybe the man on the bagpipes could do the honors.

"You're the best player I've ever seen, Officer."

"Course I am. I work the graveyard shift in Fountain Valley, and I don't have a partner."

"What do you mean?"

"In the last eight hours all I've had are two Drunk-and-Disorderlies, a stolen Toyota Corolla, and a kid get his cat stuck in a tree. So I've had a lot of time to sharpen my skills."

Thomas resumes watching. He ultimately believes the officer is a kind of Jedi, a Yoda of the Mini-Arcade, possessed of a talent so profound that Thomas would not be surprised if, after completing the game, the officer were to step back, stare at the console, and will it to levitate as if it were Luke Skywalker's crashed X-wing being lifted out of the Dagobah swamps. Such is Thomas's amazement at the performance he's witnessing that it takes a few more minutes before something else occurs to him.

"Do you have a map in your car, Officer?"

The man answers while retaining his Zen-like focus on the game.

"I got all kinds of maps, kid. Maps of the city, the county, the state, you name it. And I've got a direct line to a woman on the other end who's got all the answers that the maps don't have. You want to get to Heaven without hitting any traffic? No problem. I'll get you there in under an hour, with time to stop for a sandwich."

"Not Heaven, Officer. Just Arden Park."

"Arden Park?" the Officer says, his avatar gobbling up another ghost. "Never heard of it."

"It's in Los Angeles."

"That's a long way from home, kid. What's in Arden Park?"

"A long-lost friend of a friend, I hope."

For the first time the man removes his eyes from the screen, if only for a fraction of a second.

"Missing Persons case, eh? Alright, you've got my attention."

With that the officer casually steps away from the console mid-game, unconcerned with the fact that he'd been well on his way to what Thomas figured had to be a record score.

"You could've finished your game first."

"No worries, kid. *Pac-Man*'ll still be there tomorrow. But that long-lost friend of yours might not be."

They leave through the store's back entrance and step into the alley, where the Officer's cruiser is parked. As Thomas slides into the passenger seat, he's entranced by the rifle mounted to the dash. He's never seen a gun before. As the officer begins to thumb through a beat-up Thomas Guide, Thomas asks, "Have you ever had to shoot anybody, Officer?"

"The name's Rodriguez."

"It's nice to meet you, Officer Rodriguez. I'm Thomas."

"Good to meet you, Thomas. And yes, I have."

"You have? Who?"

"The last kid who tried to strike up a conversation while I was playing *Pac-Man*," the Officer says as he breaks into a smile.

"Arden Park," the officer adds. "Ok. Here we go."

He turns the book so Thomas can see the map as well, and places his thumb on Thomas's desired location.

"We're looking at a spot roughly 2 klicks from the Civic Center."

"Klicks?"

"Kilometers. Army slang."

"You were in the Army?"

"That I was."

"In Vietnam?"

"For eighteen months."

"Did you know Eric Channing?" Thomas asks. "He was in Vietnam too."

"There were a lot of us in country, kid."

"He was my neighbor. I used to deliver his newspaper on Sunday mornings. But he died last year."

Officer Rodriguez looks up from the map he's been continuing to study.

"You live in Sunwood, kid?"

"Yes."

"Corporal Eric Channing, 52nd Infantry. Shot himself through the right temple. Survived by his mother and two sisters."

"You did know him."

"No, but I was first on the scene. He was wearing his fatigues when he did it. Like he was getting ready to head back into the grass."

"Grass?"

"It's nothing."

"People keep saying that to me. It's frustrating."

The Officer pauses and looks out the window as Dustin empties several bags of trash into a large blue dumpster.

"Elephant grass. It was everywhere in Vietnam. Sometimes it was so thick you had to slice through it with a knife as you walked."

"That must've been scary."

"It was. Although the fear was better than the alternative. The minute the fear left you was the minute you knew you were in trouble."

"How come?"

"Because it meant you were either starting to like the fighting, or you no longer cared enough to worry about dying."

"Would you fight again if you had to?"

"That's a difficult question."

"How come?"

"Because I change my mind about it every day."

"Would you fight today?"

"No, I wouldn't. These days a war has a better chance of being another Vietnam than it does another World War II."

"That's good, because anyone who can play *Pac-Man* the way you can shouldn't risk his life in a war he doesn't believe in."

The Officer laughs.

"Good point, kid. I wish Richard Nixon had felt the same way when he picked my number out of a hat."

"My dad hates Nixon."

"Your father's a smart man."

And then remembering the map he's holding, Officer Rodriguez looks at Thomas and asks, "You working this case solo?"

"No, I'm helping a friend. He came out here from New York to look for his buddy."

"Glad to hear it. The lone wolf act gets old pretty quickly."

"Maybe you could get a partner."

"This is Fountain Valley, kid. It doesn't take two in a squad car to help an old woman cross the street."

Officer Rodriguez pulls a tablet of paper from the glove compartment and, after studying the map for another moment, begins to write. When he's finished he tears the sheet of paper from the pad and hands it to Thomas. Thomas looks to see the address of the park, as well as the main cross streets.

"I hope you find the guy you're looking for, kid."

"I hope so too. Thank you, Officer Rodriguez."

Officer Rodriguez nods and then says, "You the kid who's always on the blacktop shooting hoops?"

"Yes."

"You've got some game. Last time I saw someone with that type of court vision was when Magic first came into the league."

Before Thomas can respond the two of them notice a dog wandering down the sidewalk, casually trotting along as if he were simply out for a morning walk after breakfast.

"Are you kidding me?" the Officer says.

"What?"

"That's my dog."

A moment later the two of them begin to laugh.

"I don't know how he does it," Officer Rodriguez says.

"Does this happen a lot?"

"Often enough for me to wonder whether he actually likes me."

"Maybe he just wanted to get some exercise."

"Maybe," Officer Rodriguez says, before extending his hand for a shake. "Well, good luck in Arden Park, kid."

"I think you need it more than I do, Officer."

"You may be right about that."

After completing his route, Thomas is back in the apartment by 6:30. His mother's in the living room, eating a breakfast of strawberry yogurt, wheat toast, and a banana. She's reading a paperback novel that features the Golden Gate Bridge shrouded in a layer of fog on the cover. Thomas will never meet another soul for as long as he lives who loves to read as much as his mother. Mysteries, adventures, thrillers, science fiction, comedies, poetry. You name it, she's probably read it.

"How'd your route go?" she asks.

"Good."

"Are you going back to sleep?"

"No. I'm going to watch TV for awhile and then go across the street."

"When does Earl go back to Philadelphia?"

"Friday."

"You're going to miss him."

"He promises we can write," Thomas says, trying not to show his sadness at the fact that Earl is leaving. "What're you reading?"

"It's a book about a missing statue of a bird. Everyone's trying to find it."

"How come?"

"It's really valuable. So much so that people are willing to kill each other for it."

"That doesn't make any sense."

"No, it doesn't," his mother admits. "Life's hard enough without people making it worse for each other."

His mother sips her tea. Thomas can tell there's something more she wants to say.

"What's wrong, Mom?"

His mother takes another sip before placing the cup down onto the coffee table.

"I heard about Coach Roth."

"You did?"

"Mrs. Roth called last night after you'd gone to bed. She said you and James came to see her."

"We brought flowers."

"That was very nice of you. It meant a lot to her."

And then, after a pause, she adds, "You know, with your father gone, and Coach dying, and now Earl leaving so soon, I just....I know it's been difficult for you lately. You're too young for a lot of this."

"It hasn't all been bad, Mom. I got to go to the 4th of July Parade."

"You saw a man get shot there."

"Yeah, but there were women in bikinis there too."

"You have your father's ability to see the good in any situation."

"And yesterday Earl took me to Tower Records. He bought me a Bob Seger record and a Prince record. It was awesome."

"Tower Records, huh? That does sound like a good day."

"You've been there?"

"Of course."

"You have? Why didn't you take me?"

"Because you weren't born the last time I went, sweetheart."

He goes silent for a moment, considering whether to say what he's thinking.

"What is it?" his mother asks.

"I worry you don't have enough fun, Mom."

"What're you talking about?"

"You're always taking care of me, or working, or worrying about Dad. You know you can always go to Tower Records if you want. You don't even have to take me. You can go with your friends or something."

She puts her arm around his shoulder and squeezes him to her.

"Taking care of you is a hundred times more fun than going to Tower Records ever was. Don't worry about me. I'm happy every day that I see you. You understand?"

Thomas nods.

"I'm glad that you met Earl," his mother says.

"Me too," he says, thinking back to the day before, when Earl was the one person in the world he knew could make him feel better.

"Any word on Wings?"

"Maybe. I found two photos of him and Coach together at a court. I'm going to tell Earl about it today."

"That's great. Do you know where the court is located?"

"It's in Los Angeles."

"Which part?"

"Near downtown."

"Well," his mother says. "I hope today is the day the two of you find him."

She stands, slips into her shoes, and adds, "I'll be at work until 8 p.m. There's twenty dollars on the table for you. And remember, if you need anything, Janie is next door."

"I don't need the twenty dollars."

"Why not?"

"I have my paper route money."

"Well, take it anyway."

"Ok."

"I love you."

"Love you too," Thomas answers. "You're the best."

"You're just saying that because I always make you listen to the Beatles."

"In spite of that, Mom," he says. "In spite of that."

Two hours later, after watching back-to-back reruns of *Happy Days* and the last hour of *Heaven Can Wait,* Thomas gets ready for the day. He dresses in his go-to outfit: replica Georgetown Hoya game-shorts, a white t-shirt featuring Magic Johnson soaring for a dunk on the front and Magic's Number 32 on the back, and his broken-in Reebok high-tops. He slips the twenty-dollar bill into his sock, along with an additional twenty from the small stash of bills he has saved up from his paper route, and places his house key into the small pouch he's fastened to the top of his right shoe. After locking both locks behind him, he bounds down the steps two at a time.

Earl doesn't answer. Thomas continues to knock until, after a minute or so of consistent rapping, Earl's next-door neighbor—Stacy, a woman in her early 20s who's still dressed from whatever party she attended the night before—opens her door and says, "He isn't here, Thomas. I saw him leave early this morning."

"Did he say where he was going?"

"I just saw him from my window. He had his gym bag with him though."

"Thanks, Stacy. I like your dress."

"You always know just what to say, sweetie."

After Stacy closes her door, Thomas remains on the landing and tries to figure out what to do. He could wait for Earl to return, but it might be hours until he gets back. And Earl flies out first thing tomorrow morning. Well, he thinks, if his father could sneak back into his homeland without getting caught, he shouldn't have much trouble making it up to L.A. and back without his mom finding out. Indeed, he's almost eleven years old. It's time to start acting like it.

He descends the steps and makes his way to the bus stop at Slater and Brookhurst. He studies the schedule posted besides the bench, where an old woman dressed for mass is sitting. After a minute or so he's pretty sure he's got it figured out: take the Blue Line to the Golden West Station, transfer to a Red Line bus that'll take him to Fullerton Train Station, and from there take the Silver Line all the way to Union Station in Downtown Los Angeles.

Problem solved, he leans against the light pole until the old woman smiles at him and, scooting over, says, "There's plenty of room here, young man."

"Thank you," he says, sitting down. "Are you on your way to church?"

"I haven't missed a Sunday mass in sixty-seven years," she says, nodding.

"Sixty-seven years? How old are you now?"

"I'll be seventy-three next month."

"You never got sick even once and missed a day?"

"I've been sick plenty of times, but the Good Lord has always cured me by 9 a.m. on Sunday mornings."

"That's lucky."

"It isn't luck. It's divine grace."

"I could use some of that today."

"How come?"

"Well, I'm going to look for a friend who I haven't been able to find. Maybe God could step in and make a few phone calls."

The old woman smiles.

"I'll be sure to bring that up with him in church today."

"Thank you, ma'am. I appreciate that."

"You're welcome. Where are you going to be looking for your friend?"

"Los Angeles."

"That's a long way for you to be going alone."

"I know the way," he says, trying to convey the necessary confidence he's still only half-feeling.

"I'm sure you do. You look like a very capable young man."

He doesn't focus so much on the "young" as on the "man." part. *Man.* He likes the sound of that. After all, by the time he was nineteen his grandfather was heading off to fight in WWII. Which means, so far as Thomas sees it, he's actually a little behind in the maturation process.

The bus pulls up and the two of them stand in preparation for boarding. The woman turns to Thomas and says, "Not this one. You want the Blue Line. That's the next one. It'll be here in a few minutes."

"Ok. Thank you."

With that the woman gingerly steps onto the bus platform, the doors whooshing shut behind her. When, a few minutes later, the Blue Line arrives, Thomas takes a window seat a few rows from the back of the bus. With the exception of a trio of teenagers dressed for a soccer game, outfitted as they are in blue shin guards, black cleats, and dark jerseys, the bus is otherwise empty. As it lumbers up Brookhurst, passing the fast food joints, gas stations, pet stores, bike shops, and supermarkets, he's struck by just how much the area's changed in the short time he's been alive. The strawberry fields that used to dominate the area are almost entirely gone, other than a few stretches of farmland that his father always refers to as "parking lots in waiting." Thomas's father thinks this is a tragedy; his mother, a crime. Thomas doesn't know what to think, except that he misses those enormous baskets of fresh fruit his mother used to pick up on her way home from work.

The bus arrives at the Golden West station fifteen minutes later. Thomas disembarks and, after locating the correct bus, takes a seat on the bench out front and waits for the bus driver to finish his cigarette. He thinks about all of the things that could go wrong on this trip. The bus could break down. He could board the wrong train. He could get lost in L.A. For a few moments he begins to get nervous, but then he thinks about what his mother once told him when he asked her about the seven deadly sins. She had shaken her head and said, "There aren't seven, there's one."

"Which one?"

"Worry."

"But that's not part of the original seven."

"The original seven are ridiculous."

And yet he knows she says these things because she doesn't want him to worry the way she does; that she wants for him a freedom from the constant sense that something is about to go wrong that the Catholicism she was raised with had instilled in her. He wishes things were different, that his mother would let him do some of the worrying for her. But every time he suggests it, she says a parent's job is to worry; a child's job is to be happy.

If that's the case, he thinks, then I'm going to enjoy this adventure.

This time the bus quickly fills up, and he's soon joined by a teenaged girl wearing a Ramones t-shirt, blue jeans, and black Converse high-tops. Her black hair goes down past her shoulders, and she has a small scar along the left side of her jaw. She's listening to her walkman loudly enough for Thomas to recognize the sound of Sting's voice, although he can't tell whether it's a Police album she's listening to or something off *The Dream of the Blue Turtles*, which is a record Earl's neighbor, Stacy, listens to nonstop. As she drops down into the seat next to him and places her weathered bag between her feet, she almost immediately shuts her eyes to take a nap as the bus pulls out of the station.

He looks out the window and takes in Beach Boulevard as it passes. There are an endless supply of motels, 24-hour diners, and dive bars. There are used car dealerships, dental practices advertising in English and Vietnamese, or English and Spanish, or Spanish and Vietnamese. There are old men playing chess on the benches in a small park whose grass has not been watered in months.

It's as Thomas tries to make sense of a church marquee whose sign says, "Jesus Doesn't Save, He Keeps", that his seat-mate opens her eyes and says, "You're traveling light to be running away, kid."

It takes him a moment to realize he's being spoken to. He turns his head to look at the girl. She looks like a member of The Runaways, that teen-girl punk outfit who was all the rage a few years earlier.

"I'm not running away."

"You sure?"

"Yes."

"That's good," she says, reaching down into her bag to pull out a sandwich wrapped in tin foil. "Because now I don't have to share my food with you."

A few moments later the girl takes a large bite out of a homemade ham-and-cheese number heavy on the mayonnaise.

"Are you?" he asks.

"Am I what?"

"Running away."

"I'm not sure," she says, as if it were a question she hasn't really considered until this moment. "Maybe."

"What do you mean, 'maybe'?"

"It depends, I guess."

"On what?"

"On whether the friend I'm going to see says I can stay with him."

"Is he your boyfriend?" Thomas asks, as the bus lumbers up the onramp and merges onto the 22 Freeway.

"I'm not sure about that, either."

"My father ran away from home," he says, deciding he's asking too many questions. "He left Iran and came to America."

"That's a different kind of running away."

"How so?"

"He was fleeing an oppressive monarchy. I'm fleeing a secular tyrant."

He looks at her, not understanding what she's said.

"My father is a bastard," she clarifies.

He looks back out the window. He's happy that traffic is moving briskly. The last time he was on the 22, he and his father didn't move for two hours because one angry driver had shot another driver with a bow-and-arrow after they'd both pulled onto the shoulder after a fender-bender. His father thought it was the funniest thing he'd ever heard.

"Where in L.A. does your friend live?" Thomas asks.

"Echo Park."

"My grandfather takes me fishing there sometimes."

"Catch any bodies?"

"Bodies?"

"That's where Bugsy Siegel used to bury the bodies of the men he killed. He'd tie concrete slabs to their feet and drop them in the lake."

"Is that true?" Thomas asks, fascinated.

"Who cares? This is America. Never let the truth get in the way of a good story."

She squints and smiles at him, and then takes another bite of her sandwich. She studies her nails, all of which have been painted a light pink.

"What about school?" he asks.

"What about it?"

"You're not going to go anymore?"

"It's summer."

"But what about next year?"

"They have schools in Los Angeles too. And besides, I got kicked out."

"For what?"

"It's difficult to say. But I'm guessing the goats probably had something to do with it," she says, finishing off her sandwich.

"The goats?"

"I took three goats from our school's farm a few weeks ago," she says, through a full mouth of food.

"How did they catch you?"

"I turned myself in."

"Why?"

"I told them it was because I had a belated crisis of conscience. But the truth was I just wanted to get kicked out."

"What did your parents say?" Thomas asks, before his eyes withdraw the question, remembering what the girl has already said about her father.

The girl acts as if she hasn't heard the question. She wads the tin foil into a ball the size of a tennis ball, and places it back into her bag.

"Here we are," she says.

Beyond the window is a train depot that looks like something out of the black-and-white films his grandmother likes to watch. As the passengers begin to disembark, the girl slings her bag over her shoulder, makes sure her headphones are still around her neck, and then says to Thomas, "I guess this is where we part ways, kid."

"I'm going to L.A. too," he says, not wanting to say goodbye to the girl just yet.

She squints at him, as if trying to decide whether his previous claim that he wasn't running away should be reconsidered. Thomas is certain, were a lie detector test available to her, she'd demand that he take it.

"Yeah? What's in L.A., kid?"

"I'm looking for a friend. A friend of a friend, more like."

"And where in L.A. are you hoping to find this friend of a friend?" she asks, as the two of them descend the trio of steps and head towards the train terminal.

"Arden Park. It's near downtown."

"Your parents know you're spending the day playing detective?"

"Yes," he lies.

She gives him a sidelong glance.

"Not exactly," he says. "It's complicated."

"In other words, you didn't tell your mother where you were going."

"So maybe it isn't that complicated."

"It's alright, kid. It's like that old joke: the only two people you should lie to in this world are the cops and your parents."

"I've never heard that one."

"Well then," she says. "Come on."

Inside they purchase two tickets for Los Angeles from an old man in a booth with iron bars on it.

"Union Station, here we come," she says.

"You've been there?"

"Of course. It's the Taj Mahal of Los Angeles."

"What's the Taj Mahal?"

"It's a palace in India."

"You've been there?"

"No, but someday."

For a few moments Thomas finds himself wishing he had more than the remaining money in his sock. If he did, he would buy this girl a plane ticket to the Taj Mahal, and tell her that all he wants in return is for her to have a good time. But a few seconds later, after the girl takes his hand and says, "We don't want to miss our train," it occurs to Thomas that this is no idle daydream. It is, in fact, the vision of a young man who's just fallen in love for the first time in his life.

Though Thomas believes he's already a man of the world, Don Juan with a better first step, Lord Byron in basketball shorts, the truth is that what he knows about love could fit into his Size 5 high-tops and still leave a little extra space. Yet as the two of them board the train and settle into their seats, the girl putting her bag on the empty chair opposite them rather than into the overhead compartment, he knows enough to understand this is neither a love to be expressed nor fulfilled. After all, the girl is not only previously betrothed, but is on a quest of her own that is not to be interfered with by declarations of love from a much-younger suitor. Therefore, as the train begins to move he thinks about what Mississippi Rod once told him, that timing and luck are the dominant forces in life, rather than fate, destiny, and all of the other words Father O'Connell uses in his Sunday morning sermons. Thomas is left, then, to look across the seat at this girl, at her killer haircut, at her slim necklace from which a pendant of an electric guitar dangles, and think that if God does indeed exist, he's got one seriously dark sense of humor.

In fact, it is on this train ride that Thomas realizes the book that best explains the world is not the Bible, but *Alice in Wonderland,* and that each morning is a rabbit hole you slip through to arrive in a place where the Red Queen sends cars spinning off icy roads at night, stops good men's hearts from beating for no particular reason, and separates fathers from sons for indefinite periods of time. So that's it, he tells himself. The only sense you'll find in this life is the sense you create for yourself. Years later he will learn this is called Existentialism. But right now, in the seat of this train bound for Los Angeles, he only knows that it hurts like hell.

"You're thinking something, kid," the girl says, studying him.

"No, I'm not thinking anything."

"Come on. Brooding mysteriousness isn't a good look on you."

"Ok. I was just thinking that I don't know your name."

"Ellen Fujimoto. Yours?"

"Thomas Kabiri."

"Well, it's good to meet you, Thomas Kabiri," she says, before adding, "and that's not what you were thinking."

"I'm worried that I won't be able to find the person I'm looking for."

"Then don't look for him."

"I can't do that," he says, almost offended at her suggestion.

"Then don't waste your time worrying. Simple as that."

"Aren't you worried that things won't work out with your boyfriend?"

"No. Yes. Alright. You got me."

"You see? It isn't so easy."

"We can worry together then."

"Deal," he says.

Looking down the aisle, he adds, "I've never ridden on a train before."

"You're kidding."

"I've never flown in a plane either."

"Are your Amish?"

"No."

"Well, what do you think?"

"I think it's amazing."

"This is nothing. Some time you'll have to take a longer ride.

There's nothing like seeing America from the window of a train."

"You've done it?"

"Two years ago. My mother and I rode the Sunset Limited."

"That's a cool name. Where's it go?"

"It starts in Los Angeles and ends in New Orleans. And in between you see the kinds of places you didn't know existed. Or still existed, at least."

"That's a fun experience to have with your mother."

Ellen goes quiet, pausing before answering.

"I'll never forget it."

Thomas recognizes the look in her eyes. He saw it on Mrs. Roth's face the day before. He figures Ellen needs a little space, so he gets up and begins to do pushups in the aisle instead of asking her any more questions. A few of the other passengers look on in curiosity at what one of their fellow passengers has started to do.

"What are you doing?" Ellen asks in almost a whisper, as if his actions are a secret she's ashamed to share with the rest of the passengers.

"Pushups," he says, as he continues to slowly raise and lower himself to and from the floor.

"Yes, I can see that. But why?"

"Because I need to get stronger. I have no muscles in my arms. And I'm smaller than everyone I play against."

"That's because you're ten years old. Be patient."

"I've been patient."

"Really? For how long?"

"Nine years. And look where it's gotten me."

"That's some impenetrable logic there, kid."

"Says the girl who stole a bunch of goats."

"Not stole. Relocated."

"Yes. Because that's better," he says, getting back on his feet to take a break.

"What're you going to do next? Bench press the caboose?"

"Give me a year. And then yes."

"You men are all the same."

"Except some of us are more handsome."

"Is that right?"

Thomas shrugs his shoulders and smiles back.

"That's what my father says whenever my mom gets frustrated with him."

"He sounds like a charmer."

"He is."

"Well, get back up here and sit down. I'm getting tired just watching you. Here," she says, handing him her headphones.

"Listen to these for awhile. I'm going to take a nap."

"Do you have any Bob Seger tapes?"

"Are you serious?"

"My friend Earl says everyone should have a little Bob Seger in their lives."

"Yes, well, tell Earl I've been doing just fine without him."

"What about Van Halen?"

"Tell me you're joking."

"Prince?"

"Prince I can do."

She reaches into her bag and pulls out a cassette copy of *Purple Rain*.

"Wake me when we get to Union Station," Ellen says, before leaning her head against the window and closing her eyes. Thomas places the tape into the walkman, slips the headphones on, and listens to Prince address his congregation of one.

He looks at Ellen as she sleeps and, for whatever reason, is in awe of everything that's happened. Here it is, he thinks. Just what his father's been saying for years: that time is not a constant thing. That there are months, years even, when the clock never moves. You don't age, the world doesn't spin, and even the moon stays exactly in the same spot, night after night after night. Then it wakes back up, like a cosmic Rip Van Winkle, and is desperate to make up for what it's lost by falling behind. That's what this last week has been, Thomas realizes. Time's been shot out of a cannon and is hurtling through the air to catch up. He wouldn't be surprised if, upon returning home later this evening, the last of the strawberry fields had been paved over, their places taken by another round of filling stations and convenience stores.

As the train enters the station, Thomas feels as if he's come through some significant rite of passage: he's embarked on a journey alone, and has safely made his way through its first leg without need of major assistance. He may not feel quite like an adult, but certainly something close enough to one for him to realize some significant changes may be in order, beginning with his wardrobe. After all, even the Lakers wear suits when they're traveling, and when he saw Isiah Thomas last year at a restaurant, Isiah was dressed like James Bond, in dark gray pants, black lace-up boots, and a pressed white button-down shirt with an insignia of a man riding a horse on his left bicep. No doubt, Thomas realizes, it's time to up his game on the fashion front. Broaden his closet beyond gym shorts and t-shirts. But he can think more about this later on. Maybe ask Earl for some pointers.

"We're here," he says, gently placing his hand on Ellen's shoulder.

It takes her a moment to reenter the world as her eyes adjust to their surroundings. When she finally reorients herself, she immediately checks to make sure her bag is still between her feet.

"Don't worry," he jokes. "Two masked men tried to steal it, but I fought them off."

"Those pushups came in handy then," she says, her voice a little hoarse from sleep.

"I told you they would."

"I was a fool to doubt you."

Upon reaching the main lobby, he feels as if the train has done more than take them from Orange County to Los Angeles. It also seems as if they've somehow traveled from 1986 to 1945, as the art deco fixtures, the vaulted ceilings, the dangling chandeliers, and the maze-like floor all remind him of the kind of train station Indiana Jones might have entered before setting off on one of his adventures.

Ellen notices Thomas's wide-eyed sense of wonder.

"Pretty neat, isn't it?"

He's so awestruck by his surroundings that he finds himself incapable of summoning up a response that might do his feelings justice. He just nods instead.

When they step onto the pavement in front of the station they're surrounded by people with suitcases and overnight bags rushing past, some of them walking towards the bus stop at the end of the block, others getting into one of the many taxicabs idling at the curb.

"This is where we part ways," Ellen says. "For real this time."

"I hope he wants you to live with him."

Ellen smiles, squeezes his hand and answers, "Here's looking at you, kid."

"What's that mean?"

"It means you need to start watching more movies," she says, before turning away.

He watches as she walks off, her bag dangling awkwardly enough from her shoulder to cause a slight hitch in her walk. He wants so badly to say something that will get her to turn around, but given that he's unable to think of anything suitably romantic, he just watches her until she disappears into the crowd that crosses the street.

Still trying to get his bearings, Thomas removes the sheet of paper Officer Rodriguez has given him. After studying it for a minute, he spots a cab driver leaning against the passenger-side door of his car and reading *The Sporting News*. The man is in his late forties, with a deep tan and a full head of salt-and-pepper hair.

"Excuse me, sir," Thomas says, holding up the map. "I'm trying to find Arden Park. Do you know where it is?"

The driver calmly folds his newspaper and tucks it under his arm. He wordlessly accepts the map from Thomas and studies it for a few seconds before pointing north and saying, "Arden Park's about ten minutes from here."

"Thanks mister," he says, beginning to turn away.

"That's a ten minute *drive*, kid. Walking it'll take you an hour."

Thomas pauses and looks back towards the Union Station entrance.

"Is there a bus that will take me there?"

"What's in Arden Park?"

"I have to find somebody."

The driver looks at him, as if sizing up what the story might be behind Thomas's justification for his trip.

"Where'd you ride the train in from?"

"Fountain Valley."

The man looks at him for another few seconds before he shakes his head and says, "Alright, Marco Polo. Come on."

Thomas gets into the front passenger seat as the driver walks around the cab to slip behind the wheel. Once inside, he looks at Thomas, laughs, and says, "You've never ridden in a cab before, have you?"

"How'd you know?"

"Wild guess," the driver says, turning the ignition and navigating the car through the lot and out onto the street.

"What's your name?"

"Thomas. What's yours?"

"Eddie."

"Thanks for giving me a ride, Eddie."

"No problem. I've got a son not much older than you, and I'd have a heart attack if he was walking the streets around here alone."

"My mother doesn't know. But I couldn't wait until someone else could come up with me."

"Well, a man's got to go it alone sometimes."

"My dad says that too."

"Of course he does. Every man knows that feeling."

Thomas nods, basking in the easy camaraderie he's formed with the cabdriver. He wishes Earl were here to see how he's handling himself. He's certain Earl would be impressed. At this very moment Thomas feels like a pirate, an astronaut, and a treasure hunter all rolled up into one. A grown man doing grown man stuff.

As Eddie turns his eyes back to the road, Thomas notices the tattoo on Eddie's forearm. Though faded by what Thomas imagines is probably decades of being out in the sun, the image is still clear enough for him to make out: a Ferris Wheel spinning just beneath a crescent moon.

"That's an awesome tattoo," Thomas declares. "I'm going to get a tattoo someday."

Eddie looks down at his arm as the car eases to a stop at the light, and then looks over at Thomas.

"Why's that?"

"Because they look cool."

"Only for a little while, kid. Then you turn thirty."

"You don't like yours?"

"Let's just say it's tough to take yourself seriously when you stand in front of the mirror and realize you look like the Illustrated Man."

"How many do you have?"

"Seven."

"Wow!"

"Don't be impressed. That's seven too many."

Outside the surrounding world has suddenly changed. Beyond the car windows there seem to be an endless amount of cardboard boxes, battered tents, and dirty blankets draped across shopping carts that have been set up as shelter along the sidewalks. Thomas notices that some men wear fatigues, as if they were moving through a war-zone and trying to camouflage themselves. A few stray dogs trot up and down the street, while at the end of the block an ambulance idles as two paramedics tend to someone lying on the pavement. Thomas is almost embarrassed that he was mourning something as silly as the loss of strawberry fields less than an hour ago, considering that parts of the area he's now traveling through look like something out of a horror movie. At one inter-section a man jaywalks across the street while screaming manically about something he believes to be of serious importance; at another an old woman is washing her clothes in the gutter.

He looks at Eddie to see what Eddie thinks about all of this. For a moment it looks as if Eddie is going to try to change the subject, but instead he says, "There's a lot of great things about America, kid. The way we treat our poor isn't one of them. Our veterans too."

"Some of these men fought in Vietnam?"

"Yes. Though a lot of good it did them."

"For a war that ended a long time ago, I sure seem to hear about it a lot."

"Wars don't really end, kid. People get tired, they lose interest, they run out of money or political will or any other number of things you need to keep a war going, but they don't end. Especially not for the ones who fought the damn things."

"I wonder if I'll ever fight in a war."

"Let's hope not. And if it looks like you might have to, make sure it's one you think's worth fighting. Otherwise there's always Canada."

"What's in Canada?"

Eddie pauses, looks at Thomas and says, "So who's this friend you're looking for?"

For the duration of the drive Thomas tells Eddie the entire story from start to finish. He begins with the paper route where he first met Earl, and finishes with his decision to go it alone earlier this morning.

"A noble cause," Eddie says as they turn onto a side street at the end of which Thomas sights an unexpectedly beautiful park, just inside the entrance to which a birthday celebration is in progress. Gifts are stacked on a picnic table, a piñata hangs from a tree branch, and a group of children play soccer on the grass as the adults mingle, drink beer, and listen to Mariachi music he can hear through his open window.

"Here it is."

"It's nice. Really nice."

"That's the thing about L.A. One minute it causes you to lose your faith in humanity, then a minute later it restores it. What time's your train home?"

"4:32 p.m."

"Ok, listen. I'll meet you here at four to drive you back. Got it?"

Thomas can see in Eddie's eyes the same look his own mother gets when she wants Thomas to know it's important that he listen to her.

"Are you sure it's not a hassle, Eddie?"

"The hassle would be me having to track down and kill whoever kidnapped you after you tried to walk back to Union Station on your own. I definitely wouldn't be home in time for dinner, and my wife hates it when I'm late."

"I promise," Thomas says, laughing. "I'll be here. Thanks, Eddie."

"Alright, good. Now go find Wings."

It's been an hour since he arrived, and there's no sight of Wings. No sight of anyone at the courts, in fact. Instead Thomas has passed the time shooting on his own, using a weathered, long-past-its-prime ball that's been left near the baseline. He goes four, five, six shots in a row without missing, pausing now and then to drink from the water fountain located near the backstop whose stream shoots up as powerfully as those Yellowstone geysers he's seen on television nature programs.

For a time he does what he usually does when he's got no one to play with. He imagines he's the point guard for the Lakers, and that he has a starring role in their Game Seven showdown against the hated Celtics. This particular daydream has never failed to keep Thomas entertained and occupied. No matter where he is, or who he might be waiting for, the thought of playing in front of a sellout crowd at the Fabulous Forum, or of having the opportunity to quiet a hostile Boston Garden crowd with a couple of late-game free throws, is always a certain guarantee to lift his spirits.

But there are only so many overtimes to force. Sooner or later his mind begins to wander, ultimately settling on a thought he's not previously considered: that they might never find Wings. Maybe Wings has moved out of the area altogether. Or maybe he doesn't want to be found. It's not impossible, Thomas realizes. It seems to him that happy endings occur in Hollywood movies much more frequently than they do in the real world. But almost as soon as he thinks this, he puts it out of his mind, and remembers what Ellen told him: you can't worry about things that haven't happened yet. You'll drive yourself crazy that way. Just stay in the moment.

From down the street he can hear a ball being bounced, accompanied by approaching voices. Shortly thereafter two men enter the park. Both are in their early forties, dressed in gym shorts and tank tops, and the shorter of the two carries a duffel bag he's slung across his shoulder. Thomas picks up on fragments of their conversation:

"San Francisco?"

"Maybe. Sometimes you have to go where the work is."

"True. But the sun ain't shined there in seventeen years."

"They have the Bridge though. And the Park. Got to give them that."

"Too many hippies for my taste."

The taller one laughs.

"Too many hippies? It's 1986, man. Ain't no hippies anymore. They all grew up and voted for Reagan."

"That's even worse. Hell, at least in L.A. we've got Bradley."

"You're right about that. They shoot their politicians up north if they're too liberal."

"Harvey Milk?"

"You know it."

"God rest his soul."

"Amen."

They continue their conversation as they begin to shoot at the opposite basket. Thomas steps back to the free-throw line and begins to get up another series of shots, but within five minutes so many people have arrived that both baskets are crowded enough for it to be almost impossible to get a shot up that doesn't interfere with another shot that's been released at the same time. The newcomers ignore him, likely figuring the kid that no one recognizes will fade to the sidelines once the games begin. But instead of waiting to see if someone introduces themselves to him, Thomas approaches a man sitting on the side of the court who's tightening his ankle braces before putting on his shoes.

"Is Wings going to be here today?"

The man, who appears to be about thirty, and who has a goatee that makes him look like Magic Johnson's older brother, says, "Don't know. Wings operates on his own clock."

"When's the last time you saw him?"

This time the man looks at Thomas and begin to laugh.

"What's so funny?" Thomas asks.

"I knew it," the man says.

"Knew what?"

"You're a cop."

Thomas smiles and begins to dribble the ball.

"I'm not a cop."

"Hey Leroy," the man says, calling over to a stocky guy in his late thirties who's wearing a blue Dodgers baseball cap turned backwards.

"What?"

"Don't this boy look like a cop?"

"Hell yes," Leroy says, picking up on his buddy's joke and pushing it forward. "It's the haircut. Those flat-tops are always a dead giveaway."

"But this isn't a flattop," Thomas says. "It's a buzz."

"Even worse," Leroy says.

The man on the sidelines continues to laugh and adds, "The kid's here to arrest Wings."

"What'd he do, Detective?" Leroy asks.

"Nothing," Thomas answers. "A friend of mine's just looking for him. That's all."

"Yeah, what friend?" the man asks as he finishes with the ankle braces.

"Earl Lewis," Thomas answers.

With the mention of Earl's name both men go quiet and look at one another. Leroy comes closer to Thomas and says, "Earl Lewis? *The* Earl Lewis?"

"He's my neighbor," Thomas says.

"And he sent you to find Wings for him?"

"He doesn't know I'm here. But I heard Wings plays here sometimes and I know Earl really wants to talk to him."

"Where do you live, kid?" the first man asks.

"Fountain Valley."

"Orange County?" Leroy asks.

"Yes."

"What's Earl Lewis doing in Orange County?" a third man, wearing baggy black shorts and two red wristbands placed high up on his forearms, asks.

"Orange County's quite a drive, kid," Leroy affirms, as some of the other guys choose up sides and begin to prepare for a game. "How'd you get here?"

"Buses and trains. And one taxi."

The three men begin to laugh again, the first man saying, "That's impressive, shorty. What's your name?"

"Thomas. What's yours?"

"Cedric," he says, as the two of them shake hands. "Good to meet you, Thomas."

Leroy turns back to the men who are choosing up sides and says, "Hold up. When's the last time any of you saw Wings out here?"

Several of the men speak up in quick succession:

"'Bout a week and half back. He showed up with Helicopter."

"Maybe three weeks ago. His squad didn't lose a game all evening."

"Don't think he missed more than four or five shots the entire time too."

"Four or five?" another laughed. "Don't let Wings catch you spreading that nonsense. He'll say he hasn't missed four or five shots all year, let alone a single afternoon."

There are high-fives and laughter at this. Thomas is heartened at the fact the sightings of Wings have occurred so recently. Maybe Wings will turn up yet.

Leroy turns back to Thomas and says, "Helicopter will be here soon enough. Maybe he can give you some more info on how to find Wings."

"Helicopter's a cool nickname," Thomas says.

"It's no nickname," Leroy counters. "It's the name his mother and father gave him."

"For real?"

"Absolutely," Leroy says, but his smile makes Thomas think he's probably being played with, considering Leroy's got the same look in his eyes his father did when he told him about the sharks in the pool.

"He must be a high-flyer," Thomas says.

"It's not so much how high he jumps," Cedric adds. "But how long he stays in the air once he does."

"I heard Elgin Baylor was like that," Thomas says.

"Whoa," Cedric says. "Shorty knows Elgin Baylor."

"Not bad, kid. Not bad at all."

"Thanks, Leroy."

"Now tell me something else: you got game too, or just mad detective skills?"

"I've got so much game Maurice Cheeks calls me for advice a couple of times a month," Thomas says.

The three men fall out at this, laughing as Leroy high-fives Thomas.

"You're alright, kid," Leroy says. "You're alright."

Thomas spends the next two hours watching the games the way a conspiracy theorist would watch the Zapruder Film. He studies the way Cedric uses a pump fake to compensate for his lack of leaping ability; the way several players consistently slip the screens on prospective pick-and-rolls to get free for a series of uncontested layups; the way Leroy never fails to box out his man on the boards.

When, midway through a game, someone throws a bounce pass through traffic that reaches its intended target in perfect stride for a dunk, Thomas is so excited he stands up and claps joyously, shouting out, "Good Play!" the same way that Coach Roth used to do whenever one of his players made an especially unselfish decision with the ball.

It's nearly 3:30 p.m. when Helicopter finally arrives. What most immediately jumps out at Thomas about Helicopter is his relative youth. He's probably only nineteen or twenty, and he's wearing a pair of red-and-black Air Jordans that look brand-new. Thomas sees immediately why he's been given that nickname. Helicopter's arms are long enough for Thomas to figure that he's probably able to simultaneously open both doors of a car while sitting in the back seat. A few moments later, when Helicopter trots onto the court, he immediately picks up a ball and leaps through the lane for a one-handed dunk that seems to defy every basic law of gravity. Actually, Thomas thinks, he isn't a helicopter at all; he's a rocketship. If Thomas were assigned to come up with a new nickname for Helicopter, he'd call him NASA.

"Chopper," Cedric says to Helicopter as he begins to talk with some of the other guys. "Shorty over there needs to talk to you," he says, nodding in the direction of where Thomas is standing.

It's become clear to Thomas over the course of the afternoon that Cedric is the de facto ambassador of Arden Park. Every pickup hoops scene Thomas has ever been a part of has someone like Cedric. Any disagreements that cannot be worked out by the involved parties goes to the ambassador for arbitration, and whatever decision he makes in regards to it is accepted as final. At Matsuya, Jose Martinez—a former minor league baseball player and local schoolteacher—is the ambassador. At Mile Square, it's Bomber. Without a doubt, here at Arden Park, it's been Cedric for quite some time. Typically this unofficial position goes to an older player whose cool head and years of experience give him a level of roundball gravitas the other players implicitly respect. But Cedric doesn't look like he's more than thirty years old, Thomas thinks, which means he must be someone really special, a roundball Abe Lincoln that everyone knows is worthy of respect.

Helicopter dribbles a ball behind his back and between his legs as he approaches Thomas with such natural ease that it looks like he's commanding an oversized yoyo. When Helicopter is within a few feet, he picks up the ball, casually gives it a spin on the tip of his index finger, and somehow manages to have the ball continue spinning on his finger throughout the entirety of their subsequent conversation. Thomas doesn't think there's a miracle in the entire New Testament more impressive than what Helicopter is doing, not even the one where Christ does that trick with the loaves and fishes. Especially since there was a lot of wine being consumed at that party, which means there was probably some exaggeration going on in regards to whatever it was Jesus had been able to do. But Thomas is stone cold sober as Helicopter stands before him working his magic.

"What's up, kid?" Helicopter asks.

"I'm looking for Wings," Thomas says. "Cedric and Leroy said you might know how to find him."

If Helicopter is surprised at the question, he doesn't show it.

"Wings comes by my place once in awhile and we come here together to run, but other than that, I never see him."

"Do you know where he lives?" Thomas asks, already feeling his heart beginning to sink.

Helicopter shakes his head.

"Wings is a mysterious cat. Rumor is he took good care of the money he made back in his ABA days, and he's still living off that.

But I don't know whether that's true or not. Either way, he's like a shaman. Appears out of nowhere, does his thing, and then vanishes back into thin air just as quickly."

As Thomas considers what to ask next, Helicopter says, "Why you want to know, kid?"

After Thomas explains the situation, Helicopter responds, "Wings and I talked about Earl the last time he played here, actually. Said Earl's still the best big man he ever saw."

Thomas attempts not to get sidetracked by his wish to have had the opportunity to see Earl back in his prime, before the accident, when it sounds as if Earl was a cross between Kareem Abdul-Jabbar and Wilt Chamberlain.

"You think he'll be here today?" Thomas asks.

"Don't know. There's weeks he's here every day, and then there's weeks where he never shows."

"The next time you see him, could you tell him that Thomas was looking for him?"

"You Thomas?"

Thomas nods.

"He knows you?"

"Yes. He used to come and play at the courts across the street from where I live. He's one of the two best players I've ever seen in person."

"Who's the other one?"

"Earl."

"Glad to know Earl still's got something left in the tank."

"He does," Thomas says. "A lot, actually."

As Helicopter's about to turn back to watch the game, Thomas asks what he's been wanting to from the moment he first heard mention of Helicopter's nickname.

"Did your parents really name you Helicopter?"

"Who told you that? Cedric or Leroy?"

"Both of them."

"They're just messing with you, kid. My parents weren't crazy. Could you imagine that name on a Driver's License?"

"What's your real name then?"

"Howard."

"I like Helicopter better."

"Me too, kid."

Helicopter and Thomas bump fists, as all the while the ball continues to spin on Helicopter's index finger.

"How do you do that?" Thomas marvels.

"It's easy," Helicopter says, motioning for Thomas to hold up his finger. After he's done so, Helicopter hits the ball with his off-hand to increase the rate of speed at which the ball is spinning, and then calmly transfers it onto Thomas's finger.

For the three or four seconds that Thomas is able to keep the ball spinning, he feels like a magician, the hoops equivalent of Harry Houdini. He couldn't be more excited if he was in the process of pulling a live rabbit from a hat, or freeing himself from a series of chains while stranded at the bottom of the sea.

"Not bad," Helicopter says, as the ball finally falls from his finger and bounces away. "Keep at it. You'll get it."

After that Thomas is unable to focus on the pickup games. Instead he continuously keeps looking back down the street to see whether this is the moment when Wings might magically appear, like Willis Reed emerging from the Madison Square Garden tunnel just in time for tipoff of Game 5 of the 1970 NBA finals. But he never does. Instead, a few minutes after 4 p.m., what Thomas does see is Eddie's cab come into view. Thomas rises from his place on the sidelines and waves to Cedric, Leroy, and Helicopter, all of whom are in the middle of a closely contested game.

"See you guys later," Thomas says.

"Come again, kid," Cedric says, the others nodding and waving in agreement. "We'll tell Wings you were here."

Thomas thanks them again and then jogs towards the cab. After sliding into the passenger seat, Eddie, refolding his well-worn newspaper, asks, "Any luck?"

"No," Thomas says, the disappointment palpable in his voice.

Eddie puts the car into drive and says, "Don't beat yourself up, kid. It's not going to be the last time in your life that you didn't find what you were looking for."

"It's happened to you?"

Eddie looks at Thomas and laughs.

"Too often to count."

"It's frustrating, Eddie," Thomas says as the car swings onto the street.

"Most things worth doing usually are," Eddie responds, before turning on the radio.

"This is a good one," Thomas says a few moments later.

"Yeah? You know this one?" Eddie says, turning up the volume.

"I've heard it before, but I don't know who sings it."

"A country musician named Willie Nelson."

"He sounds like the kind of guy who hitchhikes a lot."

"That's an interesting way of putting it. I bet he is."

"Have you ever hitchhiked?"

"Once or twice, when I was fresh out of the Army and didn't have any money. But I wouldn't do it again."

"Why not?"

"Because it's one of those things that's not nearly as fun as you think it's going to be."

"What else is like that?"

"Playing golf. Buying a sports car. The state of Texas."

As Thomas laughs, Eddie changes the subject and asks, "You never told me how you snuck away without your parents knowing."

"My mother's at work until late tonight. And my father's at his mother's funeral."

"I'm sorry to hear that. How old was she?"

"I'm not sure. In her sixties, I think. Not very old."

"How come you're not at the funeral?"

"It's in Iran."

"Iran?" Eddie asks, surprised. "The Iran?"

"Yes."

"I didn't know they were booking flights in and out of Tehran these days."

"They're not. Not officially, anyway. My father snuck in."

"So this kind of lone wolf thing runs in your family?"

"I guess it does."

"Your mother must be a good sport."

"She's the best. She always says that as long as she knows where one of us is at all times, that's the best she can hope for."

"Your mother's got a sense of humor. Good for her."

"How did you meet your wife?"

Eddie whistles softly, as if it's something he hasn't thought about in years.

"I was working on a paint crew about twenty years back out in Silver Lake. A big old apartment house. This pretty woman came out to ask how long it was going to take us to finish, and I told her we'd finish up the minute she agreed to let me take her to dinner."

"Really?"

"You know it."

"What'd she say?"

"She didn't say anything. Just turned and went back inside. The next afternoon, when she came home from work, I was working on the front wall, and she walked up to me and asked when I was planning on making good on that dinner offer."

"You're like a regular James Bond, Eddie."

"No such thing, kid. Not in real life. All you can do is lay your cards on the table and hope for the best."

"Well, I'm glad she didn't turn you down, at least."

"You and me both," Eddie says, as Willie's voice floats down the Whiskey River.

At the next intersection they pass a large group of men with shaved heads in maroon-colored robes, all of whom shake tambourines as they sing and dance with a joyous abandon.

"What are they doing?" Thomas asks.

"Same thing as you. Looking for someone they may not find."

"They seem happy."

"Why shouldn't they be? There's worse ways to spend your days than believing things might still work out for the best."

"You're really smart, Eddie," Thomas says, as the car eases to a stop at a light.

"Don't spread that around, kid. I've got a good thing going here."

"Scout's Honor."

When they stop at a light Thomas watches an old man in a gray suit and black fedora walk up the block. It's at precisely this moment that Thomas realizes the opportunity to look out the window of a moving vehicle is one of the best things to do in the world, as good in its own way as watching a movie or listening to a great song on the radio. He'll never understand why this is, but the years ahead will only solidify this belief in him.

"I wonder what he's reading," Thomas says, noticing the book the old man is carrying.

Eddie looks to see the person Thomas is referring to.

"I don't know," he says, squinting. "You a reader?"

"I read *The Pearl* last month."

"Steinbeck? That's a heavy-hitter. You read him in school?"

"No, but my mother works in a library on weekends, and she checked out a few of his books for me. An 'American treasure', she called him."

"I spent three years as a Merchant Marine," Eddie says. "And the only books in the small library we had below deck were by Steinbeck. I wonder if the guy ever knew he was big with the sailors."

"What's your favorite book of his?"

"*Travels With Charley*. You read it?"

Thomas shakes his head.

"You should. It's a good one."

"What's it about?"

"It's about a trip Steinbeck takes where he drives all across the back roads of America, and then writes about the people he meets and the places he sees. There isn't really a plot, and not much happens in the way of action, but by the time you've finished the book, it feels like you understand the country a little bit more than you did before you'd started."

"Who's Charley?" Thomas asks.

"Charlie's his dog. Steinbeck brings him along."

"That's really cool. I'd like to do that some day."

"I imagine you will. You've got a lot of things to look forward to, kid."

When they arrive back at Union Station, Thomas reaches into his sock to pay Eddie for picking him up. But instead Eddie shakes his head and says, "Keep it. Buy yourself something to eat before you get on the train."

"No, Eddie. You've got to take it. I wish I had even more money to give you. If you hadn't driven me there and back I never would've made it to Arden Park."

"Tell you what. Find someone else to give some of that money to before you get home tonight. Someone who needs it more than me. Okay?"

"Okay," Thomas says, before adding, "I just realized something."

"What's that, kid?"

"You're cooler than James Bond'll ever be."

"That's what I'm going to tell my wife the next time I forget to take out the trash," Eddie says. "Now get going, kid. I don't want you to miss your train."

Thomas gets out and shuts the door behind him. He turns to wave one more time at Eddie, but he's already driven off, his cab turning out of the parking lot and merging into traffic.

Thomas re-enters Union Station and marvels at the array of people moving in and out of the sprawling lobby. It seems to him as if every single part of the world has sent an emissary here to represent their culture. It's beautiful, he thinks, the sight of three Indian women in multi-colored saris sitting beside a Catholic nun on a bench, while a few feet away two cops talk about the Dodgers with a Mexican father whose restless young son keeps attempting to squirm his way off his mother's lap. Thomas has never seen anything quite like it: this sense that the world is incapable of producing any two people who look, dress, or act alike. He wonders if this is why his father says that Los Angeles is the place that everyone wants to come to. It must be, Thomas decides.

He purchases a large submarine sandwich, a bottle of orange juice, and a Milky Way candy bar from a food cart, and carries the items over to an empty chair near the magazine-and-newspaper racks so that he can scan the covers while eating his food. It's just after he's finished eating that he sees Ellen sitting cross-legged on the other side of the lobby, reading a magazine, her bag nestled comfortably between her feet.

At first he's excited to see her, but then is reminded that her presence means things must not have worked out with her boyfriend. He wonders whether he should walk over to join her. After a few seconds of deliberation, he figures, at the very least, he might be able to cheer her up. But as he begins to walk in her direction, he tells himself not to ask too many questions, so that he doesn't accidentally wind up making her sad.

Ellen looks up to see him standing in front of her.

"Any luck?" she asks, as if she were casually picking up the strand of a conversation they'd ended only moments before.

"No," he says, shaking his head.

"It looks like we both struck out then," she says as she pats the ground next to her. "Have a seat."

"What did your friend say when you saw him?" he asks as he sits.

"He didn't say anything. His parents wouldn't let me into the house. And he didn't try to change their minds from doing it."

Thomas notices a redness around Ellen's eyes that makes him realize she's been crying. It's one of those moments where he wishes he were ten years older than he is; he pictures finding out the address of her boyfriend's house and driving out there to yell at the entire family in defense of his new friend. Maybe he doesn't even need to wait the whole ten years, he thinks. Even six or seven would do the trick. Like all boys about to enter the sixth grade, he's convinced it's only a matter of time before he transforms into the second coming of Sylvester Stallone. But since acting out his revenge fantasy isn't immediately in the cards, he decides to change the subject.

"I rode in a taxicab."

"Oh yeah?" Ellen asks, forcing a smile. "What'd you think?"

"It was awesome. I liked it more than when we got to ride in the fire truck during last year's school field trip. Maybe someday I'll drive one myself."

"That means I'll always have a ride whenever I want to go to the beach," Ellen says, squeezing his hand for emphasis.

"Or steal some goats."

"Exactly. We can tie them to the roof."

She smiles and looks like she's about to tear up again.

"Ellen?" Thomas asks.

"What?"

"If I ever move to L.A. you can come and live with me if you want. I'll have a big house with a big pool that you can swim in whenever you feel like it."

"You're a gentleman and a scholar, kid."

"Not much of one," he says, unfamiliar with the phrase. "My

teachers say I don't try hard enough."

"Good. You shouldn't. Put your effort into something that's actually worth your time instead."

"Like basketball?"

"Definitely basketball. And maybe something else too."

"My friend Earl says the same thing. I was thinking I'd learn to play the guitar."

"The women are going to love you."

"You think so?"

"Chicks dig guitar players."

"What are your two skills?"

"Well, I can take pictures. And I can speak two languages."

"That's three things! You're a Renaissance Woman. What languages?"

"English," she says. "And Japanese."

"How'd you learn that?"

"My mother was Japanese. She spoke it to me when I was little. It was our secret language."

"I can't speak Farsi. My father never speaks it around the house. And even if he did, I don't think I'd want to learn it."

"How come?"

"Because they said they'd kill him if he ever moved back to Iran. So why would I want to learn their language?"

"A government isn't a culture, kid. They're two separate things."

"What do you mean?"

"I mean never mistake the people in power for everyone else."

Thomas considers this.

"So you think I should learn the language?"

"That's up to you. But don't let some corrupt politicians make that decision for you."

As he thinks about this a bit further, he pulls the candy bar from inside the paper bag. After tearing open the wrapper, he splits the bar in two and offers Ellen the larger half.

"Thanks," she says, taking a bite.

"Whenever my father's in a bad mood," Thomas says, "he goes to 7-Eleven and comes back with a candy bar. He calls it his medicine."

"I like his attitude."

"And whenever he comes home with ice cream, he calls that his vitamins."

"How often does that happen?"

"Often enough for my mother to worry about his health."

"I bet."

As they continue to eat, Thomas notices Ellen looking at a woman selling flowers from a child's red wagon a few feet from the shoeshine stand. Thinking about what Eddie had told him a few minutes earlier, Thomas places the rest of the chocolate bar into his mouth, stands up, and heads in the direction of the stand.

He settles almost immediately on a bouquet of red roses. The woman, strands of whose gray hair fall from beneath a large hat, smiles warmly at him and says something in a language he can't understand. After he notices a small handwritten sign that says the bouquets are five dollars each, he hands her some of the money that Eddie had refused, says, "Thank you", and turns back towards Ellen, who is watching him with a look of confusion on her face.

He feels like a knight in one of those adventure stories he likes to read. Maybe one that features his favorite, Lancelot, riding out across the country in search of the Holy Grail he never seems to find. All I'm missing is the white horse, the sharp sword, and the British accent, he thinks to himself. Okay, that's a lot, actually. But still, close enough.

"These are for you," Thomas says as he hands the bouquet to Ellen.

"You sure you can afford these?"

"I'm swimming in money," he says, repeating a phrase he's often heard James say when he gets home from flipping pizzas at Dino's Pizzeria over on Newland Street.

Ellen places her nose to the flowers to inhale their scent.

"This is what Heaven smells like, I bet," she says.

"Maybe. Although I hope it smells like a quarter pounder from McDonald's. Or at least their french fries."

"Don't ruin the moment."

"People say that a lot to me."

"For good reason, I'm guessing."

They board the train and settle into their seats. After a few more minutes of conversation, which centers mostly on Thomas's curiosity as to why exactly girls like flowers so much, Ellen says, "I'll be right back. Watch my bag, okay?"

"Okay," he replies.

It's not until a minute or so later, after the train's begun to shake as it moves across a particularly rough stretch of track, that Ellen's bag falls over and some of its contents scatter on the floor at his feet. He immediately kneels on the floor to scoop up the contents, which include a silver case of lipstick, a small mirror, a travel-sized packet of kleenex, a paperback called *Goodbye, Columbus*, several music cassettes, a ticket stub from a matinee showing of *Peggy Sue Got Married*, and what looks to Thomas like a medium-sized, cast-iron vase. However, when he picks the vase up, it's heavier than he'd expected it to be. He considers opening it to look inside, but notices that the lid has been firmly latched by two metal clamps on both sides. As he places everything back into the bag, it occurs to him that he's seen this type of vase before. Janie, his next-door neighbor, has one just like it, inside of which her husband's ashes are stored.

By the time Ellen returns, he's placed everything back into the bag, this time securing it between his feet to keep it from falling over again. He doesn't say anything about the urn, but instead gazes out the windows and looks at the refineries that rise above the surrounding area like gods whose perpetual anger has paralyzed them from completing their ascension into the clouds. He imagines the men who work at these plants probably look a lot like Bruce Springsteen, and wear dark blue jeans, dirty white t-shirts, and blue bandannas in their back pockets. For some reason that he doesn't understand, it bothers him that a large American Flag has been painted onto a billboard-sized sign bolted onto the top of the refinery's tallest structure. The country should be better than this, he finds himself thinking. After all, it can't be healthy for men to breathe that dirty air day after day.

When Ellen slips back into her seat across from him, Thomas doesn't say anything at first. But a few minutes later, after Ellen's grown bored with whatever tape she's been listening to and places her walkman back into her bag, he can't help but ask, "Is that your mother in there?"

"Rule Number One," Ellen says. "Never go through a woman's purse."

"I didn't. It tipped over when you were going to the bathroom."

"Rule Number Two," Ellen says, smiling this time. "Never say you know a woman was in the bathroom."

"Why not?"

"Because we don't like boys knowing we do those things."

"Sweating too, my aunt always says."

"I was going to say that's Rule Number Three: women don't sweat. And if it seems like we are, don't say anything."

"Got it," Thomas says.

The two of them share a laugh before settling back into silence. It's not until about ten minutes later that, unprompted, Ellen says, "It's my daughter."

It takes a moment for Thomas to realize what Ellen's referring to. Once he does, he pauses and tries to figure out what to say.

"What was her name?"

"Suzu," Ellen says. "Her name was Suzu."

"That's a pretty name."

"It was my grandmother's name."

He considers offering condolences for Ellen's loss, but opts for something he heard his father say once when the wife of a friend of his from work had died of cancer.

"This sucks."

"Yes," Ellen says. "It does."

He gets up from his seat and slides into the seat next to hers. She puts his hand inside of his, and leaves it there.

Shortly thereafter Ellen closes her eyes and goes to sleep, while Thomas looks out the window and watches a world pass by that he understands less with every passing hour. After awhile he closes his eyes as well, and begins to replay some of his favorite NBA highlights: Charles Barkley dribbling the ball coast-to-coast for a slam dunk; Patrick Ewing coming from the weak side to swat a Chris Mullin layup attempt into the third row; Dr. J. taking off on one side of the basket and gliding all the way to the other side of the hoop before laying it in over his head. The images don't necessarily make Thomas feel better, but they do make him feel less alone. Why this is he'll never be able to say, but it'll never stop being true, no matter how old he gets.

When the train pulls into the station, Ellen opens her eyes. A minute later the two of them step into the aisle. As they prepare to disembark, Ellen asks, "What time does your mother get home from work?"

"8 p.m. Why?"

Ellen checks her watch. It's a few minutes before 6 p.m.

"Because I have one more thing to do today, and I could use a little help."

Though he doesn't say it, the truth is that Thomas would go with his new friend wherever she asked him to, even if it meant he wouldn't be back until long after 8 p.m.

"Are we going to steal some goats?" he asks.

"Very funny."

As they board the bus Ellen drops enough coins into the tiller for both of them. They take a seat just behind the driver, a balding, broad-shouldered man with a dark beard and ravaged ears that Thomas recognizes as signs the man has spent a significant part of his life inside a boxing ring. He wonders if he ever fought Joe Frazier or either of the Spinks brothers.

"Where are we going?" Thomas asks again.

"The beach."

"How come?"

"Rule Number Four: Don't ask too many questions. It'll make people think you're a cop."

"That's the second time someone's said that to me today."

"I'm not surprised."

"Ellen?"

"What?"

"Can I listen to your walkman again?"

She reaches into her purse and pulls out her headphones, along with the handful of cassettes she's packed for the trip.

"Knock yourself out, kid."

After looking through the possibilities, he's elated to find she has *Around the World in a Day*. Though he knows he has the same record waiting for him on vinyl back home, he puts it into the walkman and presses play. Immediately he feels as if he's entered a magical, dream-like world, full of people of all colors, fashions, and ages, where dancing seems to be the only religion, and love seems to be the only language. Though in the years ahead he'll go through phases where he'll only wear purple clothes and where he'll write imaginary love poems to Anna Stesia and Darling Nikki, for the moment it's enough to simply have Prince's music all to himself: the hypnotic drum machine, those gorgeous choruses, the guitar playing that seems to be both earthy and cosmic at the same time, as if the musician were half-shepherd and half-astronaut. These songs are like electric gospels informing him that love is stronger than grief, that joy lasts longer than loss, and that imagination is more important than experience.

"What did you think?" Ellen asks as they disembark from the bus and step onto Main Street.

"I think Prince is an angel," Thomas says. "No, I take it back. I think he's Jesus Christ."

"He isn't Jesus Christ, kid."

"How can you be sure?"

"Because Christ never wrote anything as beautiful as 'Raspberry Beret.'"

They move down Main Street in the direction of the pier. Other than a few more police officers than usual, Thomas notices the entire area is back to how it looked before the riot. The streets are clean, the windows have all been replaced, and there's even a new phone booth sitting on the corner. As they pass beneath the restored sign hanging above the Flying Zebra, he glances in the direction of the basketball courts in hopes that Earl might be there playing. He isn't. Instead there's only a pickup game of two-on-two involving a quartet of men who look like they don't get out much for exercise.

When they arrive at the intersection of Main and Pacific Coast Highway, Thomas notices that Ellen appears to be scanning the coastline to the right of the pier, as if she's looking for someone or something.

"What is it?" he asks.

"Nothing. I just always forget how beautiful it is here."

"It's all the women in bikinis," Thomas affirms.

She looks at him with an amused grin on her face.

"Don't make me regret bringing you with me."

"What? You don't agree?"

"You're too young to notice things like that?"

"It's never too early to notice things like that."

"Ease up there, Romeo."

"Who's Romeo?"

"Another guy who wasn't ready for the drama that women bring."

"Why, what happened to him?"

"Same thing that's going to happen to you if you don't stop asking questions," she says, playfully pulling on his earlobe.

"I was here last week for the riot," Thomas says, hoping such information will provide him with some street cred in Ellen's eyes.

"You were? That must have been scary."

"It wasn't," he lies. "Besides, if I'm going to be the next Rambo, I need to get used to being in dangerous situations."

"You need to be old enough for a license to drive before they give you a license to kill, kid."

"Rambo didn't have a license to kill."

"No, but he was strong enough to hold a machine gun."

"That's what the pushups are for."

They cross when the light turns green, but rather than continuing onto the pier, they instead descend the steps to the right of the pier that lead to the sand. Thomas pauses for a moment midway down the steps to watch a man ride a large unicycle while also juggling a trio of bowling pins.

On the boardwalk they slip out of their shoes, and Ellen pulls her hair into a ponytail.

"Are we going swimming?" Thomas asks.

"No," Ellen says. "Not exactly."

They walk slowly across the sand that, even as the late afternoon has slowly turned into early twilight, is still crowded with people. With the sun having softened, and the waves grown larger, it seems to Thomas as if everything and everyone, the flying seagulls, the men playing volleyball, the lifeguards standing on the decks of their towers and surveying the coast, are moving in slow motion. He will never get over this, the way that the early evening hours at the beach always seem like something out of a dream, or a spell that a benevolent genie has cast upon everyone in a moment of inspired happiness.

Once they've arrived at the shore, Ellen continues to step back to avoid the water, while Thomas remains still, allowing the whitewash to cover his feet before rolling back out to sea.

"You're lucky Suzu is with you," he says, nodding at Ellen's bag.

"Why's that?"

"Because I'd push you in otherwise."

"I bet you would, you little brat."

Thomas squats down to pick up a large sand dollar, which he then shows to Ellen and says, "It's a good luck sign."

"Says who?"

"My mother. She says anything you find in the sand brings you a different kind of good luck. Seashells mean you'll have a year of good health. A starfish means you'll have a year of happiness. Sea glass means you're going to fall in love."

"What does a sand dollar mean?"

"I don't know. She never said."

"You should have made something up, kid."

"Rule Number Five," Thomas says. "Never lie to a girl."

"And so the student becomes the teacher," Ellen responds.

A few moments later Ellen takes the bag from her shoulder and sets it on the sand. She kneels down to remove the urn, leaves the bag where it is, and stands back up with the urn in her hands. It occurs to Thomas that, except for the color, the urn looks like something a team might get for winning a championship. But rather than sharing what even he realizes might not be the most appropriate observation for the moment, he looks out at the silhouette of Catalina Island. It could be a hibernating dragon, he thinks. Or Atlantis slowly coming back to surface. No, he reconsiders. It's a slumbering giant. For sure. A gentle giant though. A giant who'd rather write poetry and play the mandolin than fight battles and cut down trees.

"You have a favorite prayer?" Ellen asks, breaking Thomas's reverie.

"I only know two. The Lord's Prayer and the Hail Mary."

"Which one do you like more?"

"The Lord's Prayer," Thomas says, as a few feet from them a husband is trying and failing to coax his wife into the water.

"Well, go ahead and say that one," Ellen says. "I'll follow along."

Thomas pauses for a moment and looks out at a man roughly his father's age who's standing on a long surfboard and riding a large wave. The man looks totally at peace, as if he'd been born to be in this exact place and time at this exact moment. Keeping this image in his head, Thomas closes his eyes and begins, "Our father, who art in Heaven, hallowed be thy name. Thy kingdom come, thy will be done, on Earth as it is in Heaven. Give us this day, our daily bread, and forgive us our trespasses, as we forgive those who trespass against us. And lead us not, into temptation, and deliver us from evil, amen. For yours is the kingdom, the power and the glory, forever and forever, amen. "

"Amen," Ellen says.

Thomas opens his eyes and says, "I never understood that part about the power and the glory. It makes God sound too much like a king. But the rest of it's really pretty."

"You said it nicely, kid. I hadn't heard it in a long time."

With that Ellen cradles the urn and begins to rock it slowly back and forth, as if she were trying to lull the ashes of her daughter to sleep, or to comfort them in these moments before they embark on their journey. A few moments later she begins to sing softly enough for it to take four or five seconds before Thomas recognizes the song: it's the same one James had been listening to the week before, about an American girl chasing after her dreams. Ellen sings the whole thing all the way through, and by the time she's finished,

Thomas thinks it's more beautiful than any prayer he has ever heard, the Lord's Prayer included.

"Are you going to scatter her ashes on the water?" he asks.

"Yes."

"The Vikings used to do that."

"No. They put the body of the dead person into a boat, set it on fire, and then pushed it out to sea."

"That's really cool."

"Let's focus here, kid."

Ellen kisses the top of the urn and says, "I love you, my sweet girl. I'll see you further along."

With that Ellen walks out into the shallows of the water. Her blue jeans get soaked to her knees, and the cloudless sky is draped before her like a transparent curtain opening onto the theater of Heaven. Soon she is waist deep, as if she were in the process of baptizing herself. After removing the urn's lid, she begins to slowly scatter Suzu's ashes across the water.

Thomas watches Ellen for a few moments. There's almost a rhythm to the way Ellen slowly moves the urn back and forth above the water, scattering the ashes evenly over the surface of the sea. It's as if she were fly fishing, or slowly mastering the art of the light-saber, Thomas thinks. He finds himself wondering whether Suzu's spirit is watching her mother do this. He hopes so. Maybe Coach Roth is watching too, making sure that Suzu is taken care of. Then Thomas takes a few steps into the water himself and cups his hands to splash water on his face. He looks north along the shoreline to see a boy a few years younger than he is flying a blue kite, the boy's eyes looking up towards the thin cloth as he breaks into a sprint, marveling at the way the kite seems to follow him no matter how fast he runs. For a split second Thomas feels as if that kite is Suzu's soul, and that the boy is an angel sent down to help her move from this world to the next.

"This is nicer than what the Vikings did," Thomas says as Ellen steps back out of the water.

"I think so too," she says, drying her eyes with the hem of her shirt.

They sit on the sand afterwards, the empty urn between the two of them. Ellen looks tired, but also happy, which surprises him.

"Why are you smiling?" he asks.

"I realized something while I was in the water."

"What's that?"

"That I'm still her mother."

Thomas thinks about this for a minute or so before asking, "What will you do now?"

"Start working more hours at the restaurant," Ellen says, shrugging her shoulders. "Save up some money to get my own apartment."

"I'm sorry you have to go back to your father's tonight though."

"I'm not going to. That's something else I realized. I don't have to. I'll stay with my friend Clare instead."

"Is Clare a Prince fan too?"

"She's the one who got me into Prince in the first place," Ellen says.

"So she's cooler than you, you mean."

"Careful, kid. Otherwise I might not introduce you to her. And you don't want that."

"Why not?"

"Because she likes to lay out in her backyard without a top on."

"When can I come over?"

"You're going to be a handful in a few years," Ellen says, and then looking at the sand-dollar that Thomas had found a few minutes earlier, adds, "Good luck, huh?", before she places it into her purse and shoulders the bag.

This time the goodbye is for real, and he knows it. They're standing at the Golden West bus stop, in the moments before he's about to board the bus that will deliver him home. Ellen looks at him for a few seconds before opening her purse, pulling out her walkman, and handing it to Thomas.

"Are you serious?" he says, a mixture of excitement and disbelief on his face.

"It still has *Around the World in a Day* in it," Ellen says. "It's a little memento of our adventure today."

Thomas accepts it from her and immediately places the headphones around his neck. He smiles and says, "You're prettier than Guinevere, by the way. I just thought you should know that."

"Guinevere? You mean the girl from *King Arthur*?"

"I used to think she must have been the most beautiful woman in the whole world," Thomas says. "But now I think it's you."

With that Ellen leans in and gives Thomas a kiss on the cheek.

"Stay out of trouble, kid. And give your mother a hug."

"How come?" Thomas asks, the skin on his cheek tingling in awestruck wonder at the fact that her lips have touched him.

"As an early apology for all the stress you're going to put her through in the years ahead."

Ellen turns and begins to walk in the direction of her own bus, which idles near the curb a little further up the sidewalk. After a few moments of watching her go, Thomas says, "Hey Ellen?"

"Yeah?" she asks, turning around.

"What'd you do with the goats, anyway?"

"I picked the lock and put them in the Vice Principal's office. Supposedly he freaked out when he found them there the next morning."

"I wish I'd been there to see that."

"I'll let you know if I ever feel the need to do it again."

He makes it home with half an hour to spare, and spends his alone time raiding the refrigerator like a Union soldier in an abandoned Georgia house in 1865. He loads a plate with cold chicken, strawberries, watermelon slices, walnuts, and a carrot large enough to double as one of those batons the men on airplane tarmacs wave in the air to signal incoming planes for landing.

When Thomas hears his mother ascend the stairs and enter the unlocked front door, he's finishing off the last of the strawberries and watching the Dodgers play the Mets.

"Who's pitching?" his mother asks as she places her purse on top of the desk.

"Fernando," he says. "And he's dealing."

"Dealing?"

"Dominating."

She sits beside him on the sofa and asks him how his day was. As he opens his mouth he is all set to fabricate a story, but after thinking about what Ellen had said to him, he instead opens with the phrase that he will later come to learn is perhaps the worst way to open a conversation with a mother. Or a girlfriend. Or any woman, for that matter.

"Don't be mad."

"What happened?" his mother says, immediately on high alert.

"Nothing. Everything's fine. It's good, actually. I went looking for Wings today."

"Did you and Earl have any luck?"

"Well," he begins. "Earl didn't exactly come with me."

"What do you mean, he didn't 'exactly' come with you?"

"Earl wasn't home when I went to see him this morning, and you know how Earl is leaving soon? So I was worried if I waited around for him to come home today we might not have had time to get up to Los Angeles and back."

As he finishes his explanation she already has her head in her hands, as if she were a gambler who has just learned that the horse she's bet on has collapsed in the final leg of the race.

"Are you telling me you went all over Los Angeles today by yourself?"

"Not *all* over," he clarifies. "Just downtown."

"That's not making me feel any better."

It's at this very moment that Pedro Guerrero hits a towering shot towards the left field fence that looks like it has a chance to leave the park. Thomas tries to change the subject by nodding towards the TV and saying, "Look at that one!", but to no avail. His mother is as dialed in on his story as a detective certain she has cracked a decades-long cold case.

"Don't worry, Mom," Thomas says, trying another angle. "I met this nice girl on the train who rode there and back with me. And then this really great taxi driver named Eddie—he has seven tattoos, but he told me not to get one, because then I'd look like the Illustrated Man—drove me to Arden Park. I saw Union Station too and ate a sandwich there. And a candy bar. So I wasn't really alone."

At this point his mother has a look on her face that Thomas has seen too many times to count, usually occurring in the wake of his father having made some catastrophically terrible decision made worse by the fact that he doesn't see what the big deal is. But

Thomas knows what the big deal is. He's just hoping the exceptional run of good luck he's had all day can continue for another few minutes, just long enough for him to talk his mother out of putting him up for adoption, or petitioning Alcatraz Island to re-open the prison on behalf of her delinquent son.

"How did you know which buses—and which train—to take?" his mother asks.

"Officer Rodriguez told me."

"Who's Officer Rodriguez?"

"He's the police officer I met this morning at the 7-Eleven."

"When were you at the 7-Eleven?"

"When the newspapers hadn't gotten delivered yet. I went over there to play video games for awhile."

"Instead of coming back home."

"I'd prefer not to think of it that way."

"No?" she asks. "How would you prefer to think of it?"

"As a good son's decision not to wake his sleeping mother."

She's not buying what he's selling. He can tell.

But a few moments later, for some reason that he, even three decades on, will not fully understand, his mother does something so inexplicably wonderful and unexpected that it is, dare he say it, a bona fide miracle.

She begins to laugh.

"Okay World Traveler," she says as she uncrosses her arms. "Did you find Wings, at least?"

"No," he says, surprised and thrilled that he appears to be off the hook. "But a bunch of guys at the park knew him and said they'd spread the word. So maybe there's still hope."

His mother nods and looks back at the television. Daryl Strawberry is up to bat. Thomas dials in on his favorite player, hoping that, even though he's rooting for the Dodgers, Straw hits one out. In this silence Thomas's mother lifts the glass from which he's been drinking and takes a long drink of water. After she's placed it back onto the table, she says, "The next time you plan on going alone, tell me, and I'l drive you."

"I will, Mom. I promise. But I needed to be Burt Reynolds today."

"Burt Reynolds *needs* to be Burt Reynolds," his mother says, poised somewhere between exasperation and laughter. "You just need to be Thomas, my ten-year-old son, who won't live to eleven if he ever goes to L.A. alone again. You understand?"

"Yes, Mom," Thomas says. "But *Smokey and the Bandit*, you know?"

"You're going to give me an ulcer," she says.

"Coach Roth used to say the same thing."

"I don't blame him."

Then she gets up, nods towards the television as she exits the room and says, "Your father is right. Baseball is unwatchable."

THE NEXT MORNING THOMAS IS ON THE COURT BY 8 A.M. He's got it to himself for the first hour, before James and Dave, returning from the direction of Mile Square Park, spot him and make their way onto the blacktop.

"Sherry says hello," James says to Thomas.

"She does?"

"No."

Dave takes the ball from Thomas's hands and immediately sprints towards another court to begin shooting on his own.

"Come on, Dave!" Thomas shouts, to no avail.

"We've got a summer league game in an hour," James says. "You want to roll with us?"

"Definitely," Thomas says.

"Cool," James says. "Sherry'll be there."

"Really?"

"No."

As James laughs Thomas lunges at him, doing his best to land a punch anywhere within the area of James's head. James ducks and slips Thomas's punches so effortlessly that Thomas can't help but begin to laugh as well.

"Stand still!" Thomas says before, tired from consistently swinging at nothing but air, he gives up and tries to catch his breath.

By this time Dave has found his way back to their court and casually begun to shoot free throws. James says, "You remember Karen?"

"Wasn't she one of the girls from the 4th of July?"

James nods.

"She got knocked up."

"You mean, like pregnant?" Thomas asks.

"No, not 'like pregnant.' Actually pregnant," James says.

"It's not yours, is it?"

"Hell no. I always glove up."

"Is she excited?"

"Not exactly."

"Why not?"

"Girls aren't typically excited to be mothers before they've graduated from high school," James says.

"You two ready?" Dave asks.

Dave's car is a '73 BMW, with a faded green exterior, a sizable dent in the driver's side door, and no remaining hubcaps. As Thomas slides into the backseat he also notices the car lacks seat belts, upholstery, and functioning windows. He wonders if it has breaks.

"Where'd you get this car, Dave?" Thomas asks.

"The 19th Century," James interjects.

"At least I have a car," Dave says.

"This isn't a car," James responds. "It's a dinosaur with wheels."

"Screw you, Bianchi," Dave says.

"I'm starting to think that should be the title of your autobiography, James," Thomas says.

While Dave bursts into laughter, James turns back and says, "You want to walk, kid?"

"It'd probably be faster," Thomas responds.

Now it's James's turn to laugh as Dave tries and fails to punch Thomas while keeping his eyes on the road.

"He's growing up right before our eyes," James says. "I couldn't be prouder."

All three courts inside the gym are full when they enter, as numerous high school teams compete against one another in a series of concurrent summer league tournaments. The local varsity team is coming off a winless season in Sunset League action, and they have lost three of their starters from that less-than-stellar squad. Other than James, the team has exactly zero proven scorers, which means it's setting up to be another long season for the Knights.

"Looks like we're a few short," Dave says, noting that only two of their teammates seem to be present. A moment later a tall man with no hair and a dark tan approaches them, with eyes so hawkish and locked-in Thomas wonders if the man is a detective arrived to arrest somebody. Only the whistle around his neck and the clipboard in his hand makes Thomas realize this is the Knights' coach. He's never seen him up-close before.

"Hey Coach," James says, as the man stands in front of them.

"Where are the others?" Coach asks, ignoring James' greeting.

"Stevie is on vacation with his family," James says. "And Wyatt's sick."

"What about Timmy, Johnny, and Seth?"

On the drive over Thomas had listened as James and Dave discussed a party they'd attended the night before, where the three guys Coach has just inquired about had eaten too many mushrooms.

From the sounds of it they were likely to be out of commission for the rest of the weekend.

"I don't know where they are, Coach," Dave lies. "I haven't seen them all week."

Coach scowls as if he were prepared to invade a country simply to release the steam that's building up inside of him.

"If they're not here in five minutes," Coach says, "we're going to have to forfeit."

"No need for that," James counters. "The kid can play. He makes five."

"What kid?" Coach asks.

"This kid," James says, pointing to Thomas.

"This isn't a kid, it's a leprechaun," Coach says.

"Half-leprechaun," James clarifies. "His father's Persian."

"Isn't that what Iranians call themselves when they don't want you to know they're Iranian?" Coach asks.

"Seriously, Coach," Dave says. "He's good. Better than Timmy. We won't miss a beat."

"We haven't won in six months," Coach responds. "All you guys do is miss beats."

"Well, then why not give the kid a shot? It can't get any worse."

Coach looks at Dave and then at James, seemingly deciding about who to yell at first, before he finally turns his gaze towards Thomas and says, "How old are you?"

"Twelve," Thomas says.

"Be serious."

"Eleven."

"When's your birthday?"

"February 26th."

"What year?"

Thomas pauses to calculate.

"Good Lord," Coach says.

"He's ten, Coach," James says. "But he sees the floor like a young Mo Cheeks."

Coach looks back at Thomas.

"Well, kid? Is that true?"

Thomas doesn't know what to say, afraid that if he opens his mouth he'll say something irredeemably stupid. Instead he simply nods.

"Speak up. I don't like quiet players. They usually choke under pressure."

"I'm more like a better-shooting Isiah Thomas," Thomas says.

"Is that right?" Coach says, impressed at Thomas's brashness. "This I'm going to have to see."

"Don't worry, Coach," James says. "How can things get any worse than last year?"

"Things can always get worse," Coach says. "Read your Socrates."

"Who's that?" Dave asks.

"The guy who coached the Lakers before Pat Riley took over," James says.

Coach looks at the door one more time, as if at any moment one of his players will arrive to at least allow him to field a typically awful team, as opposed to the all-out freak show it's about to be now that a fifth-grader is going to run the point.

"Well, kid, I guess it's your lucky day," Coach says. "It certainly isn't mine."

Thomas tries to hide his excitement. When Coach turns to walk away James looks at Thomas and says, "Just do what you normally do. Get me the ball and get out of the way."

"You got it," Thomas responds.

When they walk onto the court for the start of the game Thomas can see the players on the other team laughing amongst themselves, a few of them even arguing over who is going to get the plush assignment of guarding him. Thomas responds by ignoring the ceremonial high-fives and handshakes that always come in the moments before the opening tip, and instead tries to concentrate on the challenge that lies ahead.

"A tough guy, eh?" one of the players sarcastically says as Thomas leaves his opponent's offer of a pre-game handshake hanging.

"He's tough enough to have done your sister last night," James says, getting into position beside the two of them.

"Screw you, Bianchi," the player says.

"Tell your mother I said hello," James responds.

Thomas will forever be impressed at James's ability to effortlessly inspire hatred in people who barely know him. When the player James has just insulted shoves him, things immediately devolve. It takes the refs and both coaches two solid minutes to get their players calmed down and ready to play, with James making an armistice nearly impossible by his insistence on mentioning a particular act he's going to perform with every one of the opposing players' sisters when the game is over.

"Jesus, James," Coach says, pulling James aside. "Everyone already hates you. Hell, *I* hate you. So why insist on making it so easy for them to dislike you even more?"

"I was just standing up for my teammate, Coach," James says.

"The kid isn't your teammate," Coach responds. "He's not even tall enough to be a kid."

When the game begins Thomas immediately shows he belongs. Coach has smartly instructed his squad to play a zone defense, which enables Thomas to not get exposed on defense, where his lack of size against these older players could be a liability. Instead he does his best, closing out on shooters on the perimeter, while on the other end he takes advantage of the opposing team's certainty he shouldn't be on the floor, regularly blowing by them after they casually think they can steal the ball from him, setting up James for a series of open jumpers.

By the end of the first quarter the Knights are up six, and Thomas runs back to the bench clapping his hands and high-fiving his teammates before taking a seat.

"Not bad, kid," Coach says. "But take it easy on the hot-dog stuff."

As Coach draws up a play on the whiteboard, Thomas takes a quick scan of his surroundings. There are two other games happening simultaneously on the other courts, where middle-aged men pace the sidelines and yell out instructions to their players, while standing along both baselines and sitting in folding chairs are an assortment of parents, friends, and the occasional girlfriend. If there's a better place in the world to be on an afternoon in the middle of summer, Thomas can't think of it.

They're down one point with seventeen seconds to go. The other team has called timeout, and as Thomas and his teammates run over to the bench, James says to him, "Those poor guys. They've got no idea I'm about to break their hearts with a corner jumper."

"Alright, listen up," Coach intones, a desperation in his voice at the fact that his team, never mind that it's only a summer league game, actually has a chance to win. "Here's what we're going to run."

Coach draws up a play where Thomas will receive the inbounds pass and use a high-screen from Dave to turn the corner and get into the lane.

"Once you're in the paint, kid, kick it to James in the corner. And James," Coach adds.

"Yeah, Coach?"

"Try not to choke."

"You always know just what to say, Coach," James says.

When they break the huddle Dave puts his arm around Thomas and says, "I'll put a body on your guy, kid. Just don't blow it."

The play is busted before the ball is even inbounded. After Thomas has to scramble to get open, a defender deflects the inbounds pass, forcing Thomas into the backcourt to retrieve it. There are eight seconds remaining on the clock by the time Thomas is back in possession of the ball and has crossed half-court. But Dave, in the preceding chaos, hasn't gotten back into position to set the necessary screen that was intended to get Thomas free. So Thomas decides to improvise by crossing his man over just past half-court, but as he heads into the lane he notices James's man hasn't left him, which makes a pass to him impossible. Instead Thomas hesitates, pulls up, and looks to the opposite side of the floor where he hopes another teammate might be open for a shot. Nothing doing. The defenders are well-disciplined, and they've decided to stay home on their assignments.

Running out of options, Thomas drives deeper into the lane and rises for a floater. As he does so, his arm is grabbed from behind by the defender he has just driven by. The whistle blows at the same instant the buzzer sounds.

"Foul on Number Eight," the ref announces. "Two shots."

One second is put back on the clock. Thomas will go to the free-throw line for two shots, with his team trailing by one. He looks over to see Coach sitting on the bench with a look of anguish on his face, as if he is doing everything he can not to have a complete nervous breakdown.

"Well, kid," James says to him as Thomas prepares to step to the line. "Make these and everyone gets laid tonight."

"You think so?"

"No."

Thomas steps to the line, his eyes already fixed on the basket as everyone takes their spots on each side of the lane. The guy nearest him, a burly power forward who looks like he might have eaten his younger brother earlier in the afternoon, leans towards Thomas and says, "You suck, kid."

"Don't listen to him," Dave says from the other side of the lane. "You got these."

Thomas goes through his shooting routine, taking several dribbles before looking up at the rim, bending his knees, and releasing the ball.

No good.

As the ball caroms off the back rim and the ref retrieves the ball, James claps his hands to encourage him.

"It's alright. Just get us to overtime. I'll take care of the rest."

Thomas nods and tries to calm the nerves that are suddenly threatening to consume him. He's never come up short in a clutch situation before.

He receives the bounce pass from the ref, takes a deep breath, and goes back through his routine. "You've done this a thousand times before," he tells himself. "There's nothing to it."

He leaves the second one short, and when the ball bounces harmlessly into the other team's hands, the buzzer sounds. As the opposing team runs off the floor celebrating, Thomas remains at the foul line in disbelief.

Dave steps up to him and says, "Well, kid. You blew it."

"Don't sweat it," James says. "If you'd made those we would've had to play again in a couple hours, and I promised Sherry I'd take her to the movies."

The two of them walk back to the bench together. Coach is standing with his hands on his hips and a look on his face hovering somewhere between disappointment and resignation.

"I knew he wasn't a leprechaun," he says to James.

"How come?"

"Because leprechauns bring good luck."

When Thomas takes a seat on the bench the other two teammates don't bother giving him handshakes or telling him that he's played a good game. But James sits down next to Thomas and says, "This is part of being a player. So just forget about it and move on."

"Don't listen to him," Coach says. "The secret is to let it gnaw at you until you're so sick of what happened that you come out the next time ready to kill somebody."

"Inspiring stuff, Coach," James says.

"I tried the inspiring stuff last year," Coach says. "We went 0-12."

As Thomas and James pack up their things and get ready to leave, Coach says, "At least try not to give the kid any of your bad habits, Bianchi."

"Then I'll have nothing to give him," James says. "And I can't leave him empty-handed."

After Dave and James have dropped Thomas off back at Sunwood, he goes upstairs, eats lunch, goes for a swim, watches the first half of *Sharky's Machine*, and is back out on the Matsuya blacktop by 5 p.m. When his mother returns from work, she parks out front and waves to him before she heads up to the apartment.

Still disappointed, embarrassed, and confused by his choke-job at the foul line earlier in the afternoon, he focuses exclusively on his free throws. By 7:45 p.m., he's shot 300 of them and made 244. It's as Thomas chases down one of his misses that he sees Earl jogging across the street to join him. After Earl has climbed the fence, he runs towards the basket with his palms up, waiting for Thomas to throw him a pass. Thomas smiles and does so, raising his arms above his head in triumph as Earl leaps towards the hoop and slams the ball home.

"Working on your free throws, kid?" Earl asks. "That's already one of the best parts of your game."

"Not today."

"What do you mean?" Earl asks as he casually tosses up a fadeaway jumper.

"I missed two at the end of a summer league game this afternoon. We were down one with one second to go."

"I've been there, kid."

"For real?"

"Absolutely. I cost us a shot at the '72 Finals at the line."

"What happened?" Thomas asks, as Earl begins to take a series of short jump hooks in the paint, his left hand equally as deft as his right.

"What happened was I went 12 for 25 at the stripe in the deciding game, including missing four in a row in the final two minutes."

"Man, Earl. What did you do?"

"What do you mean?"

"You must have been frustrated."

"Frustrated? Hell, I was *devastated*. The headline in the paper the next day said 'Lewis Invents New Ways to Choke', with a photo of me clanging one off the rim."

"I can't even imagine that," Thomas says.

"You won't have to. You wind up being as good as I think you're going to be, it'll happen to you too. A few times. Maybe more."

"I don't understand it though. I'm a good shooter."

"Being a good shooter's got nothing to do with it. The hoops gods just weren't on your side today. Nothing you can do about that."

"You think God really cares about a basketball game?"

"Not God," Earl clarifies. "The *gods*. A different thing entirely."

"I don't like them."

"Hell, they don't want you to like them. They want you to fear them."

"How come?"

"Because as long as you fear them, you'll never take your success for granted."

Earl lays the ball up and then throws the ball to Thomas. When he catches the pass, Earl says, "You can't just love the game when you're winning, kid. You've got to love it when you're losing too. Otherwise it was never really love in the first place. You understand?"

"I think so."

For the next several minutes Thomas continuously feeds Earl the ball in the post, and constantly marvels at the seemingly endless array of moves Earl has at his disposal.

"You're going to dominate at your tryout, Earl," Thomas says when the two of them take a break.

"I'm just hoping I don't get run off the court."

"That's not going to happen. The hoops gods won't allow it."

Earl laughs and says, "I guess we'll see about that. Now come on.

Let's take a look at your free throw form and see if there's anything we need to fix."

It is as Thomas walks towards the free throw line that he hears Earl say, "Well, would you look at that?"

Thomas turns to see a man appearing from around the corner of the school and heading in their direction. He's wearing long black sweats, a red Chicago Bulls t-shirt, and matching red high-tops that Thomas immediately recognizes, even from this far off, as the new Air Jordans.

A few seconds later Wings raises his arm in greeting when he's about two hundred feet away, as casually as if he were simply waving to a couple of friends that he'd just seen the day before.

Thomas is almost paralyzed by excitement, afraid that even bouncing the ball might wake him from the dream he's half-certain this is. But once Wings is within fifty feet, Thomas knows that it's real.

"We've been looking everywhere for you, Wings!" Thomas exclaims.

"Don't I know it, kid," Wings says, as Earl and Wings shake hands and embrace before Wings does the same with Thomas. Thomas looks up to see that Earl appears to be in something close to shock, unable to believe that his old friend is here, in the flesh, standing in front of him. "I got to Arden Park about an hour after you left," Wings adds, "and everyone was saying some kid detective was on my trail."

"Arden Park?" Earl asks. "Where's that?"

"Up in L.A.," Wings says.

"When did you go there?" Earl asks, looking at Thomas.

"Yesterday," Thomas says. "I went by your place in the morning to tell you, but you were gone, and I was afraid that you'd leave for

Philly before we had a chance to go up there together."

Earl is smiling in disbelief at Thomas's moxie.

"How'd you get up to L.A. on your own?"

"I took the train."

"Your mother let you do that?"

"Not exactly," Thomas says.

At this Wings interjects and says, "When I got there they were laughing, saying this little white boy took off in a cab like he was The Shadow or something."

With this both Earl and Wings break into laughter.

"Damn, kid," Earl says. "Not bad. Not bad at all."

"Thanks Earl."

Earl and Wings come in for another handshake and half-hug, still marveling at the fact that, after all of these years, they're on a basketball court together, just like the old days.

"You look good, E.," Wings says. "Like you're ready to take it to Kevin McHale on the low block."

"That's the plan. What about you? People don't age in Southern California or something?"

"That's right. Why do you think I moved out here? They've got the Fountain of Youth, and it's called the Pacific Ocean."

"I hear that," Earl says, nodding, before the two of them go silent.

Thomas can tell that the conversation's about to shift into heavier topics, and that it isn't any of his business to be here when they do.

"I'm late for dinner," Thomas says. "I've got to go home."

"Come see me in the morning before I take off," Earl says.

"I will. For sure."

"I'm glad we found you, Wings," Thomas says. "I was worried we wouldn't."

Wings steps forward to bump fists with Thomas.

"I'm glad you did too, shorty. Really glad."

As Thomas is about to turn, he stops and says, "Oh, Wings?"

"What's up?"

"You should get back together with Denise. She really misses you."

Before Wings can answer, Thomas takes off towards the fence, bouncing the ball as he goes, feeling as if he were not running on the asphalt so much as gliding above it. After he's hopped the fence, he turns back to wave one more time in the direction of the two men, but they are already so deep in conversation neither of them looks in his direction.

Thomas is already shouting "Mom! Mom! Mom!" as he bounds up the stairs, loudly enough for her to open the front door while he's still ascending the final few steps.

"What? Is everything alright?"

"Wings is here! We found him."

Thomas takes her hand and leads her through the apartment to the dining room window. He points through it at the sight of Earl and Wings speaking and shooting hoops across the street.

"Isn't that something?" his mother says with a smile on her face. "After all these years."

And then, looking at her son, who continues to look out the window in amazement at what has come to pass, she says, "Nice job," and gives him a high-five. "Very well done."

She stands with him at the window for another few moments before heading back into the living room to resume reading her book. Thomas remains for another minute, looking out across the street and marveling all over again at Wings' sudden appearance.

Here, in this summer of leavings, he wants to hold onto this feeling of one man returning.

"I didn't think it would happen," he finally says, not realizing he's said it out loud.

His mother puts her book down and looks in his direction, "Sure you did," she said. "Otherwise you wouldn't have kept looking."

He's so excited that he's still wide awake well after 11 p.m. To pass the time he lies in bed, stares up at the ceiling, and replays that first sight of Wings rounding the corner, over and over again. Finally, aware sleep remains a long way's off, he slips out of bed to retrieve Ellen's walkman. But as he kneels down to pull it out of the bottom drawer of his desk, a small rock hits his window. He stands up just in time to hear a second one strike. When he opens the curtains he sees James standing on the sidewalk below, waving up at him. Thomas slides the window open as quietly as possible so as not to wake his mother.

"What?"

"You asleep?"

"No," Thomas whispers.

"A few girls are coming over. We're going down to the jacuzzi. Sherry'll be there too."

"Very funny."

"No, I'm serious. Sneak out and meet us. I figure I owe you one for not getting open earlier today. It should've been me at the line instead of you."

"I can't. My mother will kill me."

"No she won't. If anything she'll kill me."

"I'll kill you both," Thomas's mother says as she appears at the window.

"I've seen ninjas louder than you, Mrs. Kabiri."

"And I've heard machine guns quieter than you, James Bianchi."

"You're alright, Mrs. Kabiri."

"And you're waking up the neighbors, James."

"See you tomorrow, Thomas."

"See you tomorrow, James," Thomas says.

Thomas's mother closes the window and looks at him.

"Don't you have your paper route in less than five hours?"

"Yes."

"Well, then try to get some sleep. You've had an exciting day, and you need your rest."

"Ok, Mom."

She starts to exit the room, but then she stops, looks at her son and adds, "You'll be eleven before you know it. Then twenty. And then thirty. So try to enjoy this age, alright?"

"That's why I wanted to go to the jacuzzi."

"Don't push it."

After she's closed the door Thomas gets back into bed with Ellen's walkman, puts the headphones on his ears, and finally, about an hour later, falls asleep to the sound of Prince's voice in his head.

He's a man possessed on his bike the following morning, racing through the complex and throwing papers at their intended targets with the locked-in focus of a big-league pitcher working the late innings of a no-hitter. He finishes a few minutes before 5 a.m., which means by the time he pedals over to Earl's, it's 5 a.m. on the dot.

He walks up the stairs and knocks on Earl's door. A few moments later Earl opens it. He's dressed differently than usual, though, in a blue suit and red tie, with a white handkerchief sticking out of the breast pocket.

"You look like you're about to go on *The Tonight Show*, Earl."

"Got to look my best today, kid. The GM of the Sixers is picking me up from the airport in Philly."

"Are you nervous?"

"Why should I be nervous? I've only been waiting ten years for this chance."

The two of them laugh, but then Earl adds, "But that's alright. Nerves just mean you care."

"They're going to love you, Earl. They'll sign you for sure."

"I hope so. If they do, I'll be sure to leave you tickets every time we roll through L.A."

"That'd be awesome! Like I said, I've never seen a game in person."

"All the more reason for me to make sure I get a contract then."

As Earl sits on the edge of the coffee table and laces up his dress shoes, Thomas says, "Did you and Wings make up, Earl?"

Earl pauses before answering.

"Time's a funny thing, kid."

"What do you mean?"

"There wasn't really any making up to do," Earl says, standing back up after finishing with his shoes. "I told him I was sorry, he told me he was sorry, we both started to laugh, and that was that. The rest of the night we just got some shots up, reminisced about old times, and caught each other up on what we'd been doing all these years in between. Simple as that."

"Is Wings going to start playing again too?"

"You mean professionally?"

Thomas nods.

"I don't think so, kid, He's got a good thing going."

"What's he do?" Thomas asks, as Earl double-checks that his suitcase is properly latched.

"He's a cameraman for the L.A. Times. That's why he vanishes for long periods every now and then. They send him overseas to shoot wars, funerals of diplomats, the running of the bulls, anything you can think of."

"But doesn't he miss the game?"

"He said he misses the camaraderie. You know, hanging out with the guys, going out together after the games. But he doesn't miss the rest of it: the practices, the weightlifting sessions, the ice packs on the knees after workouts."

Earl fills a glass of water and drinks it down in one gulp, before adding, "He's made a new life for himself. We've all got to do it sometime. You will too someday."

"Man, I couldn't believe it when he came running around the corner."

"Well," Earl says, laughing, "that wouldn't have happened if *you* hadn't made it happen."

"I didn't do anything, Earl."

"Nice try, kid," Earl says, tapping Thomas on the shoulder as he walks back into the living room. "You got a lead and chased it down. All on your own too. Speaking of which, how'd you find out about Arden Park?"

"I saw photos of Wings and Coach Roth at Coach's house when James and I went to see Mrs. Roth after the funeral."

"Impressive," Earl says.

Earl walks over to the mirror in the dining room, making sure his tie is straight. His packed suitcase sits near the door. Thomas surveys the room and, though he's doing his best not to, realizes he's on the verge of crying. To make sure it doesn't happen, he figures the best thing to do is to keep talking.

"Hey Earl," he says, standing up and walking into the dining room to stand next to him.

"What's that?"

"You're the best friend I ever had."

Earl steps away from the mirror, looks down at Thomas and says, "Well, kid. You're the brother I never had. So I guess that makes us even."

Thomas extends his hand for a shake, but instead Earl picks him up and embraces him tightly.

"You be good, okay? Look out for your mother."

"I will," Thomas says, squeezing back.

When Earl sets Thomas back on the floor, he takes a sheet of paper out of his pocket and hands it to Thomas.

"This is where I'll be staying in Philly. And below it's my number and address in New York. Call anytime."

"You sure?"

"Most definitely."

"Okay, I will. You need help with your bags?"

"Absolutely. Take this."

Thomas slings Earl's duffel over his shoulder, while Earl picks up the large leather suitcase from the floor. They don't say anything as they walk through the complex and emerge on the sidewalk across the street from Matsuya. When they get there, Thomas is surprised to find his mother standing there with a paper bag and a thermos in her hand.

"Airplane food is terrible for you," she says, handing the bag and thermos to Earl. "And you're going to need something healthy before your tryout."

"Thank you," Earl says. "You didn't have to do this."

Earl and Thomas's mother embrace as a taxicab makes a u-turn on the street and pulls to the curb in front of them. Up the street Thomas sees Father O'Connell watering the statue of St. Mary in front of the rectory.

As the driver gets out to place Earl's bags into the trunk, Thomas steps towards Earl again and says, "Remember to pass to Dr. J. this time, Earl."

"I'll see what I can do, kid."

They bump fists, and pause for a moment before Earl turns and gets into the backseat of the cab. Thomas steps to the window and puts his palm to the glass, and Earl matches it with his own, much larger palm from the other side. As the car pulls away, Thomas raises his hand as high as possible and waves. A moment later Earl's hand emerges from the window, waving back.

EPILOGUE

"I'm telling you," James says, as he stands at the free throw line and prepares to shoot. "There's no way the Cold War lasts another ten years. At some point a bunch of teenagers in Prague, or St. Petersburg, or East Berlin are going to get tired of the fact that they can't see Van Halen in concert. And that'll be it. It's not going to be Reagan that ends Communism. It's going to be a bunch of high schoolers who want to watch the World Series on television."

"You're crazy," Mississippi Rod says, grabbing James's rare miss as it clangs off the rim and replacing James at the free throw line in the group's round-robin shoot-a-thon.

"Course I am," James says. "But that don't make it any less true. Hell, by the time Thomas here leaves for college, he'll probably be taking summer classes in Bucharest."

"Where's Bucharest?" Thomas asks.

"Romania," Arjun says, standing on the baseline and taking a drink of lemon-lime Gatorade.

"Where's Romania?" Thomas asks.

"Eastern Europe," Arjun says.

"They play basketball in Eastern Europe?" Thomas asks.

"I'm not sure what any of this has to do with me enlisting," Rod says, ignoring Thomas's question before releasing another shot.

"It has *everything* to do with it," James says.

"I don't see what you're getting at either," Arjun says.

"What I'm getting at is that pretty soon there's not going to be any need for armies. Navies either. Maybe the Air Force, but that'll be it. By the 21st century America might not even be just the 50 states anymore. It'll include most of the civilized world. One Nation, United Under Coca Cola, *Rocky IV*, and *Star Trek*."

"*Star Wars*," Rod counters.

"Okay, fine," James says. "*Star Wars*. Harrison Ford'll be President. So why put on a uniform and risk your life for a world order that's already on its last legs?"

"I'm going to get to see the world," Rod says as Arjun takes his turn at the foul line.

"There are ways to see the world that don't involve getting shot at," James says.

It suddenly occurs to Thomas that beneath James's bluster is sadness at the fact that one of his closest friends in the world is going to be shipping out in two weeks' time. James isn't pontificating; he's grieving.

"The whole point of Southern California is to stay here once you've arrived, not to leave it for some place none of us can even find on a map," James adds.

"I can find it on a map," Arjun counters.

"You know what I mean," James says.

"My father served his country," Rod says. "My grandfather too. So now it's my turn, you know?"

Thomas steps to the line to shoot, but truthfully he's finding it difficult to concentrate on his form. It's only early August and already it feels like something more than summer is ending.

"Just go back tomorrow morning and tell them you changed your mind," James says.

"Why not go to college instead?" Arjun asks.

"College'll always be there," Rod says.

"But your legs might not be," James says.

There's an extended silence as James and Rod look at one another across the kind of vast distance Thomas will come to know well in future years. The one across which he and so many of his friends will look at one another, their lives diverging in ways they never thought they would, never to be brought back together. Suddenly Thomas feels one hundred years old.

"You hear from Earl, kid?" Rod says, changing the subject.

"He sent me a letter three days ago," Thomas says. "He got signed by the Sixers. He's already rented a place in Philly and everything."

"Man, that's awesome," Rod says. "Dude's going to get to play with Dr. J."

"Moses Malone too," Arjun says.

"I'm going to see him play when they face the Lakers next season," Thomas says.

"And he was here running with us," Rod marvels. "I still can't believe it."

Rod and James exchange high-fives, whatever tension that Rod's decision has caused between them seeming to have dissolved in the happiness of this shared memory.

"He even called you the king of this court," James says.

Rod shakes his head in awe at the memory.

"It's true," Thomas says. "You are. No matter how far away the Army takes you."

"Thanks, kid," Rod says.

"Hey," Arjun says, taking a jumper from a few feet beyond the top of the key. "Did you hear that Dave's mother died?"

They all go silent for a moment. Thomas can picture her now, forever walking through the apartment complex with a blue bandanna wrapped around her head, dressed in bell-bottom jeans and a paisley blouse, a lost child of the 1960s.

"Was she sick?" Thomas asks.

"What'd you think the bandanna was for?" James asks.

"What'd you mean?" Thomas responds.

"The chemo had taken all of her hair, kid," Arjun says.

"What's going to happen with Dave?" Rod asks.

"He's got a grandmother in Tahoe," Arjun says. "I guess they're coming down to get him after the funeral."

"When's the funeral?" James asks.

"Day after tomorrow," Arjun says.

"Where?" Rod asks.

"St. Sebastian's," Arjun says, nodding towards the church.

"We should all go," Rod says.

"It's becoming a monthly thing, seems like," James says. "First it was Coach Roth, now Mrs. Hamilton."

"This is different though," Arjun says. "Coach Roth lived a full life. Dave's mother couldn't have been more than 40 years old."

"Dying that young should be against the law," Rod says, before getting up a shot that bounces off the rim.

For a minute or so no one says anything. Arjun jogs towards the water fountain, and Rod pulls a candy bar out of his bag to snack on. As Thomas drives in for a layup, James says, "I didn't know your father rode a motorcycle, kid."

"He doesn't," Thomas says, after releasing the shot.

"You sure?" James asks, nodding in the direction of Sunwood.

Thomas turns to see his father placing a helmet onto the handlebars of a gleaming bike whose chrome chassis is shining beneath the afternoon sun. He removes his jacket, drapes it across the bike seat, and then begins to walk across the street to the courts.

Thomas sprints towards his father and climbs the fence. In the middle of the empty street he wraps his arms around his father with such intensity that his father actually begins to laugh before saying, "I missed you too, kid. Anything happen while I was gone?"

About the Author

Kareem Tayyar's poetry collection, *Immigrant Songs*, will be released by Word Tech Books in 2019. Previous works include *Magic Carpet Poems* (Tebot Bach Books), *Postmark Atlantis* (Level Four Press), *In the Footsteps of the Silver King* (Spout Hill Books), and *Scenes From A Good Life* (Tebot Bach Books). A Professor of English at Golden West College in Huntington Beach, California, he holds a Ph.D. in English from U.C. Riverside. He is a recipient of a 2019 Wurlitzer Fellowship for Poetry.